PAPER HEART

BY: KEISHA ERVIN

FOLLOW ME:

IG: @keishaervin

Twitter: @keishaervin

Facebook: www.facebook.com/keisha.ervin

Pinterest: Keisha Ervin

ervinkeisha@yahoo.com

YouTube: Color Me Pynk Channel

PAPER HEART
SOUNDTRACK

PAPER HEART

Sung and Written by: Jenni Lovette

Track Produced by: RetsaM

Email: retsamworldwide@hotmail.com

SoundCloud: RetsaM

BEAST & NOT GOOD ENOUGH

Sung and Written by: Jenni Lovette

Tracks Produced by: Ozzie Clarke

SoundCloud: OzzieClarke

Bandcamp: iamozzie.bandcamp.com

ALL MUSIC ARRANGED BY:

Pancho Rucker

Twitter: @PanchoRucker

IG: @PanchoRucker

www.panchorucker.com

www.shogunmusicgroup.com

JENNI LOVETTE'S CONTACT INFO:

IG: @jennilovette

SoundCloud: Jenni Lovette

TO PURCHASE SOUNDTRACK GO TO:

jennilovette.bandcamp.com

DEDICATION

I dedicate this book to all of the people who have been rockin' with me since 2004. This is my 20th novel. I wouldn't have made it this far without each and every one of you. Your love and support overjoys me. It's mind-blowing to me that so many of you like me and my work. Each time I get the chance to write another book, I am humbled and blessed. I thank God for you and I love you.

ACKNOWLEDGEMENTS

Lord, I thank you! You are an awesome and almighty God. I thank you for your grace and your mercy. On paper, I was supposed to be a statistic. I didn't graduate from high school, was a teen mom, single mother and on welfare but you brought me through and showed the world the power of God. With you, nothing is impossible. Thank you for covering me in your blood and allowing me to see another day. Most of all, I thank you for my son. He is the biggest and best blessing I have ever received from you. Use me as your vessel, Lord. I give my all to you and love you with all of my heart.

Kyrese, mom loves you. Although you work my nerves and have given me a few unwanted gray hairs, I love you. You're my best friend. I am proud of you. The young man you have become astonishes me. You'll be sixteen this year. My God, how time flies. You were just a little baby. What am I going to do with you? You're almost a grown man. I know what I'm going to do; I'm going to cherish every moment we spend together and sit back and watch you grow into the God-fearing, loving, kind, funny, responsible, caring, hardworking man you are destined to become.

My best friends mean the world to me. Locia, Monique, Miesha and Sharissa are my rocks. Whenever life throws me lemons, they help me turn it into lemonade. We've been through it all together and I love each of them with every fiber of my being.

To my agent/friend/2nd mother, Brenda Hampton... The sky is the limit for us. We're going to take this thing to the next level. Everything that we have discussed is going to come true. God hasn't brought us this far for nothing. Love you!!!

Thank you, Jenni Lovette, for lending me your phenomenal voice on this project. The idea of the Paper Heart Soundtrack came out of a negative experience that you had with someone you called a friend. But what the devil meant for evil, God meant for good. I'm happy that the world will finally get to hear your voice and experience your writing skills. You did an awesome job. I'm so proud of you. Love you much, friend!

Pancho Rucker, you have become one of my best friends over the last year. You are the brother I never wanted but am grateful to have. Thank you for our conversations, for helping me in my time of need and your friendship. You are a true artist! The work you put in on the Paper Heart Soundtrack makes me smile. You came in and got the job done in a timely, professional manner, as always. You are an awesome rapper, lyricist, arranger and producer. You're next album - I Am Perfect - is going to be a smash hit. I love you so very much!!!

Thank you, LaMia, for another awesome editing job! I am so blessed to have found you.

Thank you, Devenchi, for an amazing cover!

Mama and Daddy, I love you. P.O.P, hold it down!!!!

"ONE LOOK AT YOU, I'M HYPNOTIZED."

-ADRIAN MARCEL, TIMELESS

CHAPTER 1

"Fuck!" Scotland shouted, bumping her knee on the side of the coffee table.

"Ooooooh... you said a bad word." Busy, the four-year-old child she was babysitting snickered.

"Don't you say it." Scotland warned, handing her a juice box.

She was already having a bad day. The kids repeating her bad words would only make it worse. After waking up ten minutes late and rushing to get dressed, her car wouldn't start. Scotland sat in the parking lot of her apartment building for over thirty minutes trying to get it to work. By the time she arrived at her job, the Frasiers, the parents she was nannying for, were pissed. Well, Mrs. Frasier understood but her asshole husband, Mr. Frasier was a complete dick about the whole entire situation and threatened to complain to the agency Scotland worked for. Suffice it to say, Scotland didn't need any more unwelcomed drama.

"Fuck." Liam, Busy's two-year-old brother repeated.

"Liam!" Scotland gasped. "No, that's a bad word. Don't ever say that again." She pointed her finger in his face.

"Say duck. Duck!"

"Fuck-fuck," Liam giggled.

"Jesus, be a fence." Scotland threw her hands up in the air exasperated. "Just play with your toys," she groaned.

Plopping down on the couch, she took a minute to breathe. She'd been running non-stop all morning. After oversleeping, she was surprised that she was able to make herself look halfway decent. Thank God that she had a 32 inch, gray sew-in with Chinese bangs in her head. All she had to do was unwrap her hair and comb it. Her individual lashes were already installed; so that only left her putting on her favorite, hot pink lipstick - Candy Yum Yum by M.A.C. She quickly threw on her gold, door knocker earrings, OBEY t-shirt, black and white striped leggings, Jordan's, grabbed her Michael Kors bag and was out the door.

After the drama with her car and getting yelled at by Mr. Frasier, she had to fix the kids breakfast, wash the dishes, give the kids a bath, get them dressed, give Busy a worksheet to do, sit Liam on the potty, go to a Mommy and Me class, come home, fix lunch and clean up the kitchen again. The rest of the day would consist of giving the kids a nap, taking Busy to French class, Liam to the doctor, coming home, preparing dinner, bathing both kids again and putting them to bed. Scotland wanted desperately to take a nap herself but she couldn't. There was no sleeping on the job.

Nonetheless, she loved her job. She'd been the kids' nanny for two years and loved them as if they were her own. This was her third family since starting with the Nanny Express Agency three years prior. The Frasiers weren't just your typical, run-of-the-mill family though. They were rich… very rich. They lived in the affluent Central West End section of St. Louis in a multi-million dollar, high-rise apartment. Their apartment had five bedrooms, four bathrooms, a spa, in-home movie theater and a rooftop deck.

Every time Scotland stepped foot inside their home she was awe-struck. Coming from the gritty streets of Pagedale, MO, she'd never seen anything like the Frasiers' home. She only saw places like it in magazines and on television. All she knew growing up was a small, two bedroom home with one bathroom. You were considered hood rich if you had two bathrooms and a finished basement. The Frasier kids didn't know how blessed they were to grow up in such a spacious, grand home.

Mr. and Mrs. Frasier only had the best of everything. Neither of them ever had to lift a finger to do anything. They had help to do everything for them. They had Scotland the nanny, Esperanza the maid, Ingrid the masseuse and Pierre the chef. Expensive paintings hung from their walls. They drove a Range Rover, Bentley Coupe and a Mercedes-Benz S-Class Coupe. In the winter they vacationed in Aspen and during the summer the Hamptons or Saint-Tropez.

A summer vacation for Scotland was going to Six Flags or Lake Ozark on a Saturday to hit up the outlet stores. To be able to have a glimpse into the good life was a blessing to her. She'd never have what the Frasiers or any of their rich friends had. All she could do is watch from afar and live vicariously through them. The reality was that when she left the safe, cozy, confines of the Frasiers' home, she had to return to the nosey, ghetto, dangerous Bentwood Townhomes in which she lived.

"Scottie, can I have another juice?" Busy asked sweetly batting her eyes.

"No, ma'am. You ain't about to piss in the bed on my watch."

"But, Scottie, I love you. You're my best friend." Busy threw herself on Scotland's legs and rested her head in her lap.

Scotland's heart couldn't help but smile. She swiftly picked Busy up and hugged her tight. Busy's soft, red curls brushed up against the side of her face. Busy was the sweetest, cutest child ever. Her porcelain white skin enhanced the red freckles on her cheeks. She had big, green eyes and always smelled like cinnamon. Liam looked like the boy version of her.

"You're my best friend too, Busy, but the answer is still no," Scotland laughed.

"Aww fuck." Busy pouted getting down.

"Busy, watch your mouth!" Scotland yelled.

"Okay," she frowned. "Can I at least watch Liv and Maddie then?" Busy asked sadly.

"Sure." Scotland changed the channel for her as her iPhone began to ring.

It was her sister YaYa.

"What up, trick?" She answered the phone.

"What you doing?" YaYa smacked on a sour gummy worm in her ear.

"I'm at work, duh. What do you want?" Scotland crossed her legs.

"Tell them gremlins I said hi," YaYa joked.

"I will not. Now what is it?"

"Guess who I saw last night at Cuetopia."

"Who, YaYa?" Scotland rolled her eyes to the ceiling.

She was not in the mood for a bunch of guessing games.

"Murda and Jamil."

"That's nice." Scotland tried to play it off like she didn't care.

Murda was her on-again, off-again boyfriend of the last two years. He'd treated her less than kind and cheated on her too many times to count but for some reason she couldn't shake him.

"Bitch, don't try to act like you don't care."

"I don't."

"Ok, since you don't care, then I guess I won't tell you that he asked about you."

"What he say?" Scotland perked up.

"Naw remember; you don't care," YaYa teased.

"Girl, what he say?"

"He just asked where you were at and how you been. I told him out on a date and that you were doing great."

"You know damn well I was at home asleep but good girl," Scotland laughed.

"Girl, when I said you were out on a date, you should'a seen his face. That nigga was tight," YaYa laughed.

"That's what he get. The last time I saw Murda was when we were coming out of Happy Hour Bar and Grill and I saw him in the car with that big bitch."

"Big bitch," Liam mumbled playing with his building blocks.

"Girl, I gotta go. You got me cussing around these kids. I'ma fuck around and get fired."

"Fuck!" Liam cracked up laughing.

"Shit." Scotland said knowing she was up shit's creek.

"Shit!" Liam clapped his hands proud of himself.

"Girl, I gotta go," Scotland tried getting off the phone.

"Hold up. Before you go, me and the girls are coming over tonight."

"A'ight. I'll see y'all then."

"Aye!" YaYa stopped her again.

"What, YaYa? I gotta go." Scotland said agitated as the front door opened.

To her surprise, Mr. Frasier had come home early. He wasn't even half way through the door and was already giving her the evil eye.

"YaYa, I'll talk to you later." Scotland hung up before she could tell her to stop and pick up some wine on the way home.

"Daddy!" Busy raced over to her father and hugged him around the leg.

"Not now, Busy." Mr. Frasier pushed her away and straightened his pants leg.

Scotland watched as Busy strolled away visibly hurt.

"Scotland, we've told you about being on the phone while watching our kids. Haven't we?"

"Yes," Scotland sighed heavily. "My bad. It won't happen again."

From the moment she was hired, Scotland always got the feeling that Mr. Frasier didn't like her. Maybe it was because she was black or lower class but he made it known that he didn't favor her. As much as Mr. Frasier disliked her, she hated him more. He was a highly successful sports agent. Mr. Frasier was quite handsome. He resembled Gerard Butler but the man was rude, arrogant and callous.

"You were already late this morning and now I catch you on the phone. What if one of the kids had put something in their mouth and choked while you were on the phone yapping to one of your friends?"

"I was watching them the whole time." She tried to explain.

"Sure you were." He shook his head and placed down his briefcase.

As he turned around, Scotland couldn't help but notice a smudge of red lipstick on the collar of his shirt. A rush of anger flushed over her body because she knew the lipstick wasn't Mrs. Frasier's. Mrs. Frasier hated red lipstick. Now it all made sense. Mr. Frasier had just had an afternoon rendezvous with his side chick and was coming home to shower.

"You might wanna take a look in the mirror. There's something on your neck," Scotland spat.

Mr. Frasier rushed over to the nearest mirror and examined his neck. He quickly noticed the lipstick stain. His face turned as red as Busy and Liam's hair.

"One of my business associates must have gotten too close as we hugged goodbye after our morning meeting." He laughed nervously.

"Mmm hmm… one of your business associates." Scotland eyed him with disgust.

"I don't know what you're insinuating but you need to be careful." Mr. Frasier came near her. "You're treading on thin ice."

"I'm treading on thin ice? You're the one playing with fire; not me. I'm simply here doing my job."

"A job that can be taken away with one phone call. You do have two strikes against you at the agency, right? One more and you're gone," Mr. Frasier grinned wickedly.

"And one phone call to Mrs. Frasier and you're gone," Scotland shot back.

She knew she shouldn't have said it but she couldn't keep the words bottled up inside. Mrs. Frasier was one of the kindest women she'd ever met and deserved much better than her slimy, cheating husband.

"You have no proof, darling." He glided his hands down her hair and smiled. "It's your word against mine."

Mr. Frasier knew that he had to play his cards right. He didn't know what information Scotland had on him. What he did know was that he and Scotland were both at a standstill with only one move to play. But if either of them played their hand, they would both lose tremendously.

"So let me tell you how this is going to go," he continued. "You're gonna take the rest of the day off and think about what has happened here today and how it will never happen again."

"It ain't even that serious. I apologize. I was out of line. Just let me finish out the day. I really need the money," Scotland reasoned.

"Kids, tell Scotland goodbye!" Mr. Frasier ignored her plea and handed her purse to her.

"Bye, Scottie." Busy and Liam raised their hands up in the air for a hug.

Scotland reluctantly bent down and hugged them both. She couldn't afford to leave early. She'd been saving up for weeks to get the repairs on her car done.

"Mr. Frasier," Scotland stood up. "Please let me stay. I said I was sorry."

"See you tomorrow, Scotland." Mr. Frasier gently pushed her out of the door and slammed it in her face.

Pissed beyond belief, Scotland gathered her emotions and marched towards the elevator. She wanted to knock on the door and beg that he let her finish out the day but she knew it would be pointless. She hated Mr. Frasier. She wanted nothing more than to expose his extramarital affair to Mrs. Frasier but if she did, she'd lose her job.

Outside of the building, the humid, August air hit her smack dab in the face. Scotland opened the door to her 1998 Lexus, threw her MK bag onto the passenger seat and got in. The tears that she'd been holding back since earlier that morning were dying to spill out. Unable to hold them in anymore, she placed her forehead on the steering wheel and began to cry. Scotland hated her life.

She was sick of living paycheck to paycheck and buying food stamps from her friends just so she could have something in her fridge to eat. Hell, she barely had $10 to get into the club on the weekends. Either she had to get there before eleven or get one of her friends to pay her way in. The little money she had left over from each paycheck went to saving up to get her car fixed because the transmission was going out.

She couldn't afford to miss a whole day of work. She needed that money like she needed air to breathe. No matter how much she wanted to sit there and feel sorry for herself, she had to pull herself together. Maybe she could use the extra time she had on her hands to go on Craigslist and look for a second job.

"Yep, that's what I'ma do." Scotland wiped the tears from her face but couldn't stop herself from crying.

Still distraught, she placed the key into the ignition and started up the engine. Unlike earlier that morning, the car started on the first try.

"Son of a bitch." Scotland hissed, not realizing that she'd accidently placed the car into reverse instead of drive.

Before she knew it, the car went flying backwards and she slammed into the car behind her.

"Oh my God!" Scotland panicked sitting frozen stiff. "That did not just happen. That did not just happen."

"Have you lost your mind?!" Scotland heard a woman scream behind her.

"Shit; it happened. It happened." Scotland winced turning the engine off.

Reluctantly, she got out of the car. As soon as she stepped out she came face-to-face with a gorgeous, butter colored woman with a dope, black, pixie cut. This chick was bad like Anika from the hit show Empire. She had slanted eyes, full lips painted red and a voluptuous frame. She looked to be only 5'3 without heels and was dressed from head to toe in an outfit from Chanel's summer 2014 collection. Scotland knew because she was obsessed with vogue.com.

"Look what you did!" The woman pointed angrily to the damage done to her Audi A8 L W12 that cost well over $100,000.

Scotland glanced to her right and saw that she'd smashed in the entire frontend of the woman's car. Her heart sank down to her knees. There was no way she was going to be able to afford the repairs. As she looked further, the backend of her car was pretty banged up as well.

"You've ruined my car!" The woman continued to yell.

"Ma'am—" Scotland began but was immediately cut off.

"Ma'am?" The woman replied appalled. "Sweetheart." She rolled her neck and placed her hand on her hip. "I'm nobody's ma'am. The name is Lennon Whitmore. What the hell were you thinking slamming into me like that? Who does that?"

"I'm so sorry. It was an accident." Scotland's voice began to quiver as tears filled the brim of her eyes. "I've just been having a horrible day. I got my period this morning. Then my car wouldn't start. I got to work late, then sent home early, now this."

"Are you crying?" Lennon squinted her eyes and stepped closer. "Oh, no-no-no-no-no." She wagged her finger in Scotland's face. "I don't have time for this. We're not about to do this. This is not the Maury Povich show. Save the drama for your mama, Bonquisha."

"What the fuck did you just call me?" Scotland snapped back to her normal self.

"Oh, I'm sorry," Lennon placed her hand on her chest. "Did I offend you? Forgive me, LaKeisha, Alizé, Tywanique or whatever your hood name is, but I am not here for your As the Ghetto Turns drama. I'm calling the police." Lennon pulled out her cell phone.

"No-no-no-no!" Scotland panicked, rushing over to stop her. "You can't do that." She tried to grab the phone.

Lennon quickly jumped back.

"If you lay a hand on me I'm going to scream," she warned.

"Girl, ain't nobody gon' touch you. Just don't call the police."

"And why not? What? Do you have a gun in there or marijuana?" Lennon looked past Scotland and at her car.

"What? No." Scotland screwed up her face. "My plates and tags are expired."

"Let me guess. You don't have insurance either; do you?"

"Nooooo… I do not. I couldn't afford it anymore," Scotland explained.

"So you mean to tell me that you've run into my beautiful car." Lennon slid her hand down the hood of her car. "And don't even have a way to pay to get it fixed?"

"Uhhh, yeah… that sounds about right."

"Before either of us go to jail today, I'm going to call my fiancé. He knows how to deal with ghetto trash like you." Lennon looked Scotland up and down with disgust.

"Ghetto trash? Bitch, who you think you talkin' to? I will bust your fuckin' ass!" Scotland pointed her fingers in Lennon's face like a gun.

"You better back up, Crazy Eyes. Remember, I can call the police," Lennon threatened.

Unwilling to go to jail for whooping Malibu Barbie's ass, Scotland stepped back and took a deep breath.

"You lucky, bitch," she snapped, getting back inside her car.

She had to get away from Lennon before she hurt her. After a fifteen minute wait, Lennon's fiancé, Knight, pulled up behind her. Lennon was leaning against the driver's side door of her car.

"Baby, you a'ight?" He asked racing over to her.

"It's alright! Baby, are you alright?" She corrected him annoyed.

"You want me to help you or not 'cause I can leave?" Knight warned.

"I'm sorry, baby." Lennon played with the lapel of his suit jacket. "This whole ordeal has just been so trying. I'm going to need a full spa day and acupuncture after this. Bonquisha here doesn't have any insurance and her plates and tags are expired. I was about to call the police but she's so pathetic. She practically got on her knees and begged me not to. I figured she'd be my charity case for the day but look at all the damage she's caused," Lennon pouted.

Knight walked around to the front of the car.

"Goddamn," he said shocked.

Both of the lights, grill and frontend of the hood were completely smashed in.

"You see. I'm going to end up paying for the damage myself," Lennon whined.

"Just calm down. Stay here. Let me go talk to her. What's her name again?"

"Bonquisha," Lennon smirked.

Knight walked over to Scotland's car and tapped on the window. Scotland looked up and locked eyes with the most beautiful man she'd ever seen. She'd never seen anything like him. He was 6'2, had milk chocolate skin, a bald head, almond-shaped, brown eyes, full, kissable, brown lips, straight, white teeth and a goatee. He possessed an athletic build and the way his Tom Ford suit kissed his body made Scotland's mouth water. He was Chad Ochocinco's long lost, twin brother in the flesh.

"Bonquisha." Knight tapped on the window again. "Can you step out of the car, please, so I can talk to you?"

Scotland snapped back to reality and got out. Knight towered over her.

"Hi, I'm Knight." He stuck out his hand for a shake.

"Hi... Scotland." She took his warm hand in hers and damn near melted.

"Scotland? Lennon told me your name was Bonquisha."

"Really?" Scotland's nostrils flared. "That silly bitch never asked me my name."

"Whoa-whoa-whoa, chill wit' callin' my fiancée a bitch," Knight warned. "I ain't here for all that."

Scotland was surprised that someone that looked and dressed like Knight spoke her language. He didn't look like he knew slang at all but that was neither here nor there. She still had to check him.

"I don't care what you came here for. You're fiancée is rude and a bitch but I'm sure you already know that."

A slight smile graced the corners of Knight's lips. He knew he shouldn't be looking at Scotland in a sexual way but she had spunk and was drop dead gorgeous. Sure, her style was over the top but he could see past all of that. Her smooth, satin, cocoa skin complimented her doe-shaped eyes, dangerously high cheekbones, pouty, succulent lips, size 34 C breasts, size 4 waist, round hips, thick thighs and small feet. She was bad and there was no way around it.

"Fuck all that. I'm just here to try and resolve all of this without getting the police involved."

"That's what's up." Scotland folded her arms across her chest. "Look, I can pay her fifty dollars a month for the damages."

"What?" Knight couldn't help but laugh.

"What the fuck is so funny?" Scotland asked feeling embarrassed. "Oh my bad. I forgot you rich muthafuckas don't know what it's like to struggle. Everybody ain't got it like you. You know what? Call the fuckin' police 'cause ain't nobody got time to be dealing wit' you two bougie muthafuckas," she snapped.

Knight stood silent and looked at her for a second before responding.

"You done? That li'l speech of yours was cute but don't let the suit fool you. I'm far from bougie, ma. Now, we can call the police if you want and they can haul yo' li'l pretty-ass off to jail."

Damn, did I just call her pretty, he thought. *Did this nigga just call me pretty,* Scotland thought as well.

"Or we can be adults about the situation and handle the situation ourselves by exchanging information so we can set up this li'l payment plan of yours," Knight compromised.

"Let me see your phone." Scotland held out her hand.

"Let me see your phone, what?" He checked her.

Scotland sucked her teeth and tried her best not to smile.

"Please."

"Much better." Knight handed her his phone.

Scotland placed her number and address into his phone and handed it back to him.

"Are we done here?" Lennon sauntered over to them and linked her arm with Knight's. "I have a late lunch date with Daddy and Mommy in 30 minutes."

"Yeah, as soon as I call a tow truck," Knight informed.

"Can I go now?" Scotland rolled her eyes. "Cause I got a lunch date with the Steve Harvey show and a bag of Ramen noodles that I can't miss."

"Yeah, you can go," Knight chuckled.

"Deuces, Ken and Barbie." Scotland chucked up the deuce and sped off.

"SHOW ME IS YOU REALLY
'BOUT YO' MONEY, BITCH, OR
NAH?"

-TIA NOMORE & KEHLANI,
OR NAH

CHAPTER 2

"I'm so glad that the day is over." Lennon exhaled, stepping out of her six inch heels. "I'm going to have Maria draw me a hot bubble bath, and then I'm going to hop in, listen to some soft jazz music and zone out."

"That sounds nice." Knight replied, untying his tie as he looked over the mail that was lying on the kitchen counter.

He was beyond proud of his home. He and Lennon shared a $3,000,000, sky-high penthouse apartment that was 1,396 feet above ground and 8,255 square feet. It had 10x10 foot windows, 12.5 foot high ceilings and solid oak floors. The penthouse held three bedrooms, three baths, and a chef's kitchen with a premium, stainless, Miele double oven, Sub-Zero appliances, dining room, laundry room, elevator, beauty and barber parlor and an indoor pool.

"I might join you." He eyed her lustfully as she slipped out of her dress.

"You want some of this, Daddy?" Lennon purred, placing her hand on her hip. "I've been a bad girl today."

"You sure have," Knight grinned.

Lennon had a body out of this world. Her physique was perfectly crafted from head to toe. She had a set of perky, vanilla, 36 B cup breasts, a flat stomach, round hips and a firm, plump ass. The black, lace, Agent Provocateur panty and bra set she wore accentuated her curves perfectly. Knight's dick was standing at full attention.

"The Dark Knight Rises." Lennon licked her lips devilishly.

"You gon' play wit' it?" Knight unbuttoned his shirt and revealed his muscular, tattooed chest.

On his shoulders were doves flying. On his right peck was a tattoo of Jesus' mother Mary with Psalms 23 written above it. On his other peck was his mother's name. Both of his arms were filled with numerous tattoos. On his left rib cage was a portrait of a knight going into battle. His entire back was filled with one gigantic tattoo of Jesus hanging on the cross with rays of sunlight beaming behind it.

Lennon hated his tattoos. She couldn't understand why someone would want to desecrate their body. Knight chalked her disdain for them up as something else they didn't have in common.

"I might." Lennon winked her eye. "I just have to take a hot bath first. Dealing with that ghetto bird today really threw me off my game. She was so ratchet." She shivered like she had the heebie jeebies.

"What were you doing over that way anyway?"

Lennon paused for a brief second before responding.

"I stopped at the Schnucks Culinaria to pick up some sushi for lunch," she replied taking off her earrings.

"But you said you were meeting your parents for lunch after the accident?"

"What can I say? I was very hungry." Lennon shrugged her shoulders.

Knight eyed her quizzically then resumed opening the mail.

"I don't know. I kinda liked her. She was a cute kid," he replied.

Lennon whipped her head around and looked at Knight sideways.

"First of all, she was a grown woman dressed like an extra in a Lil Wayne video. There was nothing cute about her, but you would like her." Lennon looked him up and down. "She is one of your kind."

"What the fuck is that supposed to mean?" Knight screwed up his face as she glided over to the wine cellar.

"OMG, Knight, calm down. Don't go into one of your little ghetto fits." Lennon pulled out a 1970 Bordeaux. "I'm not trying to be rude. I'm simply saying that you two are cut from the same cloth. You have a lot in common. Who knows, you probably come from the same neighborhood."

"You sayin' that like it's a bad thing. I'm proud of where I come from. Growing up on the West Side made me the man I am today. Everybody didn't grow up wit' a silver spoon in they mouth like you... princess. Some of us had to work hard for what we have," Knight shot.

"Umm... have you forgotten that I did five years at Brown, graduated at the top of my class, got my degree and started at the bottom of my father's firm? I worked my ass off to get that corner office. Nobody handed me a damn thing." Lennon snapped, pouring herself a glass of wine.

"Don't knock me because my parents are wealthy and you grew up in an underprivileged neighborhood."

It was little digs like this that made Knight question why he was with Lennon. They met during each of their first year at the Whitmore Agency. Both of them had graduated at the top of their class and were the firm's greatest prospects. He was immediately enthralled by her beauty, quick wit, and lethal tactics.

She was drawn to his cunningly good looks, bad boy edge and charming mega-watt smile. They were a match made in heaven businesswise but relationship-wise, they always hit a snag. The two of them came from two different worlds. Lennon lived a life of privilege and excess. She never had to worry about where her next meal was going to come from or if the bills were going to be paid on time or at all like Knight did.

Growing up, he was the oldest of five kids. He grew up in a single-parent home where his mother, June, worked as a maid at the Renaissance Hotel. June worked long, 12-hour shifts where she would come home sore with swollen legs and feet but she never missed a day of work. Neither Knight nor his siblings' fathers were in the picture, so that left everything up to June. Most times, something was cut off - whether it be the phone, lights or gas.

His three sisters, little brother and he all shared a room. Since Knight was the oldest, he got his own bed but his other siblings had to sleep two to a bed. No matter how much they cleaned, because of their nasty neighbors, they kept roaches in the house. Knight never received brand new clothes from the store, everything he owned came from the Goodwill or the church clothes bin.

On a nightly basis gun shots rang through the air. Somebody from his neighborhood was always being killed or strung out on drugs. Knight prayed to God constantly for them to be rescued from the hellhole in which they lived but no one ever came to save them. He quickly realized that he'd have to be his family's savior. He was their only way out of the hood, so Knight worked his ass off in school.

Somehow he managed to graduate school as his class valedictorian despite getting locked up a few times with his friends. He got accepted into Washington University and paid his way through college by selling weed to his rich, white classmates. All of the studying and hard work paid off. Knight was now a thirty-two-year-old, successful, talent and sports agent but he never forgot where he came from.

Whenever he had the time, Knight made it his business to go back and visit and check up on everyone. His best friends, Twan and Amir, still lived in the old neighborhood. Lennon hated his friends. She thought that they were so beneath the man that Knight was today. When it came to his family, she pretended to adore his mother and tolerated his sisters and brother.

Knight figured if he showed Lennon where he grew up she'd understand him more. The one time he took her to the West Side she freaked out and carried on so bad that he vowed never to take her back again. The reality of how the other half lived was too much for her delicate mind to handle. She couldn't relate to his life at all. It was through her nasty comments that Knight realized just how different he and Lennon were.

"I'm not doing this shit with you tonight." Knight gathered up his shirt and tie.

"Oh, I'm sorry. Did I hit a nerve?" Lennon giggled unbothered by his attitude.

"That's your problem. You think everything is a fuckin' joke. I don't find that shit funny," Knight quipped. "You're fuckin' stupid."

"Oh calm down. It's not even that big of a deal. I was just making a statement. Why are we even arguing? This whole thing started because we were talking about Bonquisha. She's ruined enough of my day. She's not about to ruin my night too." Lennon walked over to Knight and wrapped her arms around his neck.

"Let's just put all of this silly nonsense behind us. We have enough on our plates as it is. Your birthday is coming up." She kissed the side of his neck softly.

"Let's just chill. Let's get in the tub together." Lennon licked his lips. "I wanna feel you inside of me," she whispered.

Knight inhaled deep. He knew that he couldn't keep letting Lennon get away with her closed minded bullshit but his dick was hard and all he could think about was busting a nut.

After the fucked up day Scotland had, kicking it wit' her three best friends was by far the highlight of her day. She loved her girls. YaYa, Tootie and La'Shay were more than just her friends. They were her sisters. All four girls grew up in Pagedale together. They got their periods together, fought bitches together, got on niggas together and graduated school together. You name it and they'd been through it as a team. No matter what, they were always there for one another. They were each other's support system.

Scotland and YaYa had a bond like no other. When Scotland was ten, she came to live with YaYa and her family. Since birth, Scotland had been in the foster care system. She'd gone from home to home to finally land on YaYa's doorstep. The girls instantly clicked and became best friends. After two years, her parents adopted her and they became a real family.

She loved YaYa dearly. She was her friend and protector. Sometimes she took the job as protector too seriously but nobody could fuck with Scotland on YaYa's watch. She went from 0 to 100 real quick. YaYa was the hothead, loudmouth, shit starter of the crew. She only fucked with hood niggas with long paper and big dicks. She was 5'7, petite with caramel-colored skin and rocked her short hair lavender. YaYa did hair on the South Side of St. Louis. She was one of the baddest colorist in town. Everybody came to her to get their hair colored and styled.

Tootie was the sweet, mothering, peacemaker of the group. She had a smile that lit up any room she entered. Although she was caring and kind, if you crossed her, Tootie had no problem setting you straight. She was thick and had an ass that would put Nicki Minaj and Kim Kardashian's to sleep. She worked as a CNA at St. Mary's Hospital and had a one-year-old son.

La'Shay was the turn up queen. The girl loved to party. She stayed in the club. She'd never worked a day in her life. She was a single mother of three and had a body that resembled any top model's.

La'Shay was tall and statuesque. She rocked a long, platinum hairdo that accentuated her picture perfect face. People were stunned that someone so beautiful could be on Section 8 and receive cash and food benefits from the state. La'Shay got over $900 in stamps a month and sold what she had left over to her friends. She received child support from all three of her babies' daddies and would boost clothes on the weekends. She kept a pocket full of money on her at all times.

As planned, the girls sat on Scotland's mini porch throwing back Lime-A-Rita's, smoking weed and talking shit. The sun had already set but it was summertime so everybody in the complex was still outside.

"Pass me the blunt." YaYa reached her perfectly manicured hand out.

Scotland passed it to her.

"I'm tired as fuck," La'Shay yawned.

"From what? You ain't did shit all day," YaYa joked.

"I'm tired 'cause yo' man came over and banged my back out, bitch." La'Shay stuck out her tongue and hit her with the middle finger.

"Don't get mad at me 'cause I speak the truth."

"Whatever." La'Shay waved her off. "Nah for real, I'm tired 'cause I was up all night braiding Taylor hair. You know school starts next week."

"While you joking about getting your back banged out, I actually got mine cracked," Tootie said shyly.

"By who?" Scotland asked.

"Romelo." Tootie hung her head low.

"Eww… you back fuckin' wit' him again?" YaYa turned up her face.

Romelo was Tootie's son's father who was barely around and didn't help out financially.

"He said things are gonna be different this time. He really wants us to be a family. Plus, he kicked me down a few dollars to help out with RJ."

"Well that's more than what he did the last time he came around. Did you ever get the $300 he stole from you back?"

"I don't know for sure if he did it," Tootie spat. "I had a couple of people over my house that day. Anybody could'a took it."

"Don't get mad at me 'cause yo' baby daddy a thief," YaYa laughed.

"Fuck you." Tootie threw an empty Lime-A-Rita can at her.

All of the girls laughed except Scotland.

"You're quiet. What's going on with you, ladybug?" Tootie focused her attention on her.

"Y'all, I had the day from hell today," Scotland replied, replaying the accident over in her mind.

"What happened?"

Scotland took a deep breath and spilled the whole entire tea.

"I'm sorry that happened, friend." Tootie rubbed Scotland's knee.

"Not sorrier than me. I don't know how in the hell I'm going to be able to afford getting my transmission fixed, the damages to ole girl's car, my car and get my tags and plates renewed. I'm barely making it as is. This shit is just too much. Like, I just wanna disappear sometimes." Scotland said in a state of despair.

"I mean, y'all should'a seen this Lennon chick. She was dressed in head-to-toe Chanel. The bitch was bad."

"Girl, fuck her." La'Shay shot dismissively. "I can go to Frontenac Plaza tomor and boost you some Gucci shit if that's what this mini breakdown of yours is all about."

Scotland couldn't do anything but pause and laugh.

"Why don't you just ask Mama and Daddy for the money?" YaYa quizzed.

"I've borrowed enough from them," Scotland responded somberly. "Seriously, don't you guys ever think that there has to be more to life than this?" She looked at the bad-ass Johnson twins who were shooting fireworks off into the other residents' cars.

Next to them were a bunch of kids playing tag long after the street lights had gone out. Across the street, a group of teenage girls dressed in barely there booty shorts were having a twerk contest. Up the way were a click of dudes smoking weed and blasting Yo Gotti out the trunk of the car. The opposite way, several dope boys were making transactions with the local crackheads.

"What's wrong with this?" YaYa screwed up her face. "Shit is live over her tonight."

"I mean, look around you. It's a bunch of coon shit going on. I want more than this. I wanna get outta here. I wanna get out of St. Louis. Hell, I've never even been outside of St. Louis. I'm twenty-seven-years-old and I've never been on an airplane before," Scotland shrilled.

"You ain't missing shit. It ain't nothin' but a bunch of turbulence and clouds." Tootie flicked her wrist.

"Girl, you been around them white folks too long," YaYa scoffed. "You betta get yo' head out the clouds and quit all that daydreaming. This is our reality. We ain't gon' never have no million dollar home like the Frasiers unless one of us win the lottery or luck up by gettin' knocked up by a ball player. So get use to all of this 'cause this is who we are."

Scotland shook her head. Her friends would never get it. They were comfortable with the life they led but she wasn't. She'd gotten a taste of how the other half lived and she wanted in.

"I understand how you feel, friend," Tootie assured. "If you want more out of life then you have to figure out a way to get it. I used to dream about being a ballerina."

"Girl, bye; yo' ass is too fat," YaYa interjected. "You wasn't gon' be nobody's ballerina. WWE wrestler, yes, ballerina, no."

"You's a negative bitch," Tootie scowled crossing her legs.

"Don't get mad at me 'cause I speak the truth. I keep tellin' Scotland to come work at the shop wit' me. She can do a sew-in like no other. You just sittin' on money, girl." YaYa took a swig of her drink.

"Hair is your thing," Scotland sighed. "I don't wanna do sew-ins for the rest of my life."

"Then what do you want to do, Miss I Want to Have It All?" YaYa said matter-of-factly.

Scotland held her breath for a slight second before responding and looked at her friends. They were all awaiting her reply with baited breath.

"I wanna be an author."

YaYa leaned forward and spit out her drink.

"You wanna be a what?" She laughed wiping her mouth.

"An author," Scotland said self-consciously.

"Girl, if you don't get somewhere and gone wit' that. What you know about writing a damn book?"

"She did win all of those writing contest back in school." Tootie pointed out.

"This bitch won a D.A.R.E. award," YaYa sneered. "That ain't shit."

"Whatever, it was just a damn thought." Scotland sat back in her seat.

"Well, you need to quit thought'en," YaYa joked.

Feeling utterly defeated, Scotland stared absently at the ground. YaYa could see the disappointment and sadness on Scotland's face. She instantly felt horrible for going in so hard on her sister.

"Listen, ladybug." She got up and wrapped her arm around Scotland's shoulder. "I'm not trying to knock your dreams or nothing. I'm just being realistic. You ain't went to college. You've never written a book before in your life and even if you did, how would you get it published?"

"I don't know?" Scotland shrugged.

"Exactly. It's a damn pipe dream. You coming to work wit' me at the shop, now that's realistic. You gotta think smart. Stop thinking with your heart and wit' your head. We ain't nothin' but four pretty bitches from Pagedale and that's all we ever gon' be. Don't let them white folks gas you up. You gotta start making some realistic decisions about your life. You ain't gettin' no younger. You're about to be twenty-eight in a few weeks—"

"Don't remind me," Scotland cut her off.

"Speaking of your birthday, what do you wanna do?" La'Shay asked. "Cause I can get us a table at The Loft and a free bottle."

"That sounds cool," Scotland rolled her eyes.

Every year for her birthday she did the same thing. She was sick of going to The Loft.

"Oooh… can I invite Murda and Jamil?" YaYa smiled eagerly.

"You can invite Jamil. I don't want Murda nowhere around me."

"Huuuuh… you're such a party pooper. You need to invite Murda. He the one that's gon' buy out the bar."

Scotland ignored YaYa and continued to stare off into space. Maybe she was right. Maybe this was all that Scotland would ever be. Maybe she should work part-time at the shop. The mere thought made Scotland sick to her stomach. There was no way she could settle. There was nothing wrong with doing hair for a living but Scotland had plans to reach the moon. She was more than just a nanny. The world was supposed to know her name. Come hell or high water, she was going to figure out a way to better her situation.

"I GOT MY HANDS ON YO'
HIPS; NO TIME TO
BULLSHIT."

-TUPAC, NO MORE PAIN"

CHAPTER 3

A week after the accident, Scotland's car completely gave out on her. She was devastated to say the least. She hadn't been without a car in years. The only way she could get back and forth to work was to catch the bus. Scotland hadn't caught the bus since she was fifteen. She dreaded standing on the corner waiting for the bus. What if somebody she knew rode by and saw her? She would die of embarrassment.

But she had to do what she had to do to pay the bills. Scotland didn't even know how the bus system worked now. It ended up taking her three hours just to get to work because she'd mistakenly got on the wrong bus. Thank God she'd left out extra early in case something bad happened. She arrived at the Frasiers' frazzled but on time.

To her surprise, when she got there everyone was up except Mr. Frasier. The kids were in the family room watching early morning cartoons while Mrs. Frasier raced around like a mad woman getting dressed. Scotland watched amused as she ran from room to room. Mrs. Frasier was known worldwide for her home decorating skills. She'd decorated homes for Jennifer Aniston, Jennifer Lopez and the Kennedys. She'd written several New York Times Best Selling books and rubbed shoulders with the Obamas.

Even though she was rich and famous, Mrs. Frasier never let her achievements and notoriety go to her head. She was one of the most humble human beings Scotland had ever encountered. Mrs. Frasier was always there to lend a helping hand to anyone who needed help. She loved her family and friends dearly. Over the years, she and Scotland had grown quite close.

She'd shared with her on several occasions how she hated not having enough time for her family. It was hard being a working wife and mother. She tried to make it all work but sometimes the lines got blurred. She thanked God that she had someone as loving as Scotland to be there for her kids when she wasn't.

"Mrs. Frasier, you need help?" Scotland asked leaning up against the doorway to her dressing room.

"Scotland, how many times have I told you; call me Maggie."

"Uh ah, girl, we ain't playing that game. Just 'cause we're cool don't mean nothin'. You are still my boss."

"You are so silly," Mrs. Frasier shook her head and giggled.

"Where is Mr. Frasier?" Scotland looked around. "Shouldn't he be up by now?"

"Poor thing. He's not feeling well. I think he's caught that bug that's been going around."

"So he's gonna be here with me all day?" Scotland's eyes grew wide.

"Yes," Mrs. Frasier laughed putting her heels on.

"I'm pretty sure he'll be in the bed all day."

"One can only hope," Scotland mumbled.

"I heard that." Mrs. Frasier arched her brow. "Ok, now tell me." She stood up straight. "How do I look? I have a very important meeting this morning with a potential, new client."

"Oooooh… is it Beyoncé 'cause you know I'm a part of the bee hive? She is my fav!" Scotland asked eagerly.

"No, It's not mother Bey. If it was I'd be even more nervous. It's actually Gayle King."

"Oh, tell Gayle I said what's up. That's a good look for you. Shout out to you, Mrs. Frasier." Scotland raised her hand for a high-five.

"What am I going to do with you?" Mrs. Frasier high-fived her back. "Now, how do I look?"

Scotland had no idea why Mrs. Frasier was nervous about her outfit. She was a timeless, classic, beauty who could wear anything. The red, Alexander McQueen, jacquard, fit-and-flare dress she wore hugged her body in all the right places and highlighted her fiery red, shoulder-length hair and big, blue eyes perfectly. She was a perfect size two. The woman could make the ugliest outfit amazing.

"Girl, you are serving me Emma Stone realness!" Scotland snapped her fingers in a circle.

"Really? Why thank you, suga." Mrs. Frasier curtsied.

"Honey, do we have any cold medicine?" Mr. Frasier came shuffling out of their bedroom still dressed in his pajamas and robe.

His hair was ruffled and wild and the area around his nose was red from blowing his nose. The man looked a hot mess.

"It's some in the medicine cabinet." Scotland responded instead.

"I was talking to my wife." Mr. Frasier groaned, rolling his eyes.

"Excuse me. I was just trying to help yo' sick-ass," Scotland scowled. "You know what? The devil is a liar. I'm not about to do this wit' you today. Let me go fix the kids' breakfast before I say something that might get me fired." She shot Mr. Frasier a nasty look then turned and walked away.

"Why do you have to be so rude to her all the time?" Mrs. Frasier asked her husband. "She was only trying to help."

"She needs to learn her place, Maggie."

"And what exactly is her place?" Mrs. Frasier drew her head back.

"Nothing; I just want some medicine." Mr. Frasier bypassed her and headed to the kitchen.

Mrs. Frasier watched him walk away until the silhouette of his body disappeared. For months she'd been conflicted about her husband and their marriage. He was no longer the man she'd married. Lately, he'd been showing a side of himself that she'd only seen glimpses of in the beginning of their relationship. He'd always been a little snobbish and uppity but it seemed the higher they rose in society, the more he lost touch with reality. He'd become cruel and heartless.

The way he talked to the staff was appalling. She always found herself going behind him and apologizing for his rude behavior. His behavior was ridiculous and somehow began to spill over into their marriage. She was often cast away as if she were nothing. He treated the kids the same way. He barely spent any quality time with them. Liam and Busy were dying for his affection but he was always too busy to give it.

Maybe she was to blame for his sudden change. Maybe he was starting to resent her for working so much. But she was doing the best she could with what she had. Whoever or whatever was to blame, she had to figure out a way to get her marriage back on track. Divorce was not an option. When she married Paul she'd married him for life. After taking one last look in the mirror, Mrs. Frasier grabbed her Proenza Schouler striped, snakeskin clutch and headed to the kitchen.

"Bye, my loves." She kissed Liam and Busy on their foreheads. "You be good for Scotland, okay?"

The kids nodded and wrapped their tiny, little arms around their mother's neck.

"Bye, honey." She walked over to Mr. Frasier and tried giving him a kiss on the cheek but he quickly moved his face away.

"Uh ah, move. I'm sick. Don't you see I don't feel good? Why would you try to kiss me?" He snapped.

"I was just trying to say goodbye; that's all." Mrs. Frasier tried to keep a straight face.

She refused to let Scotland, the kids or even her husband see how much he'd hurt her feelings. Scotland turned her back and pretended like she hadn't seen a thing. She felt horrible for her friend.

"Ok," Mrs. Frasier forced herself to smile. "Well I'm gone. You all have a great day."

"You too and good luck on your meeting, Mrs. Frasier," Scotland smiled back.

Mrs. Frasier wasn't even out of the door before Mr. Frasier retrieved his meds and headed back to their room. He didn't even bother saying goodbye.

Twenty minutes later, Scotland and the kids sat at the kitchen island eating breakfast. The kids were thoroughly enjoying their strawberry pancakes and turkey bacon when Liam accidently knocked the entire carton of milk over onto the floor. Milk spilled and splattered everywhere. Scotland quickly jumped up and ran over to the counter to get some paper towels but there were none.

"What the hell?" She screeched.

"What the hell?" Liam mimicked her.

"Liam! Bad word! No!" She yelled, running to the linen closet to get a towel.

To her dismay, the towels were all the way up on the top shelf. She had to grab the step stool just to reach them. As she got the step stool from out of the closet, she couldn't help but overhear Mr. Frasier's phone conversation. He was inside his bedroom but the door was wide open. He obviously didn't care or didn't know how to whisper because Scotland could hear everything he was saying.

"I'm feeling better now that you called," he chuckled. "I miss you too, baby. I'll see you tomorrow, bright and early."

This nigga just don't give a damn, Scotland thought stepping up on the stool. *He just all out in the open wit' it.*

"You are so nasty," he laughed. "I love it when you talk like that."

Dirty dog, Lennon shook her head. She was eavesdropping so hard that she'd leaned forward too far and fell face forward into the linen closet causing a loud boom. Mr. Frasier came rushing out the bedroom and found her on the floor.

"I'm alright, I'm alright." Scotland shot up from the ground and fixed her clothes. "Nothing to see here."

"What are you doing?" Mr. Frasier asked with an aggravated expression on his face.

"Liam spilled some milk and I was getting a towel to get it up," Scotland shot him a tense smile.

Mr. Frasier eyed her suspiciously and resumed his conversation.

"Yeah, sorry about that. My incompetent nanny just fell." He said into the phone, closing the door behind him.

The smell of freshly brewed coffee engulfed Knight's nose causing him to awaken from his slumber. Stretching his arms and legs, he sat up wondering why the alarm clock hadn't gone off yet. Normally when he started his morning, it was still pitch black outside but the sun was shining brightly and the birds were chirping. Lennon wasn't even lying next to him. Perplexed, he looked over at his alarm clock and saw that it was 8:30am.

"The fuck?" He scratched his head.

By now he would've worked out for two hours, took a shower, got dressed, eaten breakfast and answered a few emails. Snatching the covers off of him, he got out of bed. Knight only slept in pajama bottoms. He wore no underwear to bed so his long, thick dick slapped against his thigh as he followed the smell of coffee in the air.

Knight's body was sinfully delicious. He had a set of washboard abs and muscular thighs. After a short walk, he found her at the kitchen counter talking on the phone. She was so deep in her conversation that she hadn't even heard him coming. Knight didn't think anything of her being on the phone until he noticed that she was talking in a hushed tone. Her right leg was bent back and caressing her left leg which he found odd.

"Baby." He called out for her.

Lennon jumped out of her skin and spun around.

"Honey… you scared me." She held her chest still frightened.

"My bad. I ain't mean to catch you off guard." He walked up on her and kissed her on the lips.

"Tinsley, just make sure that I have those files on my desk when I come in." She spoke in a normal tone. "Ok; thanks. See you then." She quickly ended the call.

"That was Tinsley?" Knight poured himself a cup of coffee and took a sip.

"Yeah, I have a lot of work to do today when I go into the office." Lennon placed her phone face down on the counter.

"Yeah, me too. Why didn't you wake me up this morning?"

"Cause you've been working so hard lately. I figured I'd let you sleep in. You have to take care of yourself, baby. Our wedding is right around the corner." She wrapped her arms around his waist.

"Our wedding is three months away."

"Like I said, right around the corner. There's still so much that needs to be done." Lennon removed her arms from his waist.

"Uh ah, where you going?" Knight pulled her back. "You see what you done did?" He looked down at his dick.

Lennon eyed it too. His dick was practically begging her to suck it.

"No. I have to go to work and so do you." She tried to walk away.

"Come here." Knight took her into his strong arms.

It had been weeks since they last got it in. For some reason, their sex life had gone down the drain. It didn't help that when they did have sex it was always so methodical. They only fucked in the bedroom. Lennon thought that having sex anywhere else was trashy and unsanitary. She only liked the cowgirl position because by riding him she wouldn't mess up her hair. Knight felt like it was a control thing with her. She always had to be the one in control of their relationship. It'd been that way from the start.

She'd planned out their whole entire life together. Nothing was ever spontaneous. Every day they followed the same routine unless Lennon had something else planned. Knight went along with it but he was growing tired of their mundane existence. He needed some excitement in his life. He wasn't the type of dude to be put in a box. Because of his career and his relationship with the boss' daughter, he felt like a caged animal dying to break loose.

He always had to be on his best behavior but fuck that! Right now he wanted to be on his worst behavior. Before Lennon knew it, Knight had lifted up her skirt and placed her onto the cold, marble counter top. If he didn't fuck something soon his dick was gonna break. Placing sensual kisses down her neck, he made his way down to her breasts. Just when he was about to unbutton her blouse, Lennon stopped him.

"Baby, stop. I have to go to work."

"Come on, man. My dick hard than a muthafucka," Knight groaned, caressing her hips.

"I am not having sex with you on our kitchen countertop. It's disgusting." She pushed him out of the way and hopped down. "And look what you did." She gazed down at her leg.

"You ripped my stockings! Now I'm going to have to go change them. Thanks for making me late." She shot annoyed.

"Are you really mad about some damn stockings?" Knight asked shocked.

"Yes because I told you I didn't want to."

"Get the fuck outta here wit' that bullshit," Knight waved her off. "First off, who the fuck still wears stockings? You got a million of them muthafuckas in there. One ripped pair ain't gon' make you or break you. Nah, this is about you being a fuckin' prude. Lighten the fuck up, man."

"You know what?" Lennon stared at him with venom in her eyes. "I'm going to let that little remark of yours slide because I'm late for work. But don't you ever in your life talk to me like that again. I am not one of your little slutty hoes from the old neighborhood. I am a lady and I will be treated as such." She grimaced then suddenly shot him a wicked smile. "Now, I will see you at the office."

"Yeah, see you at the office… prude." Knight shot back as she left the room.

"IT'S THE PERFECT TIME
FOR YOU TO COME
THROUGH."

-JENNI LOVETTE, BEAST

CHAPTER 4

Scotland lay snuggled underneath her black and white, flower print covers sound asleep. It had taken her hours to fall asleep due to the hunger pains inside her stomach. Earlier that day she had to choose between buying groceries or paying her light bill. The bill was past due and Ameren was threatening to turn her lights off if she didn't pay the past due amount of $204.10.

Unfortunately, after paying her cell phone bill, gas bill and putting her car in the shop, she was flat broke. She could've asked her friends or family for the money but she'd already borrowed enough from them. Scotland only had one hope and that was to race down to the Community Action Agency for help. CAASTLC was a federally funded program created to assist low-income people out of poverty conditions. Scotland had gone to them quite a few times for help. After a two hour wait, she was able to get assistance with her bill.

She was overjoyed that her electric wouldn't be turned off but after dealing with the crisis, she found herself hungry as hell. The only thing she had in her fridge was a stick of butter and a box of baking soda. Scotland cried her eyes out for hours. She didn't know how much more devastation she could take. Life was becoming too hard. She couldn't keep on living the way she was.

From the outside looking in, she looked like she had it all together. She kept her hair done all the time because she did it herself. Her makeup stayed on fleek because she did it herself as well. She stayed looking nice because she knew how to keep the clothes and shoes she had intact. Plus, Scotland knew how to dress like a million bucks on a thrifty girl's budget. She got all of her things from Forever 21, Wet Seal and if she was feeling froggy, she would splurge on an outfit from an Instagram boutique.

Lately, she didn't have enough money to by herself anything. Hell, she couldn't even buy herself a burger off the damn dollar menu. After crying and feeling sorry for herself, Scotland wiped her eyes, said a prayer to God to give her discernment and increase her territory. She also thanked Him for the many blessings he'd already bestowed upon her. Once she prayed, Scotland took a shower, slipped on a white tank top, a white, lace thong and got into bed.

Her stomach wouldn't stop growling and her head had begun to hurt because she was in desperate need of food. She might not have had anything to eat but she did have some Ibuprofen. Scotland popped two pills and put in her favorite movie of all time, *Every Girl Should Be Married* starring Betsy Drake and Cary Grant. She'd seen it over 20 times. Although she loved the movie, she had no other choice but to turn it on because her cable was off.

Scotland was so fatigued from her hectic day and lack of food that she ended up falling asleep fifteen minutes into the film. It was a little after 2:30 AM when her phone rang. Startled by the loud sound, she jumped out of her sleep and grabbed it. By the ringtone she knew it was Murda. His ringtone was Bow Wow's *Outta My System*. Scotland had been secretly awaiting his phone call for weeks.

After catching him fucking around on her for the umpteenth time with the umpteenth chick, she vowed to leave him alone for good but Murda was her kryptonite. She loved him. He would always have a special place in her heart. They'd met when she'd just turned 26. He was the nigga that every chick in St. Louis wanted.

Murda had his pick of the litter. He was unbelievably good looking. He stood tall at six feet. He rocked a low cut that had a curly texture to it. Murda's skin was the color of caramel. He had big, bushy eyebrows that complimented his intense brown eyes, strong nose and suckable lips. Murda had the kind of lips that you just wanted to kiss all day and his body was ridiculous. The boy stayed in the gym.

Most people said he resembled Trey Songz but Scotland didn't see the resemblance. Although he had boyishly, handsome, good looks, behind his charming smile lay a hustler. Murda supplied most of St. Louis with the finest heroin it had ever seen. His name rang bells in the streets. He was that dude.

In the beginning of their relationship everything was great. He treated her like a queen and spoiled her rotten then a slew of chicks started coming out of the woodwork. Every other day it was a new chick. Scotland grew tired of his playboy ways and broke up with him. But Murda always found a way to weasel his way back into her heart. She knew he was no good. Hell, she didn't even know his real name. They'd tried time and time again to make it work with no avail but there was something in his backstroke that kept her coming back for more. Scotland cleared her throat and answered the phone.

"Hello?" She answered in a raspy tone.

"Wake yo' ass up," he demanded.

"I'm up."

"You still call yo'self being mad at me?"

"Boy, ain't nobody thinkin' about you. That wasn't the first bitch I caught you wit' and it won't be the last," Scotland remarked.

"Yeah a'ight, that's what yo' mouth say. Yo' actions say different 'cause you ain't hit a nigga up in a minute."

"You ain't called me either," Scotland reminded him.

"I'm calling you now," Murda countered.

"Ooooh... you wanna brownie point? You want me to do a backflip?" Scotland replied sarcastically.

"Look, I was just callin' to check up on you. Tell you I miss you but I can see you're still on that bullshit." Murda toyed with her emotions.

"Ain't nobody mad," Scotland lied.

In all honesty, she hated that Murda couldn't be faithful. Every time he came back into her life he sold her a dream about how this time it would be different. He promised not to cheat, to take care of her and love her the way she deserved. Each time she put common sense to the side and followed her foolish heart only to be let down time and time again. All she wanted was for him to see how much she loved him. She prayed each time that he would finally see that she was enough.

"Yes, you are. You still feel some type of way. I can hear it in your voice."

Scotland poked out her lips and placed her hand up to her throat. She thought she sounded as cool as a cucumber. Maybe the hurt she felt did translate through her tone.

"You can't tell me how I feel," she scoffed.

"Ok, if you ain't mad then come open the door."

Scotland's heart stopped beating. *No way is this nigga at my door,* she thought nervously. Her heart beat a mile a minute as she tiptoed to the living room and peeked out the blinds. Sure enough, Murda's Mercedes-Benz S65 AMG Coupe was parked in front of her door.

"You bold. How you just gon' pop up at my house unannounced? I could have a nigga up in here," she grinned.

"Man, please, you ain't got nobody in there. Open the door."

"Bye." Scotland ended the call.

With the speed of lightening, she ran to the bathroom and gargled with a cap full of mouthwash. Grabbing a face towel she quickly ran it under some warm water, applied soap to it, washed under her arms, breasts and in-between her legs. There was no way she was gonna be caught slipping around Murda. Scotland's philosophy was that a woman must always be on point in the looks and smell department.

Once that was done, she put on deodorant, sprayed herself with perfume, threw on a new pair of panties and casually walked to the door as if she'd effortlessly strolled out of bed. Scotland unlocked the door and linked eyes with Murda. The seat of her panties instantly became wet. The man was fine as fuck. He rocked a white, red and black Chicago Bulls hat, matching jersey, gold, iced out chain, black, fitted jeans and a pair of Jordan Spizike sneakers.

"You gon' let me in?" He grinned.

"Yeah," Scotland stepped to the side.

She could smell the scent of his Valentino Uomo cologne as he walked by. Locking the door behind him, Scotland turned and looked him square in the eyes. Murda was drunk and high which was somehow a major turn on for her. Murda eyed her lustfully. The barely there tank top she wore kissed her hardened nipples and clung tight to her waist.

"Come here." He demanded, pulling her into him by the bottom of her top.

Scotland didn't even try to fight it. She missed him. It had been months since she'd been touched by a man so she allowed herself to be vulnerable. She was tired of putting up her guard with him. It was useless. His lips were on hers and his hands palmed her ass cheeks. Closing her eyes, Scotland wrapped her arms around his neck and allowed his tongue to explore hers. The potent taste of Hennessy danced on his lips. She quickly became drunk off his kisses.

"I knew yo' ass missed me," Murda announced proudly.

"Whatever." Scotland laughed pulling away. "Come on; let's go upstairs," she said, walking up the steps.

Murda watched enthusiastically as her bare ass cheeks bounced with each step she took. He couldn't wait to bend her over, pull her hair and hit it from the back. In her bedroom he noticed that hadn't much changed since the last time he was there. Her queen-size, wooden bed frame was still being held up by a stack of books on both sides.

Her 40 inch flat screen sat on top of her black dresser and beside her bed was a nightstand she'd found at the thrift store and painted it black. Scotland's place was nice, clean and quant. She didn't possess anything of value but she made her apartment look nice with what she had. Murda sat on the edge of the bed and looked at the television screen.

"You watching this shit again?" He asked, referring to the movie she'd fallen asleep on.

"Yes, it's my favorite movie."

"Man, turn this shit off. Turn on MTV Jams or something."

"Can't... my cable's cut off." Scotland confirmed sitting at the head of the bed.

"How much you owe?"

"$197."

Murda reached inside his pocket and pulled out a thick wad of cash.

"Here." He peeled off $500 and gave it to her. "Get ya' shit cut back on."

"Uh ah, I can't take that from you." She tried to give the money back to him.

"Man, here, take it." He vehemently placed the money into her hand.

Scotland didn't want to take it but she desperately needed the money.

"Thank you," she said, palming the money in her hand.

She was thankful for the blessing but hated feeling like a charity case. Murda kicked off his shoes and took off his jewelry. Standing up, he pulled his jersey off over his head. Scotland's eyes danced over his rippled six-pack in awe. Murda was like an edible piece of candy and she wanted a bite. Dressed in only his boxer briefs and jeans, he climbed on top of her.

She lay on her back with her legs spread open. She thought maybe they'd talk more but it was apparent Murda had other plans. His dick was hard and he wanted some after-the-club pussy. She wanted the D but after taking the money she couldn't help but to feel like a prostitute. All of those thoughts vanished once Murda placed his tongue on her nipple.

His tongue was creating magic on her breasts when she heard the familiar sound of him unzipping his jeans. Murda never wasted any time. Foreplay with him was always brief. Thank God he had a good dick game to make up for it. Scotland felt the tip of his dick rub against her clit.

"You need to put on a condom, bruh," she informed.

"Since when?" Murda asked taken aback.

"Since I caught you with that bitch," Scotland replied, twisting her lips to the side.

"Are you for real?"

"Yes."

Murda groaned and reached inside his pocket. A few seconds later the condom was on and Scotland laid face down, ass up. The sound of her ass slapping against his pelvis filled the room as she felt her first orgasm in months erupt. Murda came soon after. The two of them went another round and then fell asleep.

The next morning, Scotland awoke with a smile on her face. Flashes of the previous night replayed in her mind. She expected to find Murda lying sound asleep next to her but when she rolled over she saw that he was gone. Perplexed, she sat up and called his name but got no answer. *Maybe he left out for a minute,* she thought grabbing the phone. Scotland dialed his number. A few rings later the line picked up.

"Hello?" A girl answered the phone.

Scotland quickly took the phone away from her ear to check and make sure she'd dialed the right number. Sure enough, she'd dialed the right number.

"Hellooooo?" The girl said again.

Ok don't even trip. Maybe it's one of his sisters, Scotland told herself.

"May I speak to Murda?"

"Who is this?" The girl asked with an attitude.

"Scotland; who is this?" She shot back.

"This is Ebony; his girlfriend."

The only thing that Scotland could do was close her eyes and shake her head. She'd set herself up for this bullshit. She knew Murda was no good. Each time she came in contact with him he proved it.

"His girlfriend, huh?" She said in disbelief.

"Yeah, what y'all fuckin' around or something?"

"Nah, not anymore." Scotland hung up the phone.

Pissed that she'd once again allowed herself to be bamboozled by Murda, she lay back on her pillow and glared at the ceiling. The only thing she could think was that this was one hell of a way to start off her 28th birthday.

"YOU NIGGAS CHANGE LIKE THE SEASONS AND YOU DON'T GIVE US A REASON."

-JENNI LOVETTE, PAPER HEART

CHAPTER 5

At around seven o'clock that night, Knight, Lennon and her parents, Joan and Douglas Whitmore, sat quietly at Cielo Restaurant & Bar. Cielo was located in the Four Seasons Hotel. It was known for its modern Italian cuisine and stunning skyline views from each table. Everyone was enjoying their meal while making small talk here and there.

Knight chewed his food slowly. He was trying his best to stay awake. Being around Lennon and her parents was like watching paint dry. Her parents reminded him of Aunt Viv and Uncle Phil from the Fresh Prince of Bel-Air. Her father, especially, looked like Uncle Phil.

Once again, Knight's birthday was boring as hell. Every year he and Lennon along with her parents did the same exact thing. They had dinner, wine, talked business, ate dessert and parted ways. After dinner he and Lennon would return home. She'd give him his gift. Each year he received the same thing… a watch. It was always a designer watch but a watch no less.

He'd pretend to be surprised; they'd have sex then go to bed. Well this year, Knight was over their boring birthday ritual. He'd turned 33. He was still young. Knight wanted to party. He wanted to turn up. He wanted to be around his family and friends but his family and friends were never invited to dinner. When he wanted to spend time with them he had to do it on his own time.

Lennon's parents had never even met his mother. It was like he and Lennon led separate lives in some aspects. Something had to give though. If things kept going the way they had been, he was sure to snap.

"So, Knight, how does it feel to be the big three-three?" Mrs. Whitmore asked sweetly.

"I really don't feel any different to be honest with you," Knight replied honestly. "It just seems like another regular, old day to me." He sighed, bored out of his mind.

"How can you say that?" Lennon said astounded. "I mean, look where we are. Look how far you've come. Years ago this would've only been a dream for you." She reminded him.

"You're right, except I'm no longer dreaming. I'm wide the fuck awake," Knight responded annoyed.

"Language, please." Lennon shook her head repulsed by his behavior.

"Awww… somebody's feeling cranky." Mrs. Whitmore pinched Knight's cheek.

Knight forced himself to laugh and continued eating. It astounded him that Lennon thought they were having a good time. Being around a bunch of stuffy white folks and eating overpriced Italian food was not his idea of fun.

"You know, Knight, if you keep pulling in these A-list clients like you have been, you'll be getting your very own corner office sooner than you think," Mr. Whitmore announced.

"I'm trying, sir," Knight smiled.

He was actually pleased that Mr. Whitmore had taken notice of how hard he'd been working. Being an agent wasn't his initial dream but it served its purpose, which was to get him and his family out the hood.

"Mmm," Mrs. Whitmore swallowed her sip of wine. "How is the wedding plans coming along, dear?"

"I finally booked the venue so I'm super excited about that," Lennon gleamed. "Next week I'm going to take Mitzi and Carla to get fitted for their bridesmaid's dresses."

Knight sat perplexed. His twin sisters, Sierra and Nicole, along with his other sister Mya were supposed to be her bridesmaids too.

"Are my sisters gonna meet you there or something?" He asked.

Lennon paused and looked at her mother. Mrs. Whitmore diverted her eyes elsewhere and resumed drinking her wine.

"Umm, about that. I was thinking that my bridal party would only consist of Mitzi, Carla, Julisa, Morgan and Beth."

"So you've replaced my sisters?" Knight sat back in his seat.

"They're my friends, honey," Lennon pouted.

"You're white friends - who you barely talk to," Knight challenged.

"Yes, I do," Lennon stifled back a laugh.

She was lying through her teeth. Knight got what was going on though and was pissed. Lennon didn't want his sisters to be a part of the wedding because they weren't as sophisticated as her friends. His sisters were a little rough around the edges but they were good girls.

"I haven't asked for much but I really want my sisters to be a part of the wedding," he continued.

"I mean, honey, let's be honest here. I'm not really close to your sisters. I barely know them."

"And I'm not that close with your brothers but they're my groomsmen," Knight rebutted.

"That's different," Lennon shrugged.

"How? How is that different?" Knight placed down his fork.

"It just is." Lennon tried her damndest not to laugh in his face.

There was no way on God's green earth that she was gonna allow Knight's trashy, ghetto sisters to be a part of her wedding. If she had it her way, none of his family or friends would even be there.

"A'ight." Knight nodded his head.

He'd had enough of Lennon's bougie bullshit.

"If you'll excuse me." He scooted his chair back and stood up.

"Have a seat, son; calm down." Mr. Whitmore tried to defuse the situation.

"No, let him go," Lennon quipped, waving him off.

"Mr. and Mrs. Whitmore, it was a pleasure." Knight bid them farewell then walked off.

"Honey, go after him." Mrs. Whitmore urged her daughter.

Lennon rolled her eyes and exhaled. She knew she'd pissed Knight off but she honestly didn't care. He'd get over it eventually, like he always did.

"Lennon, this is not the way to start off a marriage," Mr. Whitmore informed.

Aggravated, Lennon threw down her napkin and followed Knight outside.

The warm, August, night air kissed her skin.

"Where are you going?" She asked.

"Can you bring my car around, please," Knight said to the valet.

"Sure." The valet said jogging off.

"Knight?" Lennon called out.

Knight stood with his back to her and ignored her.

"I know you hear me talking to you." Lennon got up in his face.

"You better back the fuck up." Knight warned.

Lennon could see the veins in his neck popping out. When he got this angry she knew it was wise to simmer down a bit.

"So you're going to leave your birthday dinner because you're not getting your way?"

"I'm gonna leave before I do something I'm gonna regret, like fuck you up." Knight looked past her.

"I'm right here not over there." Lennon forced him to look at her by yanking his face her way.

"Don't put your hands on me." Knight pushed her hand away.

Caught off guard by his reaction, Lennon stumbled back. Everyone outside could feel the tension between them.

"Have you lost your goddamn mind?" Lennon hissed, gathering her composure. "Now is not the time for you to be throwing one of your little hissy fits. Now I'm done with this nonsense. Come back inside and finish your meal. My parents are waiting on us."

"Yo, who the fuck you think you talkin' to? I'm not one of your servants. I don't work for you."

"Are you really that upset?" Lennon asked shocked. "You can't be mad because I don't want your sisters to be my bridesmaids?"

Knight ignored her once again.

"Fine, if it means that much to you then they can be in the wedding. Now stop acting silly and come back inside." Lennon tugged on his arm.

"You don't get it." Knight shook his head.

"Get what?" Lennon stomped her foot. "That you're acting like a child."

"Walk away." Knight urged feeling himself about to explode.

"Sir, your car is ready." The valet handed him his keys.

"Thank you." Knight gave him a fifty dollar tip.

"You're seriously about to leave?" Lennon folded her arms across her chest.

Knight ignored her and opened the driver side door.

"Knight!" Lennon called out for him.

Knight reluctantly stopped and looked at her. Lennon approached him and gazed up into his eyes. She figured a softer approach might work.

"Why are we fighting? It's your birthday. Let's just finish dinner. We can talk about this later." She spoke in a baby voice while caressing the side of his face.

"There's nothing to talk about. As far as I'm concerned, there might not even be a wedding." Knight shot getting inside of the car.

Staggered by his confession, Lennon watched with fear in her eyes as he drove away.

After being duped by Murda, once again, Scotland didn't even want to celebrate her birthday anymore. August 21st had officially become the worst day of her life. She couldn't believe that Murda would come over and awaken

74

sleeping feelings all the while knowing he had a girlfriend. She was over being his fool. That would be the last time he would get the opportunity to play her. At least she got $500 out of the deal but Scotland couldn't even get excited about that.

It was her birthday and she wanted to buy herself some new weave, an outfit and get her nails done but she couldn't be reckless and ignore her bills. No, she would use the money to get her cable cut back on and get her car out of the shop. Depressed over her ever dwindling finances, Scotland made it up in her mind that she didn't even wanna go out anymore for her birthday. What would be the point?

Her hair desperately needed to be redone, she didn't want to wear an outfit she already had and she couldn't even show her feet 'cause the polish on them had chipped. Thankfully, her girls came through for her in the clutch. As a present, YaYa styled her hair for free and La'Shay gave her money to get her eyebrows arched, a full set of stiletto nails and a pedicure.

Tootie felt horrible that she couldn't buy Scotland anything for her birthday but she promised to buy her a drink at the club. The only thing Scotland had to worry about was an outfit. She could've borrowed something from YaYa 'cause they wore the same size but she wanted something new, something that was hers. It had been ages since she did something nice for herself.

After pondering it, Scotland decided to forgo getting her car out of the shop that day. Instead, she was going to buy herself an outfit, wear it out that night and return it the next day. That way she'd be able to shine bright like a diamond on her birthday and get her car out of the shop that following Monday. It was a win-win situation. She couldn't lose.

Scotland walked into The Loft that night looking and feeling like a million bucks. Her face was beat to perfection. She rocked a winged eye, long, wispy lashes and a bold, red lip. Her fresh, silver, ombre weave was parted to the right. It was so long that it cascaded down her back almost touching her butt. Her outfit consisted of a black, wide brim hat, $200 white, spaghetti strap, low V-neck dress that exposed her side boob and toned back.

The only jewelry she wore was a gold, men's watch from H&M. A pair of white, lace up heels completed her edgy, angelic ensemble. Scotland was on top of the world. She and the girls popped bottles of Ciroc in the VIP section all night until a fight broke out and somebody started shooting. The club was immediately evacuated and shut down early. After running for their lives, the girls sat inside of YaYa's 2007 Eclipse debating where to go next. It was only 1:00. The night was still young and Scotland wanted to get good use out of her dress.

"Let's go to Exo," Tootie suggested.

"Uh, no." Scotland turned up her face. "Don't nobody go there no more. Hell, I don't even think it's open anymore."

"What about SoHo?" La'Shay chimed in.

"Now that's the move," YaYa high-fived her.

A short car ride later, the girls got in line and waited their turn to get inside of the club. Once they got up to the door the doorman checked their ID's and told them it would be $25 to get in.

"Twenty-five dollars?" Scotland said in disbelief. "Is it a special event going on tonight or something?"

"Yeah, Karrueche Tran is here tonight?"

"Oh, hell naw. I ain't paying no damn twenty-five dollars to see no damn Kara Coochie." She turned around. "Y'all ready to go? I ain't paying for that bullshit."

"I wanna go in. I'll pay your way." YaYa whispered so the other people in line couldn't hear.

"No, thank you. I can put that twenty-five dollars to better use."

"Huuuuuh," YaYa groaned. "Where we gon' go then?"

"I don't know, not here."

"If you're not gonna come in, I'ma need for y'all to step to the side." The doorman said.

Just when Scotland was about to step to the side she spotted Murda, his pot'nahs and some big booty bitch coming their way. He had his arm wrapped around the girl's neck. Scotland's heart dropped down to her knees. Murda walked right pass the line and headed straight for the door. He never had to wait in line like everybody else.

"Really, God?" Scotland looked up at the sky.

Her night was going from bad to worse.

"Damn, there go Murda." YaYa perked up. "You can get him to pay all of our way in." She grinned with glee.

"I will not."

"Girl, bye." YaYa waved her off. "Hey, Murda." She smiled brightly.

"Damn, what's up?" He hugged all the girls saving Scotland for last. "You look nice." He eyed her up and down lustfully.

"Thanks." Scotland replied, coldly. "You wanna introduce me to your friend?" She cocked her head to the side and eyed the girl.

"Ebony, this my homegirl, Scotland."

Homegirl, Scotland thought outraged.

"Ohhhhhh... so you're Scotland?" Ebony said unimpressed.

"Yep, live in the flesh." Scotland arched her brow.

"And that ain't sayin' much." Ebony swung her long hair to the side. "You ain't all that, mama."

"Who she talkin' to?" Scotland turned and asked her friends.

"It look like she talkin' to you, friend," La'Shay replied, taking off her earrings ready to fight.

"Oh, so you a hater? This bitch ordered an extra-large haterade wit' an extra side of hatertots. She needs to open a hatering business 'cause it's clear that she's living in Haterville," Scotland bounced back and forth like a ghetto girl.

"I'm far from a hater, ma. I just know I look better than you." Ebony pursed her lips.

"Yo, y'all coming in or what?" Murda asked to break up the tension. "This muthafucka look like it's jumping."

"Yeah, we were just about to—" YaYa spoke before being cut off by Scotland.

"Leave! We were just about to leave. You know, since it's my BIRTHDAY we're going to club hop tonight." Scotland emphasized the word birthday.

Murda could see the hurt in her eyes that he'd caused. He felt bad for playing with her heart but she knew what type of dude he was.

"You want me to pay your way in?" Murda asked.

"Why are you even offering?" Ebony said with an attitude. "This broke ho can't pay her own way in?"

"Bitch, don't worry about me!" Scotland pointed her finger in Ebony's face like a gun. "You need to be concerned wit' yourself and that each one, teach-one-ass education you have." She rolled her neck ready to buck.

"Ay yo, chill." Murda stepped in-between her and Ebony.

"Check your girl. Before I punch her in the fuckin' mouth," Scotland warned.

"Y'all doing too much. I'm about to head in. I'll holla at you later, ladybug." Murda gave her one last look then walked inside.

"Come on, y'all, let's go." Scotland walked towards the car.

"She trippin'." YaYa sucked her teeth.

"It's her birthday. If the birthday girl don't wanna go in then we're not going in." Tootie followed behind Scotland.

"Shut up, Tootie." YaYa playfully mushed her in the back of her head.

Back inside the car she turned the engine on annoyed.

"Why you ain't wanna go in?" She turned the engine back off.

"Cause I didn't want to." Scotland shrugged dismissively.

She didn't want to or feel like telling her friends about the night before. She didn't wanna hear a bunch of I told you so's. She already felt stupid enough.

"You buggin' right now." YaYa shook her head.

"I mean, if you wanna go in so bad, you can. I'll sit in the car." Scotland shot with an attitude.

"Girl, you are not about to sit in no car on your birthday," La'Shay confirmed.

"I mean, she acting like she about to diiiiiiiiie if she don't go in. Every time she see Murda she get to acting like a damn thirst bucket." Scotland spat sounding like Tamar Braxton.

"Girl, fuck you. I'm tryin' to make sure you have a nice birthday. Who knows when the next time yo' broke-ass gon' have some money to go somewhere." YaYa shot back.

"Really, bitch?" Scotland furrowed her brows.

"What? Don't get mad at me 'cause I speak the truth."

"You ain't have to say that." Scotland mean-mugged her.

"You started it and I finished it. Now what?" YaYa looked at her and rolled her neck.

"Girl, whatever; ain't nobody got time to argue wit' you," Scotland waved her off. "This shit is a wrap. Take me home."

"Y'all stop," Tootie pleaded. "Ain't nobody going home. We're about to go to another spot, have a few drinks and kick it."

"I ain't going nowhere wit' her. Fuck her." Scotland said adamantly.

"The feeling is fuckin' mutual, broke-ass ho." YaYa sneered. Y'all petty than a muthafucka." La'Shay laughed applying more lipstick to her lips. "Look, I know about this li'l hipster spot over on the South Side called Blank Space. It's pretty chill so we're gonna go there. Hopefully by the time we get there you two ig'nant bitches will be good."

"As long as she don't say shit to me, I'm straight." YaYa pulled out of the parking space.

Scotland did as she was asked and kept quiet. Instead, she hit YaYa with the middle finger and gazed out of the window.

81

"THE UNIVERSE'S ENERGY
DOESN'T LIE."

-JHENE AIKO FEAT.
KENDRICK LAMAR, STAY
READY (WHAT A LIFE)

CHAPTER 6

An eerily quiet car ride later, they pulled in front of Blank Space. Scotland looked around perplexed. They were on Cherokee Street. The block was filled with restaurants, bars and boutiques. A bunch of white hipsters and rockers strolled up and down the street. She felt out of place but comfortable at the same time.

"La'Shay, where the hell you got us at?" YaYa's nostrils flared as she got out of the car.

"Girl, hush. Give it a chance. It be some tenders up in here."

"Lies you tell." YaYa said disgusted by her surroundings.

"Come on." La'Shay pulled her in by the arm.

Scotland and the girls walked into the dimly lit bar and paid $5 to get in. It was packed inside. Scotland examined the room. Blank Space was a three-story venue. On the main floor there were wooden floors, a bar and a mini stage where the DJ was spinning Hip Hop tracks. On the walls were eclectic pieces of artwork. It was a pretty cool spot. Nobody was trying to be pretentious or bougie. Everybody was very chill and laidback. Scotland instantly felt at home.

"This is not my cup of tea." YaYa looked around suspiciously. "Where the killas at? I feel like I'm in one of SZA weird-ass music videos."

"Shut up." La'Shay playfully hit her on the arm. "It ain't that bad. Come on let's sit down."

Scotland and the girls took a seat at a white, wooden bench by the stairs.

"So you would rather be here than at SoHo?" YaYa asked Scotland.

"Yes. I like it here." Scotland pursed her lips.

"Yo' weird-ass would like this bullshit." YaYa crossed her legs and pulled out her phone.

She figured getting on Instagram would drown out her surroundings. Up the street, Knight and his boys, Twan and Amir, parked their cars. The first thing Knight did after leaving Lennon at the restaurant was hit up his pot'nahs. It had been a minute since they kicked it together. The fellas agreed to meet up with their boy. Knight asked that they give him an hour to run home and change.

At home, he changed out of his Hugo Boss suit and threw on a Diesel, dirty-wash, blue jean jacket, Givenchy t-shirt, dark, denim jeans and a pair of Nike Foamposite sneakers. A gold chain and a gold, lion head, pinky ring completed his swagged-out look. Shedding the suit felt like a 500 pound weight had been lifted off his shoulders. He loved dressing casual but hardly ever got a chance to.

Whenever he threw on a pair of J's or Tims, Knight felt more like his old self. Once he was dressed he met up with his boys at Cuetopia Billiards & Sport Bar. Twan and Amir were hood niggas to the heart. They were both former D-boys that had flipped their money into legit businesses. Despite them being businessmen, they still moved like they were supplying the streets. Twan and Amir moved in

84

silence. They never left the house without a burner. They were always prepared for a nigga to run up.

Inside of Cuetopia, Knight soaked up the laidback, down-home environment. He missed being around his people. Being around people who simply didn't give a fuck about anything else except having a good time was refreshing. Knight, Twan and Amir played a few rounds of pool, drank their faces off and left. They decided to hit up The Loft but by the time they got there the club was closed because of a shootout. After that, they swung by The City but it was wack so they bounced. Amir then suggested they hit up the South Side to see what was popping over there.

Knight had never kicked it on the South Side but decided to give it a shot. He honestly didn't care where they went. All he wanted was another drink in his system. He wasn't willing to let his buzz die down. The guys strolled past a few bars and stumbled upon Blank Space. The place was packed and seemed to be jumping. Plus, there were black people inside so they decided to go in.

After paying the cover charge and getting their hand stamped, they headed to the back towards the DJ booth. Knight leaned up against the exposed brick wall and nodded his head to the beat of Drake's *0 to 100*. Everybody on the dance floor was rapping along to the lyrics. The crowd was hype as hell. The vibe of the room reminded him of D'Angelo's *Lady* video. Knight lived for this type of shit.

"Where all these weird-ass white people come from?" Twan gazed around the room confused.

"I don't know," Knight laughed.

Twan wasn't used to kicking it around a mixed crowd.

"I'll be back." Knight announced heading to the bar.

It was time for another drink.

"Ay, let me get a vodka cranberry." He asked the bartender.

"A'ight." The tall, lanky bartender replied.

As Knight awaited his drink, Scotland turned and asked the girls if they wanted something from the bar.

"Here." Tootie dug inside her Coach bag and handed her a $20 bill. "Get us both a drink. I'll have whatever you're having."

"Thanks for the birthday drink, girl." Scotland beamed standing up. "Watch my purse."

At the bar she stood directly behind a tall, bald-headed man and awaited her turn. She hated being so close to the man but the place was so packed that she had no choice but to be. Thankfully, he smelled delicious.

"Here you go." The bartender handed Knight his drink.

Knight took the drink, handed the bartender a twenty and told him to keep the change. He had no idea that there was someone standing behind him. As he spun around, his right elbow knocked Scotland square in the jaw causing him to lose grip of his drink. Before either of them knew it, his entire drink had spilled all over her chest. Stunned by the blow to the face and cold wet drink on her breasts, Scotland stood speechless with her mouth wide open. Neither of them could believe what had just happened.

"No, God, no." She finally uttered with her head down.

"Are you a'ight?" Knight asked horrified.

"Does it look like I'm alright? You just hit me in the fuckin' face and spilled your drink all over me!" Scotland screeched, not even bothering to look the culprit in the eye.

"My bad, I ain't know you were behind me."

"You didn't know 'cause you weren't fuckin' paying attention! Look at what you did! You ruined my dress!" Scotland shouted finally giving the man eye contact.

All of the air from her lungs escaped when she realized it was Knight.

"You've got to be fuckin' kidding me! You?" She squinted her eyes. "You did this to me?"

"Damn… you're the girl that ran into my fiancée. British, right?" He smiled fondly at the sight of her.

"It's Scotland, asshole." She eyed him sideways. "Can you give me a napkin, please?"

"Yeah." Knight grabbed a handful.

Without hesitation or permission, he proceeded to rub the stain. With each stroke his hand massaged her boobs.

"So you gon' ruin my dress and molest me?" Scotland said in disbelief.

"Trust me, if I was molesting you, you'd know."

"Give me the damn napkins." Scotland snatched them from his hand. "What the fuck am I going to do now?" She spoke out loud to herself.

"I'm fucked."

The dress was her money to get her car out of the shop. Now that it was ruined she'd have to wait two pay periods to get it out. Her next check had to go towards her rent.

"Can I ever catch a break?" A tear fell from her eye.

"Damn, it's that bad? Chill, it's just a dress." Knight tried to soothe her.

"Just a dress?" Scotland fumed. "If only you knew how stupid you sound right now. I can't even afford this fuckin' dress! But today's my birthday and I wanted something nice to wear so I bought it. I was gonna return it tomorrow but now I can't because of you!"

Knight felt like shit. The look of distress and sorrow on Scotland's face tore him apart.

"That's crazy; today is my birthday too."

"Happy fuckin' birthday," Scotland spat.

"For real, I ain't know it was like that," Knight said sincerely.

"Yeah, it's like that," Scotland shot. "Where is the restroom?" She asked a random girl.

The girl pointed to the back of the bar. Inside the restroom Scotland cried and wet a paper towel. Through her tears she tried wiping the stain out to no avail.

"You're so fuckin' stupid. You should've never spent the money on this dress in the first place," she cried. "The one time I'm irresponsible and look what happens." She snapped, throwing the paper towels in the trash can.

To her surprise, when she left out the restroom, Knight was standing there waiting on her.

"What you want to spill another drink on me?" She sighed heavily, giving him the death glare.

"Come here." Knight took her by the hand.

He barely knew her but for some strange reason he felt like he needed to protect her. Their connection was weird. Staring into her eyes, he reveled in her beauty. She was absolutely stunning. Her big, brown, doe-shaped eyes entrapped him. But behind her hypnotic eyes he saw a woman that was falling apart. The tears that fell from her eyes weren't there just because of a ruined dress. There was more to her sorrow. Knight found himself wanting to ease her pain.

"You're too pretty to be crying." He wiped her tears.

Scotland continued to gaze into his eyes and found herself entranced. With each tear he wiped away she melted. Her whole entire body fell limp. She was putty in his hands. He was way too sexy to be caressing her face in such a sweet, gentle way. If he kept it up, she was sure to take him in the restroom and fuck him. Scotland knew he had a girl but from the look in his eyes she could tell he wanted her as much as she wanted him. There was a reason God kept bringing them together.

"You know that I stopped crying like a minute ago. You can stop rubbing my face now." She spoke just above a whisper.

"What if I don't wanna stop?" Knight traced his thumb across her lips.

Scotland couldn't help it. She couldn't stop herself. Before she realized what she was doing her tongue was licking the tip of his thumb. Knight watched eagerly as her tongue flickered in and out her mouth. At that moment, Lennon and their upcoming nuptials were a distant memory. He forcefully took Scotland into his arms and held her close.

Her warm breasts were pressed up against his broad chest. Scotland's arms rested at her sides. She was so caught up in the moment that she couldn't breathe. She didn't know what to do. Knight leaned forward. His face was inches away from hers. They gazed into each other's eyes, exchanging breaths. Scotland didn't know what was happening but the thrill of it all was enticing as hell. She'd never wanted another human being more in her life. It was as if they were on their own little private island where no one else existed.

"What are we doing?" She asked as her chest heaved up and down with anticipation.

"I don't know." Knight placed his lips upon hers.

She tasted like the finest wine. Each stroke of her tongue sparked a fire deep down inside of his belly. She was something different that he had no idea he'd been craving. Neither of them cared if anybody was watching as they devoured one another. Their bodies dared not to part. Knight was spellbound by her unearthly charm. She was the missing link he'd been searching for. Scotland gripped the back of his head and enveloped his lips. She never wanted to release him. They'd unknowingly become one.

"Scotland!" Tootie yelled getting her attention.

Snapping back to reality, Scotland unwillingly came up for air. She quickly stepped back and fixed her dress.

"Girl, I've been looking all over for you." Tootie looked her and Knight up and down. "I didn't know you'd found you a li'l boo." She smirked, biting her lower lip.

"Umm, Knight, this is my friend Tootie. Tootie, this is Knight." Scotland blushed.

"Knight?" Tootie said curiously. "Ain't the woman car you ran into fiancé name Knight?"

"Yeah, this is him." Scotland replied as a rush of shame washed over her.

"Ohhhhhhhhhh... excuse me," Tootie chuckled. "We ready to go. We'll be outside in the car waiting. Nice to meet you, Knight." Tootie waved goodbye, grinning from ear to ear.

Once she was out of sight, Scotland focused her attention back on Knight.

"Yo, my bad. I was out of line. That should've never happened." He apologized before she could.

Knight had no business kissing another woman when he had a woman at home waiting on him. What he'd done was unforgiveable but he wanted Scotland in the worst way.

"Right. That was weird," she agreed. "Ummmm," she paused. "I gotta go. I'll call you when I have the money for my first payment."

"Bet." Knight placed his hands inside his pockets. "Get home safe."

"I will." Scotland gave him a warm smile and sauntered off.

As she walked through the crowd, she savored the sweet taste of him that was left over on her lips. Knight was forbidden fruit. She knew she couldn't have him but every fiber of her being craved him. She'd had her first hit of him and now wanted more.

"WE KISSED; I FELL UNDER YOUR SPELL."

-MILEY CYRUS, WRECKING BALL

CHAPTER 7

The following Monday, Scotland sat on the bus gazing absently out the window. As usual, her neck, back and feet hurt from her constant on the go schedule with the kids but all of the pain faded as visions of Knight flashed before her eyes. Since their steamy run-in she hadn't been able to get him out of her mind. If she could, she would relive that night over and over again.

The touch of his hand and the comforting feel of his lips engulfed her. She'd encountered plenty of men in her lifetime but none like him. He was special but all Scotland could do was fantasize about him. He would never be hers. He was out of her league. Men like him never went for girls like her. She wasn't poised or sophisticated like Lennon.

She was from the hood. She was loud, flashy and cursed way too much. She was a broke-ass nanny for God sake. Why would he ever want her? For a man like Knight she'd be just another notch on his belt and nothing more. They were complete opposites and came from two different worlds. The kiss they shared was just that: a kiss. Nothing more would come from it.

Get yo' head out the clouds, ladybug; she could hear YaYa say that night after they left the bar. *That nigga just tryin' to fuck. Remember, he got a bad bitch at home. What he want wit' you?* Scotland hated when YaYa was right. If she hadn't ran into Lennon's car Knight would have never looked at her twice. She didn't know why he'd kissed her or held her like she was his but she had to forget it ever happened.

Getting caught up in pointless emotions was a thing of the past. Scotland was twenty-eight now. It was time to be realistic. She couldn't continue to live in a make-believe, fantasy world where Prince Charming would ride in on his white horse and save the day. She had to be her own hero because coming from where she was from, good dudes where few and far between.

They were mythical creatures that were only seen every blue moon. Instead of focusing on a man who was already promised to another, Scotland had to come up with a plan to better her financial situation. She was drowning in bills. *Maybe I should give this writing thing a shot,* she thought. She'd already written three chapters. If she continued and wrote the entire thing maybe she could submit it to a few publishing companies. But Scotland didn't even know if what she had written was dope or not. She liked it but to everyone else it could be wack as hell.

"I don't know; I'll figure it out." She mumbled underneath her breath as she pressed the stop button.

The bus driver let her off right in front of her complex.

"See you tomorrow," she smiled, getting off the bus.

Scotland reached inside her purse and grabbed her keys. A glimmer of joy shined in her heart. She was only steps away from her home. Her feet felt like needles were in them. She couldn't wait to get inside and lie down. To her surprise, as she approached her door, she found a huge box on her doorstep.

She hadn't ordered a damn thing so the delivery man must've left the package on accident. Scotland examined the box and saw that it was addressed to her. Even more confused, she checked the return address. It was from Knight. Scotland damn near passed out.

"This can't be from him." She gasped picking up the box and carrying it into the house.

Upstairs she didn't hesitate to drop her purse and keys on the floor. Scotland sat the package on the kitchen counter and grabbed a knife. Excited, she cut a slit through the top of the box. After tossing the brown packing paper to the side, she found a black and white Dolce & Gabbana box. Scotland's eyes bulged at the sight.

She'd never been so close to any designer label. Drool almost slid out of her mouth as she pulled the top off. Bewildered by what she saw inside, she stepped back and leaned up against the wall. Scotland had never seen anything more beautiful. With ease, she lifted a black, strappy, lace dress with a sheer flounce hem out of the box.

It was magnificent. Everything about it screamed rich bitch. Knight had even picked out the right size. Scotland traced her fingertips across the expensive fabric and began to cry. No one had ever bought her something so delicate and expensive.

Stunned, she looked back inside the box to see if there was more. She found a black envelope with her name on it. Scotland placed the dress down and opened the envelope. Three, crisp, one hundred-dollar bills fell to the floor and landed at her feet. Scotland swiftly picked the money up and read the small note.

This is for ruining your dress.

Knight

P.S. Happy Belated Birthday.

Scotland must've read the note a thousand times. She didn't know whether to scream, run, jump or do a somersault. She was so overwhelmed. The fact that Knight had taken the time to do something so sweet for her let her know that she'd been on his mind too. Her stomach filled with butterflies. She appreciated his gesture but she could never keep the gifts. It was all too much. She had to return them to him. Scotland pulled out her phone and dialed his number.

"You've reached the Whitmore Agency. How may I direct your call?" Knight's secretary answered.

"Hi, can I speak to Knight, please." Scotland asked taking a seat on the floor.

"Just a moment please." The woman put Scotland on hold.

A few seconds later Knight picked up the line.

"Knight Young, speaking?" He answered sitting at his desk.

Scotland cleared her throat and placed her knees up to her chest.

"Hi… it's Scotland," she said nervously.

"Hey." Knight smiled at the sound of her voice.

"How are you?"

"I'm good. I take it you got my gift." He leaned back in his swivel chair.

"I did." Scotland glanced over at the box. "The dress is beautiful and thanks for the money but I can't accept any of it. You ruining my dress was an accident. Plus, I still owe your girl the first payment for damaging her car."

"I hear you but I'm not taking no for an answer. You're keeping the dress and the money."

"No, I'm not," Scotland challenged.

"Yes, you are," Knight refuted.

"No," she giggled.

"I'm not about to argue wit' you. You're keepin' the dress 'cause I'm not takin' it back. It took me hours to pick that out for you."

"Lies!" Scotland laughed. "You ain't pick shit out."

"How you know?" Knight chuckled. "I did give my assistant a full, detailed description of what I thought you might like."

"How are you picking out dresses for me and you don't even know me?"

"Can I tell you something?"

"Yeah." Scotland said with baited breath.

"The funny thing is, I feel like I've known you my entire life," he confessed.

Scotland held the phone and inhaled deeply. Here she was again stepping into the deep end. She had no business allowing his words to kiss her soul.

"I just can't take these gifts without doing something nice for you. It was your birthday too."

"What you got in mind?"

"It might not be much, but are you free tomorrow afternoon for drinks? I'm off. I could meet you at Bar Louie in the Central West End around one o'clock."

"Sounds like a plan." Knight said excited to see her again.

"Okay." Scotland bit her bottom lip not wanting to end the call "I'll see you tomor."

"See you tomor."

The next morning clothes and shoes were thrown all over Scotland's bedroom. She had to find the perfect outfit to meet Knight in. She had to look perfect. Because of her indecisiveness, she ended up being fifteen minutes late. She'd planned on being early so she could await his arrival. She had it all planned out.

She'd be standing in front of Bar Louie looking causally cute. He'd arrive; they'd have a few drinks, share a few laughs and part ways. She'd pretend like she was heading to her car, all the while waiting for him to drive off. As soon as he was gone, she'd head to the bus stop so she could head to the repair shop and pick up her car. Instead, Knight caught her getting off the bus. To her dismay, the bus driver let her off right in front of the restaurant.

She felt like an absolute fool getting off the bus dressed in a white bandeau top, skin tight, dark denim, skinny leg overalls and leopard print, ankle strapped platform heels. A pair of gold, hoop earrings hung from her ears while a huge, fringed purse rested across her chest. Knight watched as she walked his way. She was the best dressed person he'd ever seen getting off the bus. Scotland's face burned red as he stood up to greet her.

"For a minute I'd thought you stood me up." He gave her a warm hug.

"Noooooo... I'm just about that bus life. Thankfully this shit will be over this afternoon." She felt the need to make that clear.

"I don't know if I should be saying this or not, but you look hot!" Scotland examined his Brunello Cucinelli plaid jacket, fine, pique knit polo shirt and woven, single-pleated pants.

"You look totally different from Saturday. You took it from the hood to the boardroom."

"Yeah, I came straight from work," Knight laughed at her silliness.

"What you do for a living?"

"I'm a talent and sports agent. Here." He handed her a to-go cup of strawberry lemonade. "I took the liberty and ordered us both a drink."

"Thanks but the point of us meeting up was so I could buy you a drink."

"It's nothing." He eyed her outfit.

Scotland looked fly as fuck. It just amazed him how different she and Lennon were. Lennon would never be caught dead exposing so much skin in public. Scotland didn't give a fuck. She was confident as hell which made her even sexier to him.

"Since you got us some to-go drinks and it's a nice day, you wanna take a walk?" Scotland suggested.

"Yeah, that sounds cool." Knight replied trying to play it cool.

He couldn't let Scotland know that she made him nervous. The two of them strolled leisurely down the street as cars and other pedestrians whizzed by. The Central West End was always a busy area. Wanting to get away from the crowd, Scotland led them onto a residential street. She noticed that the sun seemed to be shining brighter than usual or maybe she was happier than she had been in a while. Neither she nor Knight knew what to say but their silence seemed to say everything they were feeling.

Scotland glanced up at him out of the corner of her eye. She hadn't had a crush on anyone since high school. Knight made her feel like a school girl. She felt giddy on the inside. She wanted to reach out and touch him, kiss him, lick him… anything. She didn't care. She just wanted to be near him. Knight looked to the side and caught her gaze. Scotland quickly turned her head.

"What you lookin' at?" He quizzed.

"The houses," she lied. "I love this neighborhood." She confessed truthfully.

"I dream about owning a home over here one day. I mean, look at this house." She pointed to a three-story, brick, row home. "They don't make houses like these anymore."

"They are pretty dope," Knight agreed.

"I've always wanted to go inside one and see what they look like on the inside. I bet you've been in a million homes like these before."

"Not a million but quite a few. They really are dope as hell. When I was little I dreamed about having space. The house I grew up in was so small and there were so many of us that I felt like I couldn't breathe."

"Where you grow up at?" Scotland asked taking a sip of her drink.

"On the West Side."

"You lying." She said in disbelief. "You ain't grow up on no damn West Side. Look at you. You have on a freakin' designer suit." She flicked his lapel. "You all sophisticated and shit."

"And I worked my ass off through school to get this muthafucka too."

"Wow," Scotland said astonished. "I've never met anybody from the hood that made it out. I would've bet a million bucks that you grew up wit' dough."

"Nah, I grew up in a single parent household wit' three sisters and a little brother. Shit was tight but we made do."

"That's crazy. I grew up in the foster care system. When I was ten, I finally found a permanent home," Scotland explained. "I think I've done pretty good for

myself though, despite all the bullshit I've gone through."
She said thankful.

"I mean, as you can see, I don't have much but it
could be worse I guess."

Knight looked at Scotland amazed. The girl was
strong as hell. Hearing her story only made him grow to
care for her more.

"So what do you do?" He asked changing the
subject.

"I'm a nanny. It's not what I want to be doing with
my life but it pays the bills."

"What do you want to do?"

"It's silly." Scotland looked down at her feet.

"Tell me," Knight urged.

Scotland pondered telling him her dream. She'd
been told it was stupid so many times that she'd begun to
believe it too.

"Ok but you can't laugh."

"I won't."

"Promise?"

"Man, if you don't come on here."

"Ok … If I could, I would be a writer." She held her
breath awaiting his reaction.

"What you mean if you could? Why can't you be?"
Knight asked confused.

Scotland stopped walking and stood speechless. She'd never been hit with that question before. Why couldn't she be an author?

"I mean," she resumed walking. "I don't even know where to begin. How does someone like me become a published author?"

"What you mean somebody like you?" Knight screwed up his face.

"Let's be real. I'm not like you. I didn't go to college and I ain't got no degree. I'm a freakin' nanny that can barely pay her bills. How I'm just gon' up and write a book?"

"Easily… Write that muthafucka. You gotta stop talkin' so negatively. Never let your surroundings or circumstances define you. You can be whoever you wanna be. I'm living proof of that. I grew up with nothing; remember that," Knight declared.

"You're right." Scotland's inner being beamed with hope.

Fuck what YaYa thought. Her dreams of becoming an author weren't foolish. She would only know if she could be successful at it if she tried.

"Have you written anything yet?"

"A few chapters."

"Send it to me. I want to read it."

"Really?" She smiled.

"Nah, really." He joked.

"Shut up." Scotland playfully pushed him.

"What? I'm just tryin' to make you laugh," he chuckled.

"I don't like how well it's working. You have a fiancée, remember?" She arched her brow.

"Trust me; I remember but we're just friends, right?" Knight placed his hand on the small of her back.

"Are we?" Scotland jumped.

"I think we are."

"Friends don't buy friends expensive-ass designer dresses," she countered.

"In my world they do."

"How much was that dress by the way? Like five hundred bucks?"

"Nah."

"Less?"

"No."
"More?" Scotland said frightened by what the number could be.

"Yeah," Knight laughed heartily.

"How much more?" Scotland's eyes grew wide.

"Two grand more."

"You paid twenty-five hundred dollars for that dress?! Do you know what I could do with that kind of money?" She gasped.

"No, but I'm sure you're gonna tell me, Frugal Franny."

"You damn right I am. I could pay rent for three months with that kind of money. Damn… must be nice."

Astounded by the price, Scotland walked silently for a second until she spotted a park.

"Come on. Let's go over there." She took Knight by the hand.

Together they jogged hand in hand across the street and into the park. Scotland found a perfect spot underneath a willow tree for them to rest.

"Cop a squat." She plopped down in the grass.

"You want me to sit down in the grass? Have you looked at what I got on?" Knight eyed her skeptically.

"Fuck that suit and I want you to lie down in the grass." She grinned lying back.

"You on one." He looked around wondering if he should.

"Come on." She patted the space next to her. "Join me."

Knight shook his head and took off his suit jacket. He placed it down on the ground and lie next to her. The soft feel of the grass massaged his skin. They both took in the clear, blue sky and the sound of children playing.

"This is nice," he confessed.

"Told you," Scotland smiled proudly. "Sometimes you just have to lie back and take in God's wonder."

Knight turned and examined her face. Little did she know, but Scotland was the epitome of God's work. She was one of God's greatest creations. Her bright, sunny disposition captured him and made him hope for more. She was beauty and grace personified. Scotland could feel him starring so she turned her head and looked at him.

"What? Do I have something on my face?" She rubbed her cheek.

"Yeah... you do." Knight spoke above a whisper.
"What?" Scotland panicked thinking it was a bug. "What is it?"

Knight eased closer and kissed her lips. Scotland relished the sensation of his lips on hers. She was getting her whole entire life in that moment but they were supposed to be just friends. Friends didn't kiss friends on the lips. Once again they were crossing the line. They were heading in a dangerous direction. Nothing good would come of this but Knight had become addicted to her. She was everything he never thought he wanted but needed.

"YOU BE ON THAT BULLSHIT."

-CHRISS ZOE, HOMEBOY

CHAPTER 8

Knight felt like he was floating on a cloud. He didn't even want to return to work. He ended up spending more time with Scotland then he'd planned. They lay in the park talking about everything from love to politics. He and Scotland had so much in common. They talked for hours. The only thing that separated them was their financial situation.

If he didn't have to return to work and she didn't have to go pick up her car they wouldn't have parted. Knight dropped Scotland off at the repair shop, hugged and kissed her goodbye. He offered to stay but she insisted that she would be ok alone. On the ride back to work he bumped PartyNextDoor feat. Drake *Recognize*.

"You got niggas and I got bitches. You got niggas and I got bitches but I want you." He sang along to the track while pondering his situation.

He was literally torn between two women. He cared deeply for Lennon. Because of her, he'd been introduced to some of the most influential people in the world. Her connections pushed his career forward. He was indebted to her. They'd climbed their way to the top of the agency together. They were a perfect match businesswise.

Together they could accomplish anything. They were the Beyoncé and Jay-Z of their field. Their upcoming wedding was the talk of the town. The who's who of St. Louis and beyond would be there. So much was pending on their wedding. It hadn't been voiced, but it was understood that Knight marrying a partner at the agency would secure him a corner office as well.

He'd officially be in. Knight had worked his ass off to get to this point in his career. But now that he was almost at his goal he wasn't really sure if it was all worth it. Lennon's attitude, demanding behavior, close-minded, selfish ways was wearing thin. As a man, he couldn't sit back and tolerate her constant bullshit. She was breathtakingly beautiful, intelligent and cunning but all of the other shit that came along with her made Knight wonder could he live the rest of his life with her?

There was no joy between them. They were coexisting and faking happiness. They were nothing more than a power couple. Being around Scotland in such a short amount of time exposed all of their flaws and just how unhappy he really was. He had a lot to think about. He liked Scotland a lot but he wasn't willing to throw away everything for a woman he barely knew.

She was cool as fuck. He enjoyed every moment he spent with her. She made him smile by just being in his presence. He wanted her in a way that he'd never wanted another woman. He wanted to make her happy and ease all of her worries but he had to be mindful that he was promised to another. He knew he should've felt bad for having the feelings he had but he didn't. When it came to Lennon, he felt hollow inside.

Knight walked inside the agency and stopped at his secretary's desk to check his messages. His secretary gave him a stack full of notes of missed calls. As Knight checked through them, his colleague, Paul Frasier, approached him.

"Brain McKnight!" He joked.

"Paul." Knight spoke, not even bothering to give him eye contact.

To him, Paul was an egotistical clown.

"How you been, buddy?" He gripped Knight's shoulder and massaged it.

"I'm good." Knight shrugged his shoulder away.

"What is this?" Paul looked down and spotted a brown texture on his hand.

"Aww damn." Knight glanced back at his shoulder and saw a stain of mud.

"How did you get mud on your jacket, bro?" Paul asked taking his handkerchief out of his jacket and wiping his hand.

"I gotta flat and had to change my tire." Knight took off his suit jacket.

"Hello, boys." Lennon strolled their way.

Paul couldn't take his eyes off of her. Everything about Lennon was put together perfectly. Her hair was styled immaculately. Her makeup was filled with peach and nude tones. She wore a black, Victoria Beckham, flared, mini dress that highlighted her toned legs and ankle strapped Alexander McQueen heels. Paul wrapped his arm around Lennon's waist and gave her a warm one-armed hug.

Lennon savored their brief contact. For months she and Paul had been having a torrid affair. Whenever and wherever they could get their hands on each other they did. The day of the accident they'd met outside of his apartment building for a quickie. They'd been doing a damn good job at hiding their affair but that day they'd become dangerously close to being caught. Lennon couldn't have that.

Their secret love affair could never make the light of day. He was married with children and she was engaged to Knight. Plus, her father would have a fit if he found out she was seeing a white man. Mr. Whitmore didn't have a problem with white people in general; he just preferred that his daughter not date one. He'd made it perfectly clear that she would be disowned if she ever brought a white man home. He wanted her to marry a black man so Lennon satisfied her taste for heavy cream on the low.

She loved white men. She was sexually attracted to them more than black men. Black men didn't rile her up like white men did. Lennon found most black men to be degenerate, uneducated, thugs who wanted nothing out of life but to be a serial baby daddy. Fooling around with Paul gave her the best of both worlds. She had Knight who was the Will to her Jada. The two of them together was unstoppable. He gave her the edge and street cred that she needed when dealing with rappers and athletes.

Throughout the years she'd tried polishing him up but with a man like Knight there was only so much that could be done. He came from the streets. There would always be a rough, dirty edge to him. The way he talked, the way he dressed and the music he listened to was all wrong. She tried to get him to stop sagging his jeans and rapping lyrics that called women bitches and hoes but Knight wasn't having it. It just wasn't his steeze.

He hoped that Lennon would come around and accept him for who he was but she couldn't. She didn't understand him. The way he grew up, his mannerism, the way he spoke and his frame of mind was foreign to her. Outside of his dashing good looks, charm, dick game and drive, they were incompatible.

Although they were incompatible, with Knight by her side she'd be able to take over the world. She'd be able to push her father to the side and run the Whitmore Agency. She'd have it all - a husband that would raise her to a position of power and a lover in Paul that could satisfy her sexual needs.

"Paul," she replied, casually.

"What is that on your hand?" She grimaced. "And please tell me that whatever it is that you didn't get it on my dress."

"It's mud from the back of Knight's suit."

"How did you get mud on you?" Lennon questioned perplexed.

"I caught a flat and had to change the tire," Knight lied.

"No-no, honey," Lennon wagged her finger. "We don't change tires. That's what AAA is for."

"I can do it myself." Knight shot annoyed by her logic.

"Whatever, if you want to act like the help instead of the boss, then that's all on you. Father wants to see us in his office." She walked off unbothered.

Knight followed behind her. Lennon tapped on her father's door.

"Come in, dear." Mr. Whitmore waved them in. "You two have a seat."

Every time Knight entered Mr. Whitmore's office he was always flabbergasted. It was huge and looked like something straight out of Elle Décor. The walls were a charcoal gray while the boarders of the windows and door were painted white. In the center of the room was his wooden desk. Surrounding his desk were several built-in book shelves. Mr. Whitmore had over a thousand books in his office. He'd even let Knight borrow a few. Knight placed his suit jacket back on and took a seat.

"It's time to seal this shoe deal between Nike and Ba'Sheer Turner. He's the biggest star in the NBA right now so this deal between him and Nike will take him over the edge. It's a must we secure this deal. There are just a few more things to go over before Ba'Sheer signs so we're going to fly you two down to Miami tomorrow to meet with Nike and Ba'Sheer so we can wrap this thing up."

"Sounds good." Knight nodded his head ready to go.

"Unfortunately, I won't be able to go," Lennon confirmed.

"And why not?" Mr. Whitmore situated himself in his seat.

"I already have meetings set up with a few of my clients this week that cannot be rescheduled. Knight can go by himself." Lennon told a half-truth.

She did have work that needed to be attended to but she also didn't want to be bothered with Knight. Things between them were already strained. She was over the tension. It was bad enough that she had to deal with him at work and at home. She didn't want to take a business trip to Miami and be miserable there too. They desperately needed space and she wanted time to freely be with Paul.

"Knight, are you ok with that?" Mr. Whitmore asked.

"Yes, I can handle it," he assured.

"Great. Well you two get back to work," Mr. Whitmore focused his attention on the paperwork on his desk.

"You have a good day, sir." Knight stood up and left the room.

"Knight?" Lennon called after him.

"What's up?" He asked stopping mid-stride.

He prayed to God that she wasn't about to start an argument.

"Where have you been all day? You've been missing from your office all afternoon," she quizzed.

"I had lunch at my mother's house. I ended up staying longer than I thought," he lied.

"How is Jean?" Lennon folded her arms across her chest.

Knight glared at her.

"What?" She asked confused.

"My mother's name is June. June."

"Jean, June, Jody Watley, whatever," Lennon waved him off, frustrated. "It was a mistake," she huffed. "You take everything so seriously."

"Are you done?" Knight said annoyed by her presence.

"Yeah, because there's no talking to you. I'll see you when I get home." She flicked her wrist dismissively and stormed off.

"If I come home!" Knight shot.

"Don't come home. I don't care." Lennon yelled over her shoulder.

Knight could give two fucks about her attitude. He didn't care so much that he walked to his office and picked up the phone. He was determined not to let Lennon ruin his day. He was on a high and planned on staying lifted. A few rings later Scotland answered the call.

"Hello?" She said surprised to hear from him so soon.

"What you doing?"

"Just got home." Scotland pulled her purse off over her head.

"What you doing tomorrow?"

Scotland thought about it for a second.

"Ummmmmm…working. Why what's up?"

"Take off and come to Miami wit' me."

"Boy, don't play wit' me."

"I'm dead-ass serious. I gotta go for business and I wanna take you wit' me," Knight said sincerely.

Scotland's heart began to beat a mile a minute. She'd always wanted to go to Miami but never could afford it. With the way her life was going she thought she'd be stuck inside of St. Louis until she died. Scotland pondered the notion for a second. She had a couple of sick days on deck that she could use. It was a free trip she assumed. She'd be able to get on an airplane for the first time. She'd get to go to sunny Miami and see the ocean and the best perk of all, she'd get to be with Knight. There was no way she was gonna say no.

"Ok, I'm down."

"A'ight be ready at 8:00a.m."

"I'll be ready." Scotland squealed hanging up.

"THEY SAY I DON'T LOVE YOU, WE FINNA SEE."

-FANTASIA FEAT. JAZZE PHA, DON'T ACT RIGHT

CHAPTER 9

"Can you eat my skittles? It's the sweetest in the middle, yeah," Scotland sang into a brush that she used as a pretend microphone.

La'Shay and Tootie were her backup singers. Beyoncé's *Blow* played while they danced around her room. Everyone was having a good time except YaYa. She lay on Scotland's bed unfazed by their playfulness. She wasn't in the mood for a bunch of silliness. She had more important things on her mind, like why her sister was being so dumb and naïve.

"I'ma lean back don't you worry it's nothing major." Scotland rocked her hips from side to side. *"Make sure you clean that; it's the only way to get the flavor."* She got in YaYa's face and sang.

She was trying to get her to laugh or participate but YaYa wasn't having it. Scotland ignored her pissy attitude and kept on dancing. She had worked up quite a sweat but her feet wouldn't stop moving. When Beyoncé came on she immediately morphed into Sasha Fierce. She was the baddest bitch in the land that couldn't be beat. Once the song went off the girls fell into a heap on the floor. They were all out of breath but cracking up laughing.

"Remember when we were kids and used to do this shit all the time?" Tootie held her stomach she was laughing so hard.

"Girl, I'm tired as hell," Scotland tried to catch her breath. "I think I pulled a muscle."

"My ass gon' be sore as fuck tomorrow," Tootie replied.

"Hell, I'm sore as fuck now," La' Shay confirmed.

"I gotta stop playin' wit' y'all and start packing." Scotland eased her way off the floor.

"Yeah, I need to call and check on my kids", La'Shay pulled out her phone.

"Who got RJ, Tootie?" Scotland asked.

"His daddy," Tootie smiled brightly. "They at my house."

"No tea, no shade but you let that nigga stay in yo' house while you're not there?" Scotland quizzed.

"I told y'all! I don't know if he stole the money!"

"Ok, girl," Scotland threw her hands up in air. "If you say so."

"What are you going to take with you to wear?" La'Shay asked getting off the phone.

"I don't know. You know all I got is a bunch of black shit."

"I still can't believe this nigga takin' you on a trip already." La'Shay sat up against the wall. "It ain't even been a week yet. *And* you ain't even gave up the box or have you?"

"No, I haven't fucked or sucked him yet but I might while we're gone." Scotland stuck out her tongue.

"I know that's right!" La'Shay gave her a high-five. "Get you some!"

"No, she needs to close her legs to an almost married man." YaYa shot them both a stank look.

"Ugh, why you always hatin'?" La'Shay threw a pillow at her.

"I'm far from a hater, ma." YaYa dodged the throw. "Don't get mad at me 'cause I speak the truth. Let's keep it real." She sat Indian style.

"Oh, Lord. Here we go," La'Shay rolled her eyes. "What you got to say, Dr. Phil?"

"He's taking you to Miami; that's cool, I guess. I mean, it's nothin' but whatever." She down played Scotland's trip.

"Shaaaaaaade, honey!" La'Shay laughed hiding her face.

"I know right?" Scotland agreed. "Bitch, I don't see nobody takin' you to Miami." She shot rolling her neck.

"Girl, whatever; I'll take my damn self to Miami." YaYa hit back.

"Yeah, cause you're just ballin' out of control. Okay, girl." Scotland dismissed her.

"AT THE END OF THE DAY." YaYa bobbed her head from left to right to get her point across. "When you go and come back he's still gon' be engaged to ole girl. She gon' always come before you. You side pussy, ma."

"I ain't side shit 'cause I ain't fuckin' him," Scotland checked her.

"But you just said you might." YaYa challenged.

"And I just might if I decide to. I'ma grown-ass muthafuckin' woman. I can do what I wanna do. What you mad for is the question?" Scotland quizzed.

"You can stop wit' the mad shit, girl. I'm stating facts. You my sista and I don't wanna see you out here lookin' crazy. Quiet as kept, I'm happy you found you a nigga wit' some paper. Maybe he can help you get this bed fixed." YaYa glared at Scotland as if to say checkmate.

"Nigga, that wasn't even shade, that was a whole palm tree." Tootie exclaimed stunned.

Scotland stared at YaYa. They were looking at each other square in the eyes. There was no denying that YaYa was feeling some type of way. Since they were kids she'd gotten her li'l smart shit off and Scotland ignored it. She chalked it up to YaYa being YaYa. She was always bossy and assertive but Scotland wasn't gonna put up with her slick shit anymore.

"Damn, bitch, you really mad. My bed ain't did shit to you but if it's bothering you so much, get yo' miserable-ass up off of it."

"Girl, please; this bed comfortable than a muthafucka," YaYa laughed trying to ease the tension. "I'm just sayin', sister, be smart about the situation 'cause I can see the stars in your eyes. You feelin' this nigga; ain't you?"

"I am." Scotland softened some. "There's something different about him. We have this crazy connection. It's weird and I know he got a chick. Y'all know I normally wouldn't even involve myself wit' a dude that got a woman but everything about him says he's supposed to be mine."

"Supposed to be and is are two different things, ladybug," YaYa declared. "He's engaged. What you think Mommy and Daddy would do if they found out about this? They would be so disappointed in you. I mean, we all know you're the golden child. Just do me a favor. Go to Miami and have a good time but keep your feelings back here in St. Louis. Trust me; it'll be the best decision you've ever made."

"Mmmmmmmm...yessssss." Lennon sucked in air through her teeth as she bounced up and down on Knight's dick.

Her eyes were closed. With every roll of her hips jolts of electricity ran through her body.

"Mmm... this feels so good," she moaned, oblivious to the fact that Knight was lying there uninterested.

His mind wasn't there with her or on her. Visions of Scotland's sweet face danced in his mind. He couldn't wait to see her again. Their flight couldn't leave fast enough. Going to Miami was a much needed and welcomed distraction from his and Lennon's problems. Things were getting worse between them by the day.

Being around her was starting to make his skin crawl. He never realized how self-absorbed and cynical she was. Being in her presence was exhausting. The longer she rode his dick the softer he became. Lennon was so self-absorbed that she didn't even realize he wasn't into it.

"Ooooh… I'm gonna miss you." She massaged his chest. "You gonna miss me, baby?" Lennon leaned forward and attempted to kiss his lips.

Knight ignored her question and jerked her head back with his hand instead of kissing her.

"Owww, that hurt." She pushed his hand away. "You know I don't like it rough."

"Yo, we gotta finish. I got a flight to catch." Knight gripped her hips and made her rock back and forth at a faster pace.

Startled but turned on by his touch, Lennon went along with the flow. Knight rocked her hips at a feverish pace. Lennon could barely keep up. When she rode him she liked to take things nice and slow. Lennon was delicate or so Knight thought. She didn't like to sweat or get a hair out of place. The way she was moving, her edges were sure to sweat out and get nappy.

"Baby," she whimpered. "Wait. You're going too fast!"

Knight heard her cries but refused to slow down. He needed her ass to hurry up and cum.

"It hurts! You're too big!" Lennon gasped for air as her breasts flopped in the air.

"You wanted to fuck, right?"

"Yeah," Lennon shrilled.

"Then act like a big girl and take this dick." Knight slapped her on the ass hard.

"Don't be slapping me on the ass! I'm not a damn donkey!" Lennon hit him on the chest as she felt herself about to cum.

"Oh my God," she roared, convulsing.

Lennon's body shook out of control. She hadn't even come all the way down from her orgasmic high when Knight roughly lifted her off of him.

"Well damn." Lennon panted pulling the sheets over her body. "What's wrong with you?"

"You know I got a flight to catch and I'm not even done packing." Knight threw on a pair of hooping shorts.

"We always make love before you go out of town. It's our tradition." She caught her breath.

"Maybe we need to start a new tradition. The ones we've been doing are gettin' kind of old."

"You know you've been really moody since your birthday. Why can't we get past what happened and move on? I'm tired of the negative energy. It's draining me." Lennon massaged her temples. "I had to get two massages this week alone."

"Poor, you. Poor, little rich girl. Polly wanna cracker?" Knight mocked her.

"You can be such an asshole sometimes." Lennon sneered, wrapping the sheets around her.

Pissed, she hopped off the bed and stormed into the bathroom, slamming the door behind her. Knight proceeded to grab his suitcase and finish packing. He wasn't at all fazed by Lennon's temper tantrum. His mind was focused on one thing and that was getting to Scotland as fast as he could.

"I WANT YOU BUT WOULD YOU PLEASE BE CAREFUL WITH MY PAPER HEART?"

-JENNI LOVETTE, PAPER HEART

CHAPTER 10

It was a foggy, muggy, hot, August morning but the depressing weather could not dampen Scotland's happy mood. She'd been smiling since she woke up that morning. One of her biggest dreams was coming true. After 28 years she was finally getting out of St. Louis and getting on an airplane!

She was nervous as hell, especially since planes were going missing but she trusted that God would keep her safe. She stood on her porch patiently awaiting Knight's arrival with her bags in tow. They would only be gone a few days but Scotland packed like she would be out of town for a month. She didn't know what the vibe would be like in Miami so she had to be prepared.

"Girl, what you doing out here? It's hot as hell." Her loud, noisy, older, next door neighbor Lisa stepped out onto her porch.

Scotland took a deep breath and exhaled slowly. Talking to Lisa was like having a nail drilled into her skull. She was forty-seven-years–old and always up in somebody's business and spilling unnecessary tea that nobody cared to hear. It didn't help that she was outside looking a hot mess. Like always, a cigarette hung from her lips, her wig was filled with rollers, and she had on an old, pink, tattered robe, bunny slippers and a cup of coffee in her hand. No matter the time of the day, Lisa always had a cigarette and a cup of coffee. Scotland didn't understand why she needed so much energy. She didn't do shit all day but look out the window all day to see what everybody else was doing.

"Hey, Lisa, girl. How you doing this morning?" Scotland shot her a fake smile.

"Obviously not as good as you. What's all the bags for? You ain't gettin' put out is ya'? Oooooh... you going on a trip? Where you going, girl?" Lisa said at once.

"No, I'm going out of town." Scotland couldn't help but laugh.

"Where you going?"

"Miami," Scotland beamed.

"Bitch, what?" Lisa shrieked. "How you going to Miami? Hell, the other day you just asked me could you borrow a loaf of bread."

"A friend of mine is taking me." Scotland shot her a look that could kill.

"That's one hell of a friend." Lisa popped her lips.

"Speaking of friends, here he come right now." Scotland smiled proudly.

She and Lisa watched as a black Lincoln Navigator turned the corner. The palms of Scotland's hands instantly began to sweat. Knight always had that effect on her.

"Girl, this you?" Lisa stepped off the porch so she could get a better look.

The car pulled into the parking lot and parked. The driver got out and opened the back door. Knight stepped out looking like a GQ model. It wasn't even fair that a man could be so fine.

It was as if time slowed down as he approached her. She could hear her heartbeat through her chest as she examined the way his NY Yankee fitted cap rested on his head. The gray t-shirt he donned clung to his chest. The fitted, dark denim jeans he rocked sagged just enough and the Nike Air Jordan VI's were a nice added touch of hood-boy chic. His tattoos were on full display. She loved it. It was nice to see him out of a suit and tie. Knight walked up and placed a soft kiss on her forehead. Scotland felt like a puddle of water in his embrace.

"You ready, beautiful?" He asked.

"Mmm hmm." Scotland responded unable to get a word out.

"Uh mmm!" Lisa cleared her throat loudly. "Scotland, introduce me to your friend." She looked Knight up and down like he was a piece of meat.

Scotland rolled her eyes.

"Knight, this is my next door neighbor - Lisa. Lisa, this is Knight."

"How you doing, Knight?" Lisa said in her Wendy William's voice. "You got a brother, Knight?"

"As a matter-of-fact, I do," Knight chuckled.

"Tell you brother I keep it tight." Lisa winked her eye. "Whew, you fine as hell!" She wiped an invisible bead of sweat from her forehead. "God only knows what yo' brother look like."

"Ok, it's time for us to go." Scotland pushed Knight towards the car. "Lisa, keep an eye on my place while I'm gone, please."

"You know I got you, girl. Knight, don't forget to tell yo' brother I said hi!" Lisa yelled as the driver placed Scotland's bags in the trunk. "Y'all be safe now, ya' hear!" She waved goodbye as they got in the car and left.

The flight from St. Louis to Miami was a long one but Scotland enjoyed every minute of it. She never thought in a million years that she'd be so close to God. Being so high up in the sky amongst the clouds was blissful. She wanted to reach out and touch every last one. The entire plane ride she hadn't stopped smiling. Scotland gazed out of the window with her earphones in her ear. She was jamming out to Big Sean's smash hit *I Don't Fuck Wit' You*. Scotland sang along to the breakup anthem not realizing that she was singing louder than she thought.

"You little stupid-ass bitch! I ain't fuckin' wit' you! You li'l dumb-ass bitch! I ain't fuckin' wit' you!" She raised her hands in the air and danced.

She'd completely forgotten where she was. The other passengers in first class were looking at her like she was an imbecile.

"Bitch, I don't give a fuck about you or anything that you do!" She threw up the middle finger and Crip walked in her seat.

Knight sat next to her amused and mortified all at the same time. He knew she didn't mean any harm but

Scotland had to chill before she got them kicked off the plane.

"Scotland." He softly nudged her arm to get her attention.

The other passengers were angry as hell because some of them had been awaken by her loud singing. Scotland continued to dance and sing oblivious of her surroundings.

"Will you shut her up?" A man behind them asked furious.

"I'm tryin'," Knight laughed.

He found the whole thing funny as hell. Lennon would've never let loose like this.

"Scotland!" Knight tapped her thigh urgently.

Scotland jumped. She quickly focused her attention on him and pulled her earphones out of her ear.

"Huh?"

"You're loud." Knight pointed his head towards the other passengers.

Scotland glanced around at everyone. A ton of angry faces shot her dirty looks. One man shook his head at her while an elderly lady told her to have some class.

"My bad," Scotland apologized mortified.

Embarrassed, she slumped down in her seat. She prayed to God that she would evaporate into thin air and disappear.

"I'm so embarrassed." She hid the side of her face with an US Weekly magazine.

"You was over there gettin' it." Knight cracked up laughing. "Shit, I was about to join in wit' you."

"What you know about Big Sean, Mr. Conservative?"

"Scotland, all I listen to is Hip Hop. You gotta get past the suit and tie, ma. I does this." He stated pulling out his iPhone.

Knight scrolled through his music app.

"You got that new School Boy Q? I've been wanting to listen to that," Scotland exclaimed.

"Uh yeah, that muthafucka go hard."

Scotland began to scroll through her playlist of music too.

"You ever heard of G-Eazy?" She asked.

"I got a few of his songs. I like that joint I Mean It by him. I've been listening to a lot of PartyNextDoor, Pancho Rucker and Kanye."

"I fucks wit' PartyNextDoor heavy. I would've never thought we had the same taste in music. I assumed you only listened to like Barbra Streisand, Taylor Swift or Sam Smith," Scotland joked.

"Don't sleep on Sam Smith. That white boy can sing," Knight grinned. "But I listen to a lot of shit though. I like R&B and Neo-soul. Sometimes I even dabble off into a li'l country and rock and roll."

"Me too." Scotland became serious. "Thank you again for bringing me on this trip. I didn't expect this shit at all."

"Me either. It was a last minute thing."

"Well, it was very sweet of you. I assume Lennon doesn't know that I'm here with you?" Scotland quizzed nervously biting her bottom lip.

"Nah." Knight confessed staring off.

"Oh." Scotland stared off as well.

Suddenly she felt uncomfortable. *What the hell am I doing,* she thought. *You should have your ass at work. You missing money for a nigga that gotta bitch. YaYa is right. You ain't nothing but a piece of pussy to this nigga.*

Scotland folded her arms across her chest. She wanted off the plane. She wanted to go home. She realized that she was making a huge mistake by being there with Knight. He wasn't her man. He would never be.

Knight could tell that her entire energy had changed. It seemed like all of the joy had been sucked out of her. He knew what she was thinking. He was thinking the same things too. He didn't know what he was doing by bringing her to Miami. He couldn't promise her that they'd be together. He honestly didn't know if he wanted her to be his. All he knew was that he loved being near her. She made him happy. He could relax around her and be himself.

Until he could figure out his emotions, that's what he wanted to focus on, being happy. Knight reached out his arm and held her hand. He had to calm her fears. Scotland turned and looked at him then down at their hands intertwined. His hand enveloped hers but somehow they still fit perfectly together. It amazed her how the mere touch of his hand eased all of her worries. What she felt between her and Knight wasn't imaginary. It was real. It might not have been perfect but it was the beginning of something real.

"YOU JUST CAN'T GET OVER
HOW GOOD MY FRAME
LOOKS IN THE MOONLIGHT."

-JENNI LOVETTE, BEAST

CHAPTER 11

The potent, intoxicating smell of the Atlantic Ocean engulfed Scotland's nose as soon as she stepped off the plane in Miami. Scotland couldn't stop cheesing. Her cheeks hurt she was grinning so much. She'd never been this happy before in life. Being in Miami was like being transported to a whole new atmosphere. To be there in real life versus seeing it on television was surreal.

Miami was like a tropical hideaway right in the United States. It was magical. Things got even better once they arrived at the hotel. The Delano Hotel was located right in the center of South Beach. She and Knight were staying in the penthouse suite. Upon entry, Scotland was hit with all white, custom, Starck-designed furniture, a walk-in wet bar, sitting area, dining area, billowing white curtains and stunning light.

The extraordinary, luxurious bathrooms were crafted of imported Italian marble and each featured an enormous marble soaking tub. The penthouse also included a spacious, private balcony where she could enjoy discreet sunbathing and unparalleled ocean views. Scotland's heart was overwhelmed with joy as she stood on the balcony and overlooked the ocean. She watched as the waves crashed upon the shore. She would be remiss not to stop and take a moment to thank God.

"Lord, thank you," she whispered.

Knight gave the bellboy a $20 tip for bringing up their bags and closed the door behind him. He was immediately captured by the silhouette of Scotland's body as she stood on the balcony. Knight crept up behind her and wrapped his arms around her waist.

Scotland smiled and took in the moment. Life, at that second, was perfect. She wanted to pinch herself. She couldn't believe all of the wonderful things she was experiencing. She felt like a princess. Knight brushed her hair to the side and placed a small kiss on the back of her neck. Scotland closed her eyes.

"St. Louis feels so far away," she whispered.

The feel of his lips on her skin was tantalizing and pleasing. Knight placed small kisses all over her neck, making his way around to her lips. Scotland looked up into his eyes. A look of lust and hunger resonated through his gaze. This was it. The moment both of them had been anxiously anticipating. They were about to make love for the very first time. Scotland's legs became jelly as he tugged on her hair and kissed her passionately.

As their tongues did the merengue, she could feel her clothes slip off piece by piece. The afternoon sun beamed down onto her cocoa skin. Knight paused and took a minute to take in the visual of seeing her naked. Scotland's body was a work of art. She was petite in frame but her full breasts sat up at full attention. Her nipples reminded him of two chocolate morsels.

He couldn't wait to place them into his mouth so they could melt with each lick of his tongue. Knight pulled his t-shirt off over his head and revealed a chest full of tattoos. His body was ripped with muscles. With one glance Scotland was turned out. Knight was the truth. Even before penetration she knew that from that day on he'd be her drug of choice.

Knight took his shirt, placed it around Scotland's eyes and tied it from behind. He wanted her to experience everything he was about to do to her through touch and sound. Scotland had never been blindfolded before. She didn't know what to expect. Knight got down on his knees and placed Scotland's legs on his shoulders.

Her pink clit called his name. Knight swirled his tongue around her clit causing her to moan. A tidal wave of pleasure ran through Scotland's veins. She wanted so bad to watch as Knight assaulted her pussy with his tongue. He was doing things that should've been illegal in all fifty states. Moans of ecstasy escaped her lips. She didn't care if anybody could hear. She had to convey how Knight was making her feel.

Knight flicked the tip of his tongue across her clit feverishly. His mind was racing with thoughts of him entering her wet slit. He had plans of having his way with her but first, she had to submit herself to him.

"You like that?" He spoke in the lips of her pussy.

"Yes," Scotland panted.

"Tell me how much you like it." Knight sucked on her clit.

"Oh my God!" Scotland whimpered. "I love it. Shit!" She massaged his head.

It was only a matter of minutes before she came. Knight was dangerous to the touch. He enticed her senses. She had to have him inside her.

"Knight, fuck me... Please... fuck me," she begged.

"Not until you cum." He ignored her cries.

Scotland was right where he wanted her. She was on the brink of losing all control. She would soon realize that Knight liked to be dominant during sex. He liked to have full control at all times. Seeing his partner in such a vulnerable state turned him on. It gave him a rush. Lennon never let him exercise that right. He would never have that problem with Scotland. She went along with the flow and allowed him to lead.

With each stroke of his tongue her body spasmed. Knight was breathing life into her. She was going mad. Her quivering flesh enticed him to only torture her pussy more. The sweet honey nectar dripping from her honeycomb hideout filled him up. With each lick he wanted more. Fire raced down Scotland's spine as her body convulsed. A sensuous orgasm roared throughout her core.

"Knight!" She screamed out his name as a single tear slipped out the corner of her eye.

Scotland had never experienced an orgasm so intense that it caused her to cry. She didn't know how she survived it. This was only foreplay. Knight hadn't even entered her yet and he already had her going insane. Scotland uncovered her eyes and looked at him. Laughter welled in her chest.

"Goddamn, nigga. You really expect me to take some dick after that?" She giggled as her head continued to spin.

"Oh you gon' take this dick." Knight placed her down onto her back.

Scotland opened her legs wide and prepared herself for liftoff.

A slow harmony of classical music played as Knight and Scotland made their way inside of Scarpetta restaurant. Scotland looked around in awe. The place and people in it screamed money. The ambiance and atmosphere was stunning. Scarpetta had a wraparound veranda and floor-to-ceiling glass windows that offered a breathtaking view of the Atlantic Ocean.

Scotland felt so out of place. Everyone dining looked so fancy and sophisticated in their designer duds. She thought she looked cute at first but as she looked at the other women that wore simplistic makeup and understated jewels she realized she was dressed all wrong. Knight told her to get dressed for dinner and drinks. He never told her exactly where they were going though.

It was Miami and everyone she'd seen so far was dressed really flashy and sexy so Scotland pulled her weave back into a bun, put on her big, Trust No Bitch earrings, threw on a black blazer with the sleeves rolled up, black, lace bra, baggy, ripped, boyfriend jeans and black gladiator style heels. She figured the more skin the better. Her entire chest and stomach was exposed. She had the body to rock the outfit but it was a cute outfit worn at the wrong time. Scotland felt like an absolute idiot. She looked like a chicken-head.

"Why didn't you tell me this was the kind of restaurant we were going to?" She whispered to Knight as they waited to be escorted to their table.

"My bad; I thought you knew. I told you we're going to dinner with my business associates."

"Bruh, you know in the hood associate means somebody you don't fuck wit' like that. So we're about to meet people you work wit'-work wit'? Like, important people?" Her eyes grew wide.

"Yeah," Knight answered, dressed appropriately.

He donned a 3-piece, shawl-collar, Dolce & Gabbana suit.

"Oh my God," Scotland said mortified. "Take me now, Lord. If I would've known, I would'a wore the dress you bought me. That would've been perfect."

"Follow me." The hostess said.

"Well, we're here now. Don't worry about it. Everything will be fine." Knight tried to make light of the situation.

When they left the hotel he was taken aback by her outfit choice but figured it was her personal style. He thought the outfit was inappropriate for where they were heading but didn't want to offend her. Knight and Scotland approached the table where Ba'Sheer Turner, his manager and two Nike execs were awaiting their arrival.

"Oh my God is that Ba'Sheer Turner?" Scotland whispered out of the side of her mouth.

"Yeah."

"You didn't tell me we were having dinner with Ba'Sheer Turner." Scotland said about to pass out.

"Cause I didn't want you to freak out like you're doing right now."

"Ok, Scotland, pull it together." She said to herself.

"Good evening, gentleman." Knight smiled and shook everyone's hand. "This is my friend Scotland."

Scotland quickly looked up at him. Her feelings were hurt. She hadn't expected him to introduce her as his girlfriend but she for damn sure hadn't expected just to be his friend either. Friends didn't do the nasty, freaky things they did to one another the night before. Playing it cool, she shook the guys' hands.

"What an interesting hair color." Carlos a Nike exec eyed her curiously.

He'd never seen anyone with gray hair.

"I've never seen anything like it."

"Thank you. I guess." Scotland replied unsure if she was being dissed or complimented.

"Damn, Knight. You ain't tell me you had friends that look like this." Ba'Sheer shook Scotland's hand slowly.

He took his time to admire her exposed assets. Scotland instantly felt cheap. She wanted to disappear but instead she shook his hand and smiled. On the up side, she was shaking hands with Ba'Sheer Turner. He was the biggest athlete in the world. Everyone wanted a piece of him. He was not only handsome but smart as well. He graduated college at the top of his class.

Ba'Sheer was 6'4, weighed 220 pounds and was chocolate. He rocked a low cut with spinning waves and a beard that would put Rick Ross' to shame. The man could most definitely get it.

"Where is Lennon?" Ted the other Nike exec asked Knight.

"She's in St. Louis swamped with work. She's so sorry that she couldn't make it but sends her love," Knight replied pulling out Scotland's chair.

He had no idea that his response had pierced her heart. Scotland had no idea that she was second choice. She thought that he'd intended on bringing her the whole time. It was becoming clearer and clearer by the minute that YaYa was right. She was nothing more than Knight's side ho.

"Ohhhhhh, I see you, playa," Ted winked his eye.

"No, it's not like that," Knight assured.

He was beginning to think that bringing Scotland to dinner wasn't such a good idea.

"Scotland is the homegirl. Ain't that right?" He asked her.

Scotland swallowed the tears in her throat.

"Yeah, we're just friends," she declared.

Knight could see that he'd hurt her tremendously. He'd never meant to put her in such a fucked up situation. After that, Scotland sat back silent. She had nothing to say. While the men talked over drinks, she sat back deep in thought.

Why am I even here? I should've stayed my black ass at home. No, what you need to do is toss that damn drink in his face for disrespecting you. Got you at this damn table lookin' like a video ho. They all think you're his whore. Well, aren't you? Y'all are just friends, right?

"Scotland, your dinner is getting cold." Knight got her attention.

Scotland snapped back to reality and looked down at her plate.

"What is this?" She furrowed her brows.

"It's short ribs, bone marrow and gnocchi. Try it. It's delicious," Knight insisted.

"What is bone marrow?" She asked in a low tone so that no one else could hear.

"It's the soft, mushy inside of the bone."

Scotland tried her best not to throw up. The shit looked and sounded disgusting. She didn't want to eat bone marrow at all but she didn't want to come across uncultured. She didn't even know how to eat it. Self-conscious, she picked it up with her hand and tried sucking the substance out. Everyone at the table looked at her like she was crazy as she sucked loudly on the bone.

"Slurp!" She sucked hard to no avail.

"It ain't coming out." She got frustrated and hit the bone on the plate repeatedly causing a loud clanking noise.

Other people in the restaurant were starting to stare at them.

"Scotland," Knight laughed nervously. "Put the bone down. That's not how you eat it." He took the bone marrow from her hand and placed it back down onto her plate.

Scotland wanted to cry. She was so embarrassed.

"You take your spoon," he instructed.

Scotland picked up her spoon and followed suit.

"Scoop out the inside and eat it." He showed her.

Scotland felt like a stupid, uneducated child. She looked like a complete and utter fool in front of Knight and his business associates. She didn't even know why he'd brought her. She wasn't on his or the people he worked with level.

"Thanks, I got it." She zoned everyone at the table out.

Scotland placed the spoon up to her mouth and tasted the marrow. The shit tasted like lard. There was no way she was going to be able to swallow it so she spit it out back onto her plate.

"Uh ah... no!" She wiped her tongue clean with her napkin. "Ain't no fuckin' way. What the hell you got me eating? They ain't got no fried chicken up in here?"

"No." Knight said totally humiliated.

He couldn't believe that she'd spit her food out in front of everyone as if it were nothing.

"Shit, I'm like you Scotland," Ba'Sheer chimed in. "I ain't down wit' all this bougie shit either."

"Where a Popeye's at in this muthafucka?" Scotland raised her hand for a high-five. "Give a bitch a three piece and a biscuit."

"Ya' heard." Ba'Sheer gave her a five.

"Ooooook." Scotland laughed.

She didn't care that Knight had a look of bewilderment on his face. It was what he got. He'd embarrassed her so she was going to embarrass him.

"When this wrap up, me and you should go get a bite to eat for real," Ba'Sheer said seriously.

"We might just have to. I'm sure my buddy here wouldn't mind." Scotland roughly massaged Knight's shoulder.

Knight wanted to kick her ass for showing out in front of everyone.

"Actually, I do mind. We have an early morning tomorrow." He responded with an attitude.

He didn't like the chummy banter between Scotland and Ba'Sheer at all. He knew Ba'Sheer was on her and he wasn't having it.

"Damn, y'all leaving tomor? I was tryin' to get up wit' you." Ba'Sheer cupped his hand over Scotland's.

"No, we're here for one more day." Scotland replied, loving the attention.

"So uh, Ba'Sheer, back to this deal." Knight tried to get the meeting back on track.

"Hold up," Scotland stopped him. "We're not done talkin'. What did you have in mind for us if we kicked it?" She asked Ba'Sheer.

"Is this your first time in Miami?"

"It is."

"Well, I'd love to show you around. Take you to dinner and get to know you better." He flashed his megawatt smile.

Knight's blood was boiling. He knew Scotland was trying to make him jealous and it was working. She was his and now that he'd gotten a taste of her sweet kitty he would never be able to let her go.

"Sounds like a plan to me," Scotland smirked.

"Give me your number so I can give you a call." Ba'Sheer handed her his phone.

Scotland took the phone and said, "Gladly."

"I BARELY UNDERSTAND IT.
NOT THE WAY I PLANNED IT.
WHY CAN'T IT JUST BE
WHAT IT IS?"

-MARIO, NO DEFINITION

CHAPTER 12

"What the fuck was that?" Knight barked as they entered their hotel room.

"What was what?" Scotland played coy, throwing down her purse.

"Did you really give ole boy your number?" Knight took off his suit jacket.

"Who?" Scotland continued to walk towards the bedroom.

"Yo, stop fuckin' playin' wit' me. You know who the fuck I'm talkin' about! Did you give him your number?" Knight untied his tie.

"I sure did." Scotland took off her blazer.

"So that's what you on? I bring you here wit' me and you give another nigga yo' number and in my face no less," Knight fumed.

"We're just friends, right?" Scotland spun around and faced him. "I mean 'cause that's what you said." She folded her arms across her chest.

"C'mon, man, you know I had to say that. Everybody at that table knows that I'm engaged to Lennon. I had to tell them we were just friends."

"And you really think they believed that? Look at how I was dressed." Scotland looked down at her outfit.

"I look like a high-priced hooker! You know how dumb I felt dressed like this? I could've worn the dress you bought me! It was right here in my bag!" She reached inside her suitcase and pulled it out.

"If I would've had this on then those arrogant-ass, Nike execs would've respected me more! But nooooo... instead I looked like some uneducated, ghetto bitch that you fuck on the side!" She threw the dress at him.

"Why did you even bring me here anyway? You could've fucked me back in St. Louis," she snapped.

"I bought you here 'cause I wanted to spend some time wit' you but obviously that was a mistake."

"That's the first thing we've agreed on all night," Scotland shouted.

"Yeah, 'cause you was actin' like a fuckin' bird!" Knight barked.

"Oh, so now I'm a bird?" Scotland placed her hand up to her chest appalled. "Fuck you! I should've stayed my ass at home. You got a whole bitch that you're engaged to and call yo'self having a damn attitude. Nigga, please."

"But who I'm here wit'?" Knight countered. "You!"

"Don't act like you doing me no favors. It was by fuckin' default, my nigga! The only reason I'm here is because yo' bitch couldn't come. So let's not pretend that it's more than what it is. You fuckin' humiliated me tonight." Scotland kicked off her heels and threw them down onto the floor.

"I humiliated you but you were all up in another man's face? Yeah, ok." Knight scoffed. "Sell that bullshit to somebody else. Just admit it. You got in yo' feelings 'cause I said you were my friend but that's what we are, Scotland. Ain't no title to this. You're not my girl. You're just my friend."

Knight knew that his words would sting but it was the truth. He dug the shit outta Scotland but he had a whole life before he met her that he just couldn't put aside. He needed time to figure out his feelings and figure out what role he wanted her to play in his life, if any.

Scotland licked her bottom lip and nodded her head. Everything in her wanted to cuss him out but she couldn't because she'd done this to herself. She'd fallen for somebody that never made it clear what his intentions were with her. She'd jumped in feet first based on the hope that they'd somehow be together. But Knight didn't know what he wanted. She didn't have time to play games with another indecisive-ass nigga.

"I wanna go home." She turned around and stomped towards her bags.

"What?" Knight screwed up his face.

"I wanna get the fuck outta here!" Scotland began to throw her things into her suitcase.

"Our flight doesn't leave for a whole, 'nother day." Knight unbuttoned his shirt and took it off.

"I don't give a fuck! I wanna go home now!" Scotland ran into the bathroom and grabbed her toiletries. "Do what you gotta do so I get the hell outta here."

"I ain't doing shit. If you wanna leave early find your own damn way home," Knight shot, unfazed by her dramatic behavior.

"I can't stand yo' black ass. Fuck you," Scotland hissed.

"Fuck me?" Knight repeated enraged.

That was the second time she'd said that to him that night. He'd let it slide the first time but now he was gonna have to dig in her ass for being disrespectful.

"Word? Fuck me? Nah, fuck you!" He grabbed Scotland by the wrist and yanked her towards him.

"That's really how you feel? Fuck me?" He held her wrist tight.

"Let me go." Scotland tried to wiggle away.

"Nah, answer the question." He held her wrist even tighter. "You bold enough to let it come out yo' mouth. Back yo' shit up. Fuck me? For real? After everything?"

"Everything? It ain't been nothin' but a week," Scotland remarked as if he were insane.

"I don't give a fuck how long it's been. Don't ever say fuck me unless you mean that shit. Now, I'ma ask you again. Is that how you feel?" He pulled her into his chest and unhooked her bra.

Scotland's breasts spilled out into the open air.

"What are you doing?" She inhaled deeply.

"You really wanna go home?" He leaned down and twirled his tongue around one of her harden nipples.

"Knight, stop." Scotland clinched her pussy walls. "I'm not about to fuck you."

"You really wanna leave me?" He lifted her up into the air and threw her down onto the bed.

Scotland's head hit the pillow. Knight stood before her unbuckling his pants. Seconds later, he was naked. She marveled at his toned physique. His body resembled an African god. Knight had muscles in his arms, chest, stomach and thighs. The Ken Doll slits on his hips made her mouth water. Looking at that region of his body only made her focus her attention on his long, thick, chocolate dick.

It was hard and pointing in her direction. All thoughts of leaving had completely vanished. She'd completely forgotten why she was mad in the first place. Knight crawled on top of her with his belt in his hand.

"You bet not hit me with that," she warned.

Knight had a crazed look in his eyes. She didn't know what he was up to. Without uttering a word, he took her arms and lifted them above her head. Scotland breathed heavily. Knight took his belt and tied her hands to the headboard. Scotland was right where he wanted her. She was helpless and unable to leave. He was going to make her regret ever telling him she wanted to go.

Using his teeth, he unbuttoned her jeans and slid them down. Scotland eagerly kicked them off. Knight pushed her panties to the side and toyed with her clit with his thumb. Scotland watched, coming undone. Knight was a master at manipulating her pussy. He knew exactly what to do to make her cream. Knight slipped two of his fingers inside her warm slit while continuing to thumb her clit. Scotland drowned in his touch. She was losing her mind.

"Oh my God." She met each thrust of his fingers with a roll of her hips. "Why do you keep doing this to me?"

"Cause you like it?" Knight replaced his fingers with his dick.

Scotland's eyes rolled to the back of her head as she gasped for air. She wanted to protest and beg him to stop because they still hadn't solved anything, but having him inside her felt like home. The pull of her hands by his leather belt and the stroke of his dick pounding into her were almost too much to handle. The leather burned into her skin. She was experiencing a combination of pleasure and pain. She liked it. Knight was turning her into pools of liquefied passion.

"You still wanna leave?" He asked, holding her legs up in the air.

Scotland eyed him through the V-shape of her legs. She knew the game Knight liked to play so she didn't say a word.

"Answer me." He demanded, stroking harder.

"Ahhhhhhhh…" Scotland moaned.

"You still wanna leave me?" He went deeper, hitting her G-spot.

"Noooooooo!"

"You gon' be a good girl?"

"Yessssssssss." Her breasts jiggled back and forth as he rocked her pussy to sleep.

"PHONE CALLS OUT THE BLUE ASKIN' HOW I BEEN."

-ALGEBRA BLESSETT, BETTER FOR ME

CHAPTER 13

Scotland and Knight made love for hours. They made love until they each were physically exhausted. Her wrists were sore and red but she didn't care. The scratches and bite marks on Knight's body made up for it. Together they lie chest to chest wrapped up in each other's arms. The balcony doors were open. A cool breeze swept into the room.

Scotland never wanted to let him go. She hated that they'd fought. Knight felt the same way. He never wanted Scotland to see that angry, jealous side of him. He loved that things between them were normally peaceful. Scotland made him undeniably happy.

After seeing her flirt with Ba'Sheer, he realized just how much he cared for her. He didn't want to admit it because of the repercussions, but he was falling for her. The feelings he had for her were unlike any other. He was engaged to Lennon but he never felt the way he felt towards her like he did for Scotland.

Scotland was a different breed. She was witty, sassy, funny, energetic and fun to be around. She never complained and was grateful for every opportunity she got. To see her eyes light up over the simplest things made him happy.

She was a strong beacon of hope. She showed him what life could be like if he just let go. He no longer wanted to coast through life. Being in Scotland's presence made him want to live life to the fullest. He wanted to feel completely fulfilled, like he did when he was with her, all the time.

"Guess what?" He said, holding her in his arms as he gazed at the moon.

"What?"

"You make me happy?" He admitted.

Scotland looked up at him and smiled.

"Really?" She blushed.

"Yeah." He kissed her forehead. "You're my baby."

"I like the sound of that." She closed her eyes and inhaled the scent of his skin.

He smelled like blackberries and oak. She loved that when she talked to him he seemed to adore her every word. She could tell him how she felt and he never judged her. He never made her feel stupid or ghetto. He understood her which made her want to open up to him even more.

"I'm sorry for flirting with Ba'Sheer," she whispered.

"It's cool. I deserved it."

"No you didn't. You've done so much for me in such a short amount of time. For that alone, you'll always hold a special place in my heart," she confessed. "Can I tell you something?"

"What's up?"

"This thing between me and you is scaring the hell outta me."

"Me too," Knight chuckled. "I swear to God I wasn't expecting this shit. I'm buggin' out for real."

"I know. You only see stuff like this in the movies. I mean, I loved the guy I was seeing before you a lot but I'm starting to question if that was even love. I'm starting to think it was just a deep infatuation."

Knight lay quiet. Had she just confessed to being in love with him? Knight didn't want to ask the question in fear of what she might say.

"How long were y'all together?" He asked instead.

"Off and on for two years. It was a mess. He cheated on me with so many girls."

"Why did you keep going back?"

"I don't know," Scotland shrugged.

"I guess 'cause I wanted to believe that he cared for me as much as I cared for him. I got sick of being alone and just wanted someone there to hold me at night. It's hard being single nowadays. It seems like the more sense you have, the harder it is to find a stand-up guy. I truly believe that if I was just out here giving up the pussy, I would have niggas all over me. But since I keep my legs closed, have morals… well not in this case," she laughed. "I find myself alone."

"Damn, I would've thought you had niggas knockin' down your door," Knight said surprised.

"I mean, I got a few friends but they ain't talkin' bout shit. As soon as I say I want a relationship, they on some, I'm tryin' to stay focused bullshit."

"That's crazy. So you sure you're over your last dude?" Knight died to know.

"I'm very sure. That shit been dead a long time ago. I just kept trying to bring life back to it. I got a question for you though." Scotland sat up on her elbow and rested her chin on the palm of her hand.

"Shoot." Knight lay on his back.

"Why are you still wit' ole girl? It's obvious you're not happy."

"You know what? I've been questioning that myself. She's cool sometimes. She just do too much and we're so different. She wants me to be somebody that I'm not. You know, I've never told anybody this, but I don't even wanna be a sports agent." He looked at her.

"Really?" Scotland said shocked.

"Nope. I wanna own a restaurant. Cooking is my thing," Knight smiled.

"That sounds dope. Why don't you do it? I'm sure you have the money."

"It's a huge financial risk and I got my family to take care of. I wanna make sure that they straight for life."

"Hold up, you ain't got no kids do you?" Scotland asked alarmed.

"Nah," Knight grinned. "I'm talkin' about my moms, my sisters and they kids. I got a li'l brother but he out in the streets doing his thing. We barely speak."

"That's fucked up."

"Yeah, but it is what it is. Can't save everybody," Knight sighed.

"He on drugs or something?"

"Nah, but he sell'em and it's fucked up 'cause he's smart too."

"What's his name? I might know him."

"Omari."

"Oh, nah. I don't know no Omari." Scotland shook her head. "So what's gonna happen when we get home?"

"I wish I had answers for you, baby girl, but I honestly don't know. I got so much I need to think about. Just know that I fuck wit' you heavy. The energy that you're getting from me ain't fake. What we share is real."

Scotland sat quiet and allowed his words to sink in. Basically, they were still in limbo. She hated this part. She wanted to move forward but so many things stood in their way. She wished that she could hit restart and start all over again. Maybe then she'd do better at hiding her emotions but here they were. She was deep in her feelings and he was still unsure.

The girls sat four to a booth at Panera Bread enjoying their iced coffee and bagels. Scotland had been back in town a few days. It was her first time talking to or seeing the girls since she left. She was extra excited to tell them about her trip.

"Look at you lookin' like an easy, breezy, beautiful, bad bitch." La'Shay snapped her fingers in a circle in approval of Scotland's look.

"Is that a Hermès cuff bracelet he bought you?" She examined her wrist. "And why yo' wrists so red?"

"You don't wanna know," Scotland giggled. "And yes, it is."

On their last day in Miami, Knight took her on a huge shopping spree. Scotland told him that the trip was enough but Knight insisted that she let him buy her a few things.

"You want some of my cinnamon bagel?" La'Shay placed it up to Tootie's mouth.

"No! You know I'm on a diet. I gotta get this weight off of me."

"Didn't you just eat a slab of ribs last night?" YaYa pointed out.

"Who asked you?" Tootie threw up the middle finger. "Y'all know I'm going through it."

"Going through what? What happened?" Scotland asked confused.

"That day when we were over your house helping you pack… When I got home, why were all my electronics gone? My flat screen, my tablet, my microwave, my DVR, you name it; it was gone."

"Was Romelo there?" Scotland asked still perplexed.

"Yeah."

"He was in the house the whole time?"

"Yeah."

"Where he say everything went?"

"He said he never saw none of the stuff," Tootie shrugged her shoulders, sadly.

"And you believe him, Tootie? Please tell me you don't," Scotland begged, hoping her friend couldn't be that dumb.

"I mean—"

"Tootie, noooooooo!" Scotland threw up her arms in distress. "Girl, you know damn well that crackhead had some niggas come over and rob your shit. While he was there!"

"I know…," Tootie sighed.

"I know that's RJ's daddy but fuck that," Scotland said furiously. "Don't let that nigga around shit of yours, including RJ. Hell, you keep it up and yo' ass gon' come up missing."

"I'm not; that was the last straw," Tootie assured.

"I hope so."

"Now, back to you, bitch," La'Shay interjected. "What else you get?"

"He bought me so much stuff, y'all. I kept tellin' him no but he just kept on buying shit."

YaYa sipped her drink and eyed Scotland enviously. She looked better than she ever had before. Scotland was laced from head to toe in designer gear. She rocked a semi-sheer sweatshirt with two color block stripes, black, skinny jeans and 3.1 Phillip Lim suede mule sandals. Her entire outfit was well over two grand. YaYa didn't understand why Scotland always lucked up and got the dudes that were caked up.

"He copped me some stuff from Givenchy, Alexander Wang and Balmain. Y'all, I was overwhelmed. I didn't know what to do. Hell, this Alexander Wang top I got on right now cost $595. I'm used to paying $13 for a shirt at Forever 21. My shirt is a used car, y'all," she joked.

"And guess what? He bought me all that stuff and then said that I didn't have to worry about paying Lennon back. He said he'd pay for the damages. He's gonna give her the money and act like I paid him," she beamed.

"That's what up." Tootie nodded her head in approval.

"You must've gave him some, girl," La'Shay teased.

"I did and as soon as we got there too," Scotland laughed.

"Was it good girl?" Tootie asked in a hush tone.

"A-MA-ZING. The things that man did to me," Scotland sighed heavily, falling back against the seat. "I couldn't keep my hands off of him."

"Girl, I have never seen you look this happy," Tootie said, happy for her friend.

"If I were you, I wouldn't be braggin' about gettin' gifts and fuckin' an almost married man." YaYa said displeased with her sister's behavior. "That shit ain't cute. Mama and Daddy raised you better."

"How she braggin' when I asked her a question?" La'Shay challenged. "Sit yo' petty-ass back and be quiet." She waved her off.

"Right, Petty Crocker." Scotland responded unfazed by YaYa's sour attitude. "You know I'ma give y'all some of the stuff 'cause I can't keep it all for myself." She confirmed as she received a text message.

Scotland checked her phone. It was a text from Murda. The message read:

<Messages   **Trash**   Contact

IMU... How u been?

"Boy, bye." She tossed her phone back down on the table.

"Who was that?" Tootie asked.

"Murda," Scotland rolled her eyes.

"What he say?" YaYa's upper lip curled.

Scotland passed her the phone. YaYa read the message and slid the phone back.

"Mmm." Her face grew hot.

"I swear it's like this nigga can sense in the air when I'm happy."

"The devil is a lie. Don't let that nigga take away your joy 'cause I have never seen you this happy," Tootie professed.

"I really am happy. I had so much fun with him, you guys. We had a slight hiccup but other than that it was chill."

"What happened?" YaYa asked intrigued.

Scotland stirred in her seat. *Why did you say that,* she thought? She knew YaYa fed off drama. She thoroughly enjoyed making Scotland look like a fool.

"We worked it out but at dinner with his business associates he introduced me as his friend and my feelings were kinda hurt," she confessed.

"How were your feelings hurt? He spoke the truth." YaYa shrugged her shoulders dismissively.

"Yeah but we're not just friends; that's the thing," Scotland rebutted.

"So what? You wanted him to introduce you as his side piece? I mean, 'cause that's what you are. You act like you want him to glorify that shit."

"I don't want him to do or say anything he's not comfortable with. That's why we had a discussion clarifying exactly what we are," Scotland spat.

"And what are you?" YaYa sipped on her drink and cocked her head.

"We're taking things slowly." Scotland played with her straw.

She knew she sounded ridiculous.

"We're gonna take our time and figure this out 'cause we both really care about each other."

YaYa damn near spit out her drink she was laughing so hard.

"Girl, you sound 'bout crazy. Y'all takin' things slow? That nigga hit you wit' the infamous side bitch line. Scotland, listen to yourself. You sound stupid as fuck. That nigga playin' you, ma. He's gassing yo' head up and buying you a bunch of expensive-ass shit to keep yo' ass pacified. He's trying to keep you distracted from what's real. That's why y'all still tryin' to figure things out." YaYa made air quotes with her fingers.

"You obviously didn't listen to a damn thing I said to you before you left. You came back sounding even dumber than before."

"First of all, I'm not dumb." Scotland checked her. "You haven't even met him so how you know how he feel about me? Only he and I know what we have and what we share. You can't judge that. I know Knight cares for me. And yeah, shit is moving fast but what we have is real. So you can keep your li'l opinion to yourself."

"Ok, Karrueche Tran." YaYa rolled her eyes. "Believe what you wanna believe but when he breaks your heart don't come crying to me."

"MAYBE I NEED TO TUCK IN MY THIRST."

-JENNI LOVETTE, NOT GOOD ENOUGH

CHAPTER 14

*"I'ma make her scream my name, baby. She gon'
wanna marry me."* Adrian Marcel's *5 Minutes* bumped
softly as Scotland climaxed. She lie on her back spent. As
soon as she got off work, she met Knight at her place so he
could have his way with her. All day long they'd been
sending sexy messages to one another. By the time
Scotland made it home, she was hot and bothered.

She and Knight didn't waste any time tearing each
other's clothes off. The two of them went at each other like
two wild animals. They hadn't physically seen each other
since they came back from Miami. A week had gone by.
They missed each other like crazy.

How much they missed each other was shown
through their love making. Scotland pulled the covers up
over her breasts and watched as Knight stood up and placed
on his pants. She wondered where he was going.

Knight zipped his pants and looked around her
place. It was his first time being inside her crib. It wasn't
horrible but it wasn't great either. None of the fixtures or
appliances was up-to-date. Some of the paint on her walls
was chipping.

He was kind of frustrated because he couldn't even
get to fuck her like he wanted to because of her broken bed.
He didn't want it to collapse so he took it easy. Easy wasn't
his thing. He liked it rough. Fucking at her apartment was
definitely not an option anymore. Knight sat on the end of
the bed and placed on his dress socks.

"I'm 'bout to get outta here in a minute." He put on his shoes.

"You leaving already?" Scotland asked, disappointed.

"Yeah, I gotta get home." He stood up and put on his shirt.

"I thought you would at least stay a little while. I haven't seen you in a week. I didn't think you were just gon' smash and dash." Scotland sat up and combed her fingers through her hair, frustrated.

"I'll try to stay a little longer next time."

"Next time?" Scotland eyed him in disbelief. "So that's what this is gonna be? You just gon' come over, fuck me and leave?"

"What are you talkin' about?" Knight said annoyed. "I can't stay as long as you want one time and it's a problem? This my first time coming over here. You act like this is a continuous thing."

"But it will become a continuous thing if I don't put a stop to it now. I'm not gon' be the girl that you fuck on the side," Scotland declared.

"Who said you was gon' be? What the fuck is wrong wit' you?"

"You! You're what's wrong with me. I'm starting to feel like this ain't nothing but a game to you."

Scotland felt herself cracking. Everything YaYa said was coming to fruition. Scotland had just been too foolish to see it.

"You about to come on or something 'cause you trippin'?"

"No, I'm not about to come on. My period ain't got shit to do with this. I'm starting to fall in love wit' you, Knight, and I'm not trying to get my feelings hurt."

Knight dropped his hands down to his sides. She'd finally come out and said it. He thought she loved him but wasn't sure. Or maybe he was sure and just didn't want to face the truth. He could tell she loved him by the way she looked at him, the way she held onto him at night. It was written all over her face.

He knew he cared for her deeply. He didn't wanna lose her but things between he and Scotland was getting too heavy. He told her he needed time to think. He couldn't understand why she was trying to rush him by throwing her emotions out on the table. It wasn't fair because now if he didn't tell her he loved her back he'd be the bad guy. Knight took his hand and rubbed his eyes.

"Why did you have to say that?"

"Cause it's true. I'm not gonna lie about my feelings." Scotland wrapped the covers around her body tight.

She felt overly exposed. It was obvious by his reaction that Knight didn't feel the same way. *I'm so fuckin' stupid. What am I doing?*

"How you know you love me? We've only known each other a few weeks."

"Love doesn't have a time limit, Knight. Look, it's cool. It's ok. You don't love me back. I'm a big girl. I can handle it. I didn't expect you to anyway."

"Don't put words in my mouth." He rose and threw his suit jacket on. "You don't know how I feel about you."

"Scoot over," he said.

Scotland reluctantly moved over. Knight sat beside her. She wouldn't even look him in the eye she was so upset.

"Look at me." He turned her face towards him. "When I told you, you were my baby, I meant it." He cupped the side of her face with his hand.

"You're not just somebody I'm fuckin' so get that shit out yo' head. I have feelings for you and just because mine aren't moving as fast as yours doesn't mean that they aren't as strong."

Scotland blinked away the tears in her eyes. She was so confused she couldn't think straight. The genuine feelings she felt from Knight mixed with the doubts YaYa had implanted in her mind were driving her mad. She wanted Knight but she also wanted her dignity. She couldn't risk winding up on the losing end of the stick but the selfish part of her wasn't ready to give him up either.

"Now stop acting like a spoiled brat and give me a kiss."

Scotland was still torn but kissed him anyway. There was no way she could say no to Knight.

"I REALLY CAN'T BE TOO MAD; THE CRAZY BITCH STILL HAD YOU FIRST."

-JENNI LOVETTE, NOT GOOD ENOUGH

CHAPTER 15

"Let's practice our numbers in Spanish." Scotland sat Indian style on the play room floor of the Frasiers' home.

Busy and Liam sat before her playing with their toys. They were barely paying her attention but she was determined to get them to learn.

"Busy, say uno," she encouraged.

"Một trong những." Busy said in Vietnamese instead.

"We're practicing Spanish today, sweetie, so say uno."

"Uno," Busy groaned.

"Dos." Scotland encouraged Liam to say as well. "Liam, say dos."

"Hooooo," Liam cracked up laughing.

"No! That is a bad word," Scotland shrieked.

"Ho-ho-ho-ho-ho-ho!" Liam covered his mouth and laughed hysterically.

"I'm gon' whoop you," Scotland warned.

"No you not," Liam giggled.

Scotland couldn't even get mad 'cause she knew she wasn't going to spank Liam either. Besides it being against Mr. Frasier's rules, she was too tired to spank him anyway. Her shift was over but she'd agreed to work overtime. The Frasiers were having dinner guest and needed her there to keep an eye on the kids until they went to sleep. Scotland couldn't wait to get home and lie down.

It didn't help that she was missing Knight like crazy. She'd only seen him once since he came over to her house. It had been almost two weeks. The reason they hadn't seen each other is because he said that he was swamped with work. Scotland tried to be understanding but dating someone to only barely see them wasn't what she signed up for. They talked every day, all day, nonstop but there was nothing like seeing him face-to-face. Wanting to hear his voice, she called him. She was disappointed when he didn't answer.

Scotland poked out her bottom lip and placed her phone down. Seconds later Knight text her back.

<Messages **Bae** Contact

Hey, boo! What's up?

A little perturbed that he decided to text her back instead of call she responded:

<Messages **Bae** Contact

Nothin'; just wanted 2 talk. Y u textin' me back?

Cuz I'm in a meeting

Scotland found it kind of odd that he would be in a meeting that late at night but went along with his story.

<Messages   **Bae**   Contact

Ok, well, I ain't want shit. Just hit me up later.

Knight replied back and said a'ight.

"Ok, gremlins," Scotland sighed. "It's time to take a bath." She got up off the floor.

She left the kids to play while she went to the linen closet to grab some towels. Mr. and Mrs. Frasier were down the hall in the living area getting prepared for their guest. They both looked like movie stars. Mr. Frasier wore a Berluti, soft plaid jacket, crème colored, fitted tee, linen-cotton blend, flat-front trousers and Berluti brown, Gaspard, slash-toe, leather shoes.

Mrs. Frasier matched his fly by wearing a black, La Petite Robe di Chiara Boni, off the shoulder, peek-a-boo jumpsuit. The chic jumpsuit accentuated her long legs and modelesque frame. Her red hair was up in a sleek ponytail which showcased her 5 carat diamond earrings. The two of them looked fabulous together. They could've easily been featured in Vogue magazine.

If you didn't know any better, you would think they were the perfect couple. They weren't however. Mr. Frasier hardly ever talked to Mrs. Frasier unless he absolutely had to. He acted as if she got on his last nerve. Mrs. Frasier felt the cold shoulder he was giving her. However, that didn't stop her from trying to breakthrough to her husband. She was determined to get their marriage back on track. She felt that deep down inside, he had to still love her.

As Mr. Frasier tried his best to avoid Mrs. Frasier, Chef Pierre cooked up a fantastic meal. The house was filled with the aroma of sautéed onions, garlic and mushrooms. Scotland was hungry as fuck and wanted some. Chef Pierre always looked out for her and sat her aside a plate to take home. The kids had already eaten dinner. All Scotland had to do was bathe them and put them to bed then she could go home. As she pulled two face and body towels from the linen closet, the doorbell rang.

"They're here." Mrs. Frasier sang doing a quick jog to the door. "Hiiiiii!"

"Hi, love!" Lennon air-kissed each of her cheeks.

"How you doing, Maggie?" Knight gave her a warm hug.

"Come on in." She stepped to the side.

Lennon walked in and smiled seductively at Paul. All she could imagine was tearing his clothes off and fucking him right then and there. Whenever she and Knight had dinner with the Frasiers', she and Paul's sexual chemistry filled the air. Lennon played it cool and sauntered towards him.

"Paul." She said sweetly, air-kissing his cheek.

"Lennon." He wrapped his arm around her waist and held her a little longer than he normally would have.

"You look beautiful." He gushed, finally let her go.

Maggie smoothed her hair back. She hoped the pain she felt on the inside didn't seep out onto the surface. Paul hadn't even acknowledged how she looked. Maggie couldn't even hate on Lennon though. She looked phenomenal. She wore a fitted, red and white printed cardigan, white crop top and a long, red and white, flower print, flowing skirt. Maggie diverted her attention from the hole in her heart and on Scotland whom she saw in the hall.

"Scotland, honey, come meet our guest," she called.

Knight's eyes instantly flashed towards the direction of the silhouette coming down the hallway. *It can't be,* he thought as Scotland neared. His heart sank down to his knees. He had no idea that Scotland was the Frasiers' nanny. Scotland tucked the towels underneath her arm and prepared herself to act as if she was interested in meeting the Frasiers' guest. The bright smile on her face vanished as soon as her eyes connected with Knight's. Her heart almost fell out of her chest as she spotted Lennon standing beside him.

"Knight and Lennon this is our nanny, Scotland. Scotland meet Knight and Lennon, Paul's colleagues." Maggie grinned oblivious to the awkward tension in the room.

"Don't I know you?" Lennon squinted her eyes. "You look oddly familiar." She focused in on Scotland trying to remember where she knew her from.

"I crashed into your car back in August." Scotland replied wanting to die.

"Now I remember you." Lennon looked at Scotland as if she smelled.

"Nice to see you again, Scotland." Knight held out his hand for a shake.

Scotland swallowed back her tears in her throat and placed her small hand inside his. She wanted to slap fire out of him not shake his damn hand. He'd lied to her. Scotland was furious. She'd never be able to look at him the same way again.

She now questioned everything he had ever told her. All of the nights he said he was busy with work she now wondered was he just laid up with Lennon. It was becoming crystal clear that she was nothing but a glorified side chick. Scotland felt like a dummy. She couldn't continue to allow Knight to play her. She could no longer be blinded by his mesmerizing eyes or poetic words. It was all bullshit.

It didn't help that she looked a hot-ass mess. She didn't have on a stitch of makeup. Her hair was in two braided pigtails. She wore a ratty, old, OBEY t-shirt, black leggings and Jordan's that she'd had for years. Every time she was in Lennon's presence, she looked like a ghetto banshee.

"So you all know each other?" Paul asked surprised.

"Sort of," Lennon replied. "Like she said, she and I got into a finder bender. Austria here backed into my car."

"You mean Scotland?" Maggie corrected her.

"Did I say Austria?" Lennon laughed knowing damn well she'd butchered Scotland's name on purpose. "Forgive me. Names escape me."

"I have to go give the kids a bath." Scotland said to Mrs. Frasier.

"Sure, go ahead."

Scotland didn't bother giving Knight or Lennon a second glance. She had to get out of that room before she broke down in tears. She quickly got the kids in the tub, closed the door behind her and allowed herself to cry. Hot tears scorched her cheeks. She couldn't tell if all the things Knight had told her were a lie or the truth. *Did he truly care for me like he said he did or was it all game?*

"Fuck this," she said underneath her breath, wiping her face.

Sniffling, she began to bathe the kids. Back in the living room the couples made small talk while drinking wine.

"Mmm," Lennon placed down her wine glass. "Paul, I hate to talk business right now but I need your advice on a client of mine. Maggie, do you mind if I steal your husband for a minute?"

"He's all yours." Maggie said draining her glass.

"Paul, do you have somewhere we can talk privately?" Lennon asked with a devilish look in her eye.

"Yeah." He rose from his seat.

"Baby, I'll be right back." Lennon assured Knight by placing a soft kiss on his lips.

Paul led her to his home office. The two of them didn't waste any time getting physical. Lennon fervently bent over his desk. Paul unbuckled his belt and unzipped his pants.

"Fuck me," Lennon ordered.

Paul lifted her skirt. She wore no panties just like he requested. Paul grinned and inserted himself deep inside her walls. Lennon sunk her teeth down into her bottom lip. She was in sheer agony. Each thrust of his dick made her want to scream out his name but she couldn't. His wife and her fiancé were only a few feet away.

Lennon held onto the desk and willed herself not to make a sound. Paul watched as her ass cheeks jiggled. He pounded her pussy at a feverish pace. He loved the way her cream covered his dick. Paul closed his eyes and relished the feel of the electric currents soaring through the limbs of his body.

He didn't even bother pulling out as he came. He came long and hard inside of Lennon like he always did. Cumming too, Lennon soaked up every drop of his semen. Her body had been craving that quickie. With Paul, she felt like they were equals. He was on her level in every way. If she had it her way, they'd be getting married and living happily ever after.

"That was fantastic." She turned and kissed Paul passionately on the lips. "If we had enough time I would suck your dick right now."

"You know how I like it when you suck it." He slapped her hard on the ass. "C'mon and clean up before Maggie or Knight come looking for us." He handed her a few tissues.

Lennon wiped the leftover juices from in between her thighs and threw the tissues in the trash. After straightening their clothes, she and Paul left the office as if nothing had happened.

"There you two are." Maggie plastered on a fake smile. "Dinner is ready."

"Good 'cause I'm hungry. I've worked up quite an appetite." Paul rubbed his stomach.

"Me too, I'm famished." Lennon winked her eye at him and took a seat at the table.

"Lennon, are you okay? You're sweating profusely." Maggie questioned.

Lennon patted her forehead so she wouldn't ruin her makeup.

"I think I'm just having a hot flash or something." She fanned herself nervously.

Knight wondered how he could make his way towards the back to talk to Scotland. He had to explain to her why he'd lied.

"Excuse me. I need to go wash up before dinner."

"You remember where the bathroom is right?" Maggie asked.

"Yeah, down the hall and to the left," Knight responded.

"Yep."

"And hurry up. We're ready to eat," Paul declared.

Knight shot him a quick thumbs up and walked down the hall. He didn't know which room Scotland was in but he was determined to find her. Scotland was in Liam's room. She'd already put Busy down for bed, now it was Liam's turn. She stood at his changing table applying lotion to his legs. Knight silently crept in the room and closed the door. Scotland didn't even know that he'd entered the room.

"I need to talk to you." He said in a low tone scaring her.

"You scared the shit outta me." She jumped holding her chest.

"Look, I was wrong for lyin' to you. I just didn't know how to tell you what I had going on tonight. I knew you were gonna get mad and I ain't wanna argue wit' you again," Knight said truthfully.

"You ain't gotta explain nothin' to me. We good," she said nonchalantly. "We ain't together."

"You ain't gotta front. I know you mad. You got every right to be." He tried to come near her.

"Uh ah, move back." She softly elbowed him in the stomach to push him away. "You better get back in there with your fiancée. We don't want nobody to get suspicious, now do we?" Scotland shot sarcastically.

"C'mon, Scotland, don't be like that." Knight tried to reach out for her arm.

"I told you to move." Scotland shot him a death glare.

If he touched her she was sure to black out and hit him. Knight caught the hint and backed away reluctantly. He didn't want to leave but he had to get back to Lennon. He was under enough stress as it was. He didn't need any more unwanted problems that night. Knight shook his head, heated, and left the room. He would have to deal with Scotland after dinner.

"Thank God. He's back." Paul raised his hands in the air. "Now we can grub. Get down wit' the get down. Ain't that how y'all say it?" He teased Knight.

Knight eyed Paul sideways as he sat down.

"I don't know what you're talkin' about." Knight replied not amused by Paul's humor.

Lennon could since his tension.

"Calm down, baby. It was just a joke," she whispered.

"Joke my ass." He placed his napkin in his lap.

Knight was not in the mood for Paul's racist-ass comments.

"Dinner smells delicious, Maggie," Knight said warmly.

"Yes it does," Lennon agreed. "I can assume you didn't make it." She quipped with a laugh.

Stunned by her backhanded comment, Maggie took a sip of her wine before responding.

"No, Lennon, I didn't. Cooking isn't my thing."

"That's what Paul tells me," Lennon smirked.

Maggie looked at her husband devastated. She couldn't believe that he'd discussed their marriage to another woman.

"Oh, really?" She cocked her head back dismayed.

"I mean, you can't cook, Maggie," Paul scoffed. "It's not like I lied."

Maggie didn't even bother responding. Her feelings were beyond hurt. She worked a full-time job then came home and took care of their kids by herself while he sat on his ass and watched Sports Center. She tried her best to be superwoman and cater to his needs. All he did was put her down every chance he got. Maggie didn't know how much more she'd be able to take.

"Dinner is served." Chef Pierre placed their food before them. "Tonight, I've prepared braised short ribs, creamy polenta and mushrooms. Enjoy." He nodded and backed out of the room.

"This looks delicious." Paul said ready to dive in.

Lennon looked down at the food and immediately felt sick to her stomach. Out of nowhere she felt queasy. Knight couldn't concentrate on eating either. All he wanted to do was talk to Scotland.

He couldn't imagine what was going through her mind. They'd just spent a magical few days in Miami. They'd confessed their hopes, dreams and fears to one another. He felt himself falling for her. Pangs of love filled his chest. He didn't know how much longer he'd be able to hide it.

"Knight, you haven't touched your food," Maggie noticed. "And neither have you, Lennon. Is something wrong with the food? We can have Chef Pierre prepare you something else if you like."

"Nah, I'm good. I just have a lot on my mind," Knight replied.

"I hope you're thinking about our wedding. There is still so much that needs to be done." Lennon took a sip of her drink. "Who knew that planning a wedding would be such a headache?"

"I loved planning me and Paul's wedding." Maggie smiled fondly at the thought. "It seems like ages ago."

"It feels like it too," Paul chuckled.

"Excuse me." Scotland entered the dining room with her purse in hand ready to go.

Knight looked over his shoulder at her. Scotland avoided his eye contact and looked the other way.

"The kids are asleep so I'm going to head out."
"No, join us. Stay for dinner." Maggie got up and pulled out a seat next to her.

"I don't wanna intrude. Plus, it's late," Scotland shook her head no.

"Nonsense, I insist." Maggie pulled out a chair next to her.

"Maggie, this was supposed to be an intimate dinner with just us and our friends, not the help." Paul said disgusted by the thought of breaking bread with Scotland.

"First of all, she's not the help. Scotland is practically family," Maggie insisted.

"I should go before things get out of hand. Lord knows I don't wanna turn up in here tonight," Scotland said ready to blow.

She was not in the mood for Mr. Frasier's bullshit. It was bad enough that the man she secretly loved was only inches away from her and she couldn't even acknowledge her feelings for him.

"I see her mouth is still reckless," Lennon remarked, rolling her eyes. "I swear finding good help nowadays is nearly impossible."

"Chill," Knight warned.

"What?" Lennon shrugged.

"Chef Pierre, can you bring Scotland a plate?" Maggie said over her shoulder. "She's joining us for dinner."

Maggie made Scotland sit down. Scotland reluctantly sat at the table. She leaned back in her seat with her purse in her lap. She wasn't about to eat a thing. She felt sick to her stomach just being there.

She did everything in her power to avoid eye contact with Knight. If she looked at him once she was sure to break down and cry. It was hard enough to comprehend that she was about to share a meal with the man she loved and his fiancée. Scotland was a tough chick but she wasn't built for this shit. Chef Pierre placed a plate in front of Scotland and gave her a look of encouragement. He knew she needed it. The tension in the dining room was so thick you could cut it with a knife.

"So you two." Maggie pointed her fork back and forth between Scotland and Lennon. "Got into a car accident? That's how you all know each other?"

"Well, I don't really know her. She and I obviously don't run in the same circles," Lennon said defensively.

"You'd be surprised." Scotland said with a sudden fierceness.

"No, honey, you run with the Mike Browns of the world." Lennon folded her arms across her chest.

"What the fuck is that supposed to mean?" Scotland fumed.

"Yeah, clarify that shit." Knight ice grilled her.

"Let's be serious here. She and I are not on the same class level," Lennon said firmly.

"No, we're not 'cause I have more integrity in my pinky finger than you have in your whole entire body!" Scotland sat up straight.

"Bougie bitches like you make me sick! You think 'cause you got a little bit of money that makes you better than me or less black! The zeroes in your bank account don't mean shit 'cause like Mike Brown and Treyvon Martin, yo' ass will still get killed just because of the color of your skin! You better wake up, bitch!" Scotland snapped.

"How dare you to speak to our guest like that?!" Paul threw down his napkin furiously. "Who do you think you are? Do you not know your place?"

"Whoa!" Knight scooted his seat back. "What exactly is her place? You talk to her like she's a damn slave!"

"Let's not make this a racial thing 'cause it's not that at all!" Paul clarified.

"Then what is it?" Knight challenged.

"C'mon, Knight, she's not like you. She's not like us," Paul reasoned.

"Paul, you sound absolutely ridiculous," Maggie said flabbergasted.

"No, I'm being realistic. We're all college educated, cultured, individuals. People like her just wanna listen to 3 Chainz, get a head full of gray weave, smoke weed and let people like us finance their ghetto lifestyle! I'm sick of it! I've worked too hard while people like her sit on their ass and do nothing with their lives!"

"And then they wonder why the police shoot them," Lennon shot Scotland a mock-glare and grinned.

Before any of them knew it, Scotland leapt across the table and grabbed Lennon by her throat. Glasses, plates and floral arrangements flew everywhere. Struggling to get away, Lennon waved her arms and kicked her legs frantically causing her chair to fall back. She and Scotland fell to the floor in a thud. The fall didn't cause Scotland to lose her grip on Lennon's throat though.

"Scotland!" Maggie screamed in a panic.

"Get your hands off of her!" Paul raced around the table and tried grabbing Scotland.

"Fall back, homey!" Knight pushed Paul out the way. "You ain't gon' put your hands on her!"

"Scotland, let her go." Knight pulled her off of Lennon.

Lennon held her neck and gasped for air.

"You crazy bitch. I'm gonna sue you for everything you have!" Lennon declared.

"You ain't gon' get much 'cause let you two racist muthafuckas tell it, I ain't got shit no way, which I don't!" Scotland spat.

"Mommy? What's going on?" Busy entered the dining room rubbing her eyes.

"Baby, what are you doing up?" Maggie rushed over to her and picked her up.

"I heard you all yelling and I got scared."

"You a'ight?" Knight looked Scotland over to make sure she was ok.

"Are you seriously asking her if she's okay?" Lennon said in disbelief still on the floor. "She just attacked me!"

"And you deserved it, bitch!" Scotland lunged at her again.

Knight held her back.

"Knight, why are you sticking up for her?" Lennon yelled. "You barely know her! You should be over here with me! I'm your fiancée!"

"Did you not just see what she did?" Paul questioned.

Scotland looked at Knight. This was his chance to tell the world that he loved her and wanted to be with her, but instead, Knight looked at her with sorrowful eyes and said, "Cause I understand where she's coming from. I get it."

Scotland nodded her head. A million tears filled the brim of her eyes. He'd just disrespected everything that they'd built. Scotland was better than this. She didn't deserve to be treated like a dirty, little secret. Hell, Knight was no better than Paul and Lennon. He might've cared for her but his actions showed that he was ashamed of her.

"Fuck this bullshit. I quit!" Her voice trembled.

"No, Scottie! You can't go!" Busy began to cry.

Scotland looked at Busy with tears in her eyes. She didn't want to leave but she had to. She would not be disrespected by anyone for a paycheck. Scotland was done being the victim. She didn't utter a single word. The look of pure disgust on her face said it all as she grabbed her purse and stormed out the door.

"THE DEVIL IS A LIE. YOU WON'T GET TO HAVE YOUR CAKE AND EAT IT TOO."

-JENNI LOVETTE, NOT GOOD ENOUGH

CHAPTER 16

Knight was so heated after the crazy dinner from hell that he didn't even bother taking Lennon home. He was so pissed off that he didn't wanna look at her face. The dumb-ass, ignorant statements that she made instantly made him look at her differently. He knew exactly who she was. She was an uppity, spoiled princess that looked down on the lower class. She didn't like certain types of black people and the certain types of black people she didn't rock wit' were people that grew up just like him.

It didn't matter that he was a multi-millionaire and wore Ferragamo suits and ties. He was still the same little, black boy that grew up on the West Side of St. Louis. He could feel the hunger pains in his stomach from the nights he didn't have food to eat. Privileged people like Lennon would never understand that.

She never knew what it was like to struggle which was ultimately causing the demise of their relationship. Lennon didn't even see that the things she said were wrong. She also didn't understand why Knight refused to take her home. Knight didn't give a fuck how she felt or about the fingerprints that were imprinted into the skin of her neck.

He had to go see Scotland. He had to go make things with her right. The whole ride over, he'd tried calling her and she wouldn't answer the phone. Knight pulled in front of her building and parked his car. He didn't even bother to turn off the engine. He jumped out and ran down the walk way. Frantically, he rang the doorbell and pounded his fist on the door.

Scotland sat at the top of the steps. She knew he was coming. Each pound of his fist against the door caused her heart to skip a beat. She knew if she answered the door he'd say something to pull her back in and she couldn't chance it. It was time to end whatever it was she and he had. Seeing him with Lennon confirmed her quiet fears. He could never truly love her or be hers.

Although they came up the same, they were completely different. She would never be smart or classy enough. She would never fit into his social circle of friends. She didn't have what it would take. Paul and Lennon were right. She was useless, ghetto trash.

"Scotland, open up! I need to talk to you!" Knight yelled. "Baby, I'm sorry! Let me explain!"

"You gon' need to shut up all that damn noise!" Lisa stepped outside smoking a cigarette and drinking a cup of coffee. "What the hell is wrong wit' you? Folks tryna' watch Scandal. Scotland, you better come get'em for I call the police!"

Scotland let out a long, deep sigh. She would rather pull her teeth out one-by-one then face Knight but she got up anyway. She didn't need the police knocking on her door, especially with all of the racial tension in St. Louis. Hesitantly, she unlocked the door and opened it. Knight's hand immediately fell to his side once he saw her face. Scotland's eyes were swollen with tears.

"Girl, what the hell you done did to this man?" Lisa asked standing back on her leg.

She was in her robe and slippers like always.

"He don't know niggas get shot for disturbing the peace?" She looked Knight up and down.

"It's ok, Lisa. He won't make any more noise," Scotland said exasperated.

Lisa looked at her and saw how distraught and swollen her face was.

"This nigga ain't hit you did he? You ain't gon' be Chris Browning my girl, nigga. Scotland, say the word and I'll call the homies from up the street." Lisa said ready to pop off.

"No, he didn't hit me," Scotland replied.

"Yo, can you give us a minute?" Knight said with an attitude.

"Oop." Lisa clutched her invisible pearls. "Excuse me, choosy lovah. You ain't said nothin' but a word and turned me on all at the same damn time." She winked her eye and walked back inside.

"What's up?" Scotland asked with a stone expression on her face.

"Don't what up me. You already know what it is. I've been hittin' yo' phone and you ain't answering. That's what we do now?" Knight mean-mugged her.

"What you mean is that what we do? We ain't shit. You made that clear tonight, bruh, so I don't even understand why you're here."

"I'm here 'cause I love you. I'm sorry that I didn't say it when you wanted me to but I needed some time to figure this all out."

"Now you love me? Ok." Scotland massaged her forehead.

She was starting to get a headache.

"And figure what out, Knight? There's nothing to figure out. We met, we kissed, we fucked and pillow talked a little bit, that's it. I don't know why I made myself believe that you were going to leave ole girl and we were gonna be together. I don't know why I'm so fuckin' stuck on stupid. All of my life I have been waiting on someone to save me. Whether it be my birth parents, my friends or some damn man but I always end up at the same place, here with a cracked face and a broken-ass heart. I can't keep doing this to myself. I won't do this to myself anymore 'cause it hurts way too fuckin' much. So please, Knight, do us both a favor and turn around and leave. Let's just act like neither one of us ever existed."

Knight hung his head and licked his bottom lip. He could never do that.

"I can't do that."

"Well, you're gonna have to." Scotland refused to budge.

Knight eyed her quizzically.

"You and I both know that there ain't no forgetting this. How could I forget you? You're perfect. I couldn't pray you away even if I wanted to." He massaged her cheek with his thumb.

"You're a part of me now. I ain't expect this shit to happen but it did and now I can't let you go. I don't give a fuck how mad you get, how much you get in' yo' feelings or try to push me away. You're mine. Ain't shit gon' change that."

Scotland gazed deep into his smoldering, brown eyes. She could see herself wrapping her arms around his neck and hugging him with all of her might. She imagined the feel of his warm breath on the side of her neck as he held her close and she allowed herself to believe his words. Maybe she was jumping the gun by giving up so soon.

She could tell he was being truthful about his feelings. His lips spoke nothing but the truth but she'd played the fool one too many times for men like Knight before. She was over being any man's second choice. It was either all or nothing.

"I'm done." Scotland stepped back. "Please respect that and leave me alone."

She took one last look into his sorrowful eyes and closed the door in his face.

"WHEN I SAID I DIDN'T NEED YOU, BOY, YOU KNOW I WAS JUST FRONTIN' HARD."

-BRANDY, WITHOUT YOU

CHAPTER 17

Scotland lay in her bed with her phone up to her ear. The sound of the phone ringing was killing her softly. This had to be her fifteenth time calling Knight. He hadn't bothered to pick up any of the times. Scotland felt like she was going insane. It had only been a few days since she quit her job and told Knight that she was done with him.

She'd been sick ever since. She never thought in a million years she'd miss him so much. They'd only known each other a short amount of time but the impact that he had on her life was profound. He'd opened her up to the possibility of real, true love.

She'd been in and out of her tumultuous relationship with Murda for so long and been disrespected on so many occasions, that she'd forgotten what a healthy relationship looked like. Her biggest fears were falling back into that rut with Knight. Her heart could no longer take shock and disappointment. She yearned for a slow and steady love.

The question still remained - could and would Knight give her that? After only one night she'd begun to regret her decision. She missed him so much it hurt. She tried hitting him up so they could talk things out but he wouldn't answer. After all of the beautiful words he'd spoken to her, she never expected him to shun her. Maybe he was just spitting game to her the whole time.

Maybe she was the only one that had fallen so deep. Scotland never thought she'd be in this space again. She'd jumped too soon to say fuck it and now had to suffer the consequences. She'd acted on emotion instead of thinking about long-term repercussions. The love sick, nauseating feeling in her stomach was equivalent to death. She just wished he'd answer the phone. The silent treatment he was giving her was too much to bear.

The fact that she was not only man-less but jobless, was killing her even more. Mrs. Frasier had called and apologized profusely for Mr. Frasier's behavior but Scotland wouldn't accept it. Mrs. Frasier apologizing on the behalf of her husband wasn't going to fly. She'd done nothing wrong.

Mr. Frasier owed her a personal apology but she'd never get it. Mr. Frasier was a delusional bigot. Although she'd been fired by the nanny agency for her poor behavior, Mrs. Frasier begged her to return to work but Scotland refused. She could never work there again. Mr. Frasier didn't respect her. She'd miss the kids terribly but being treated like dirt wasn't worth her self-respect or her dignity.

Scotland would work at McDonald's if she had to. From the looks of her damn near empty wallet, she was going to have to. Scotland lay on her back gazing at the ceiling. She hadn't left her bed in days. It had become her safe haven, her sanctuary. Clothed in her favorite Victoria Secret Pink pajamas, she closed her eyes and tried to erase visions of Knight from her mind. She tried to think about anything but him; nothing was working. He kept invading her memory bank. Scotland popped her eyes open.

"Fuck this shit." She groaned, placing a pillow over her face. "Get over it. It's over. You said you were done fuckin' wit' him so deal with it. He ain't even answering your phone calls no way. Keep it pushin', ma. The dick wasn't even that good anyway." Scotland tried to convince herself.

"Bitch, please. Who you foolin'? That shit was magically delicious. Damn, I'ma miss that shit." She glided her left hand across her breasts.

"You gotta get over this nigga. You fucked up your whole life behind this shit. What the fuck were you thinkin'?" Scotland asked herself sitting up.

Her knees were up to her chest.

"Knight and Lennon are gon' be good. You the dumb one sittin' up here wit' no man and no job. This is by far the dumbest thing you've done." Scotland closed her eyes again.

A single tear slipped out of the corner of her eye. Flashbacks of the first time she and Knight kissed, them lying side by side in the park, and making love on the balcony in Miami tortured her. She wanted to scream but if she screamed the whole world would hear her cries.

"Lord, I want him back. I don't care. I just want him back." She cried into the palms of her hand.

Then suddenly, her cell phone began to ring. The sound of Alex Isley's *Set in Stone* ringtone caused her to nearly jump out of her skin. It was Knight. Scotland's heart began to pound like a bass drum. She wasn't expecting God to answer her prayers and especially not so fast. With a sweaty hand she answered the call.

"Hello?" She said barely able to breathe.

"Come outside." Knight demanded then hung up.

Puzzled, Scotland held the phone for a second. She wondered what he was up to. Maybe he wanted to tell her to stop calling him face-to-face. Scotland slid out of bed and threw on her leopard print house shoes. She'd never been more afraid in her life. She knew she'd told him it was over but she was just angry at the moment and didn't really mean it.

She had to make him see that she was just trippin'. She understood now that he needed time to make such a detrimental decision. Sure she loved him, and she was sure he loved her too, but loving each other didn't out-trump a relationship he had for years, or did it? Scotland stepped out into the afternoon sun. She hadn't felt the rays from the sun in days. Knight sat inside his Mercedes-Benz S-Class Coupe. It was obvious by his slouched posture that he wasn't getting out to open her door. Scotland pulled the door handle and got in.

"Hi." She spoke softly sliding into the passenger seat.

Knight didn't speak back. He turned up the volume on the radio and speed off. Scotland turned the volume down and asked, "Where we going? I ain't even lock my door."

"Fuck that door." Knight turned the volume up high and gripped the steering wheel tightly.

The veins in his forearm protruded through his skin. Sex appeal and anger oozed from his veins. Scotland examined the side of his face. From the serious expression on his face she could tell he had a lot on his mind. He looked stressed out. He hadn't shaved. He wore a simple, white tee, jeans and Tims.

The intoxicating scent of his cologne filled every crevice of the car. He hadn't looked her way once but she didn't care. He was there next to her. That was all that mattered. It didn't matter where they were heading or that she looked a hot mess, as long as they were together.

Drew Anthony's *FYIWW (For You I Will Wait)* played as he drove. The song had a cinematic romantic feel to it. The singer talked about taking things slow for the woman he loved. He promised that he would always be there for her. Scotland wondered if Knight felt the same way. Fifteen minutes later, they pulled into a residential neighborhood in the Central West End. Knight parked the car.

"Get out," he demanded.

Scotland eyed him sideways and rolled her eyes. She could only take but so much of his bossiness. Feeling some type of way, she did as she was told and got out of the car. A middle-aged, white woman jogged down the street. She looked at Scotland curiously. Scotland immediately remembered that she was dressed in her pajamas during the middle of the day. She also didn't have on a bra. Scotland quickly folded her arms across her chest.

"Come on." Knight took her by the hand and led her up a flight of steps that led to a three-story, brick, row home.

Knight pulled out a key and unlocked the door. He escorted Scotland inside the empty house and turned on the lights. Scotland looked around in awe and bewilderment. The house was everything she'd ever dreamt or prayed for. She wondered why Knight had brought her there. Was he trying to throw up in her face that he'd bought him and Lennon a home?

"Whose house is this?" She asked strolling around the living area.

"It's ours." Knight said at once.

Scotland spun around and looked at him.

"It's whose? Ours?"

"That's why I haven't been answering any of your calls. I've been busy securing this for us."

"You lyin'?" Scotland twisted her lips to the side in disbelief. "You didn't buy this house for real."

"Here's your set of keys." Knight reached inside his pocket and handed them to her. "You can start moving your things in today if you like."

"Knight, like seriously. Wait a minute." Scotland said feeling faint. "I can't afford this. I just quit my job and even wit' a gig I still couldn't afford this."

"It's already bought and paid for. You always said that you wanted a house like this so I got it for you. I got it for us." He stepped closer. "That's how serious I am about me and you. I told you I don't play about how I feel. When I said I loved you, I meant it. I'm cuttin' things off wit' Lennon. I wanna be wit' you. So what's up? You down or what?"

"Hold up," Scotland paused. "What brought all of this on? Just a minute ago you weren't sure."

"When you told me you were done fuckin' wit' me, that messed me up for real. I couldn't have that. So I had to make a choice - respect your decision and be miserable without you or man up and step up to the plate. Like you said, love doesn't have a time limit. And no matter how hard I tried to fight it, love kept creepin' in. You're the one for me. You're the woman I need."

Scotland's entire face lit up. She couldn't contain herself. Tears of joy filled her eyes.

"I love you." She leapt into his arms.

Her arms and legs were wrapped around him as she kissed his face repeatedly. Knight held her in his arms and laughed. He hadn't felt this good about a decision in a long time. Leaving Lennon to be with Scotland was a no brainer. She filled every need he ever desired.

She made him undeniably happy. Being without her, if only for a few days, was excruciating. He never wanted to feel that kind of pain ever again in life. She was his baby. He wanted to tell the whole world about their love. He wasn't the type of dude that believed in love at first sight but from the moment they met, he knew there was something special about her. She was the missing piece to the puzzle of his life. Now that he had her, everything felt right.

"I love you so much," Scotland said sincerely.

"Yo' fake ass. Now you love me? Get the fuck outta here. The other day it was fuck me," Knight mocked her.

"I do love you," Scotland grinned.

"Act like it then. Don't ever come out ya' mouth and say you done fuckin' wit' me. You understand?"

"I understand. Now give me a kiss 'cause I missed you."

"I ain't giving you shit," Knight chuckled.

For Lennon it was just another typical day. She'd finished work and was now heading home to unwind. Never in a million years did she expect to walk in on Knight packing his things. They hadn't really been talking since the altercation at the Frasiers' but that wasn't new. She and Knight were always at odds. Just as displeased as he was with her, she was equally displeased with him.

It had been hard for her to even be around him. He made her look like an idiot in front of Paul and Maggie. No matter what happened or how he felt, he was supposed to have her back. She would never forgive him for that. She never thought he would be so mad he'd wanna pack up and leave. Lennon placed down her keys and purse slowly. Knight didn't even bother to look in her direction. Lennon wasn't in the mood for a fight but if Knight wanted a showdown, he was about to get one.

"So you're not going to even speak to me? I know you see me standing here," she spat.

Knight continued to pack his things in silence, pretending that Lennon wasn't even there.

"Are you going on a trip that I don't know about?" She walked over to the opposite side of the bed he was on.

"Nah, I'm moving out." Knight grabbed another stack of his shirts from out of the closet.

"Excuse me? What do you mean you're moving out?"

"What I mean is," Knight paused for a second and looked at her. "Is that this," he pointed back and forth between him and her. "Is a wrap. I don't wanna be wit' you no more."

Lennon stood speechless. She couldn't have possibly heard him right. Knight couldn't possibly be breaking up with her. She was Lennon Whitmore. Nobody dissed Lennon Whitmore. Lennon was a woman that always got what she wanted. No one ever turned her down or said no to her. This had to be some kind of joke.

"Knight," she chuckled. "We're not breaking up. We're engaged. We're about to get married." She tried reasoning.

"You might be gettin' married but I'm not."

"Is this still about the other night? I told you I was sorry. It was the wine talkin'. I didn't mean any of it," she lied.

"A drunk always tells the truth," Knight shot.

"I'm not a drunk." Lennon corrected him offended by his comment. "Knight, you really have to learn how to forgive and forget. I've apologized to you and so has Paul. Carrying all of this anger inside of you is not healthy."

"You and Paul can kiss my ass. I don't fuck wit' either one of y'all. Like I told Paul today at work, respect me and I'll respect you. Other than that, stay the fuck away from me," Knight warned.

Lennon felt her face become hot. She was about to have a stroke. The wedding she'd been planning for months was only two months away. All of her friends and family would be there. It was the social event of the year. She would look like a complete loser if she had to call it off.

"You can't do this to me." She panicked as her chest heaved up and down. "What will everybody think?" She massaged her temples.

"See, that's your problem. You always worrying about what somebody else gon' think. Fuck what everybody else thinks! What about what I think or how I feel? Don't you think I get tired of hearing that shit?" Knight barked.

Lennon's mind raced. In her mind there had to be another logical explanation to why Knight was behaving the way he was. It couldn't have possibly been because she was a selfish bitch.

"No-no-no! You will not do this to me! I won't stand for it!"

Knight sat on the side of the bed facing the wall. He tried his best to drown out Lennon's screams. He was mentally drained. He was tired of fighting with Lennon. He didn't have the energy to anymore. She was delusional. She was more concerned with them having to call off the wedding versus him leaving her.

Knight didn't care though. He had one bag left to pack and he was up. He was ready to move on from her and her toxic attitude. He deserved to be genuinely happy with a woman that didn't put him down or treat him like he was less than she was.

Their relationship was doomed from the start. She never appreciated him. She always looked down on him and his upbringing. She never took the time out to fully understand him. She never wanted to become closer to his family. Knight should've known their relationship was doomed when his mother didn't like her. He figured if he loved her enough, she'd grow to love him just the same. Years later, they were still right where they began.

He couldn't take pretending to be happy anymore, especially when he had somebody as sweet and caring as Scotland by his side. In a matter of a month she'd come and completely changed his entire existence on earth. His job was to love her with every fiber of his being.

A woman like her deserved every ounce of love he had to give. If given the chance, he wanted to spend the rest of his life figuring out ways to show her just how much she meant to him. She no longer had to worry about him being indecisive and playing with heart. She was what he wanted.

Knight knew Scotland's heart was fragile. He often imagined it being like paper and torn into a million little pieces. With time, love and patience, he'd mend those tattered pieces back together like she'd done for him.

"I can't believe you're doing this to me!" Lennon cried pacing back-and-forth.

The hem of her hoop skirt twirled with each turn. She was so distraught she couldn't breathe.

"What did I do to deserve this? You just up and decide one day that you're done? Who does that? You! Because you have no regard for anyone but yourself!"

"You sound fuckin' stupid," Knight shook his head.

"You really think this came outta nowhere?" He looked over his shoulder at her. "Where the fuck have you been this entire relationship?"

"Here! Supporting and grooming your ungrateful-ass for success! Do you know all the things I have had to put up with just to be with you? I had to suffer through that horrid music you like to listen to, your ghetto boy, flashy clothes, heart/artery clogging fried foods, your illiterate homeboys and let's not even talk about your ratchet mother and hood rat sisters!"

"Yo, you say one more thing about my family and I swear to God I'ma fuck you up," Knight warned, feeling like his head was about to explode.

Back in the day, he would've fucked somebody up for saying some disrespectful shit like that. He wasn't trying to go to jail but if Lennon kept it up, he was sure to end up there.

"My reputation is ruined because of you! I'm going to look like a total loser and Lennon Chanel Whitmore is not a loser!"

"I'm up." Knight grabbed his duffle bag and headed towards the door.

"I'm not done talking to you!" Lennon raced behind him and grabbed him by the arm.

"What have I told you about touching me?" Knight looked down at her hand on his arm.

Lennon could see the venom in his eyes. She quickly removed her hand from his arm and composed herself.

"I just wanna know what I did wrong. Tell me, what did I do?" She pleaded.

"When I told you it was over, did you ever stop to say I love you, don't go, I'm sorry, let's try and work this out?" Knight quizzed.

Lennon tried to think of a quick comeback to explain why she hadn't done any of those things but couldn't think of anything quick enough.

"I'll answer that for you," Knight remarked. "No, you didn't. Everything that has come out of your mouth has been me this, me that. This relationship has been all about you! It was never about us and that's why I'm done fuckin' wit' you!"

"That's some bullshit and you know it! You know how I feel about you! I love you!"

"Let's be real, Lennon. You don't love me. You feel sorry for me. I'm like a charity case to you. Fuckin' with me is like slumming for you."

"That's not true," she lied. "We can fix this, Knight. I'll change. I'll do better. Just don't leave me." She said as a stream of tears fell from her cheeks.

"Please don't leave," she wept. "Oh my God, I think I'm gonna be sick." She held her stomach.

The room had begun to spin. Lennon had to sit down or else she was going to faint.

Slowly she slid down the wall and sat down. For a minute, Knight almost believed she was sincere. He'd never seen Lennon so broken. She never cried or showed real emotion. Once the room stopped spinning, Lennon looked up at him and said, "Our wedding is around the corner, Knight. I can't look like a fool. We can get married and then annul it. I just can't look stupid."

Knight shook his head and scoffed.

"You're fuckin' insane. I gotta go." He turned to walk away.

"Is it somebody else?" Lennon eased her way off the floor.

Knight stopped dead in his tracks.

"Yeah, it is." He answered without hesitation.

"Who is it?"

"That ain't important. The fact that it ain't you is all you should be concerned wit'."

"No, tell me. I can handle it," Lennon lied. "Is it Jill from accounting? No it's not her." Lennon answered her own question.

"Is it your assistant? She continued to guess.

"It's not anybody we work with," Knight sighed heavily.

"Then who is it?" Lennon stomped her foot.

"It's Scotland."

Lennon blinked her eyes. Stunned weren't the words to describe how she felt. She truly felt as if she'd been kicked in the stomach with a steel toe boot.

"The chick that ran into your car. The Frasiers' former nanny. The girl who whooped yo' ass the other day. Scotland; that's who I'm leaving you for. Now if you'll excuse me, I gotta go. She's waiting on me." Knight turned and walked out the door.

"You bastard!" Lennon picked up a crystal vase and threw it at his head.

As Knight closed the door behind him the vase went crashing into the wall breaking into a million pieces.

"THE WORLD SAYS THAT
THIS LOVE IS NOT DEFINITE
BUT MY HEART SAYS THAT
IT IS."

-FANTASIA FEAT. BIG KRIT,
SUPERNATURAL LOVE

CHAPTER 18

"Turn right onto Eagle Valley Drive." The GPS system instructed Lennon.

She looked around wearily as she made a right turn into the Bentwood Townhomes complex. She'd never been on that side of town before. Never had she seen so many thugs and scantily clad dressed young girls in her life. There was trash on the sidewalks. Children were outside running in the streets. She almost hit a little girl as she drove. The little girl had the nerve to get an attitude for almost getting hit and threw up the middle finger at her.

Horrified, Lennon wondered had she made the right decision by paying Scotland a visit but there was a conversation between them that needed to be had. Lennon pulled up to Scotland's address and parked. She was troubled to see a woman next door sitting on the porch, sipping on what Lennon hoped was coffee, and smoking a cigarette while dressed in a pink robe and slippers. Six kids played around her. The children were wild like banshees running and screaming. The woman seemed unfazed by all of the chaos going on around her.

Lennon grabbed her Jimmy Choo, leopard print clutch and got out. A group of African American, teenage boys with their pants sagging down to their knees eyed her as she chirped the alarm on her Rolls-Royce Wraith. Lennon flashed the can of mace on her key chain at the young boys. She would gladly use it on them if they got out of line.

Little did Lennon know, but the boys weren't thinking about her. They only looked her way because she was a bad chick stepping out of an even *badder* car. It wasn't typical to see a Rolls-Royce pull up in the hood. Lennon carefully walked up Scotland's walk-way with a look of pure disgust on her face. She felt dirty by simply being in that neighborhood. At any moment she thought she was going to be attacked. She had to give Scotland a piece of her mind and get the hell outta there before she got shanked or shot.

"Who you here for?" Lisa eyed Lennon suspiciously. "If you're a bill collector, Scotland don't live here no more. She's gone on to The Lord," she lied.

"What are you and why are you speaking to me?" Lennon clutched her purse close to her chest. "This isn't a thing where if I talk back to you, I get jumped into a gang is it, because I am wearing red?" She asked nervously looking down at her red, Donna Karen New York, shift dress.

"What? Girl, whatever. You must be a Jehovah's Witness." Lisa waved her off and went back to doing her crossword puzzle.

Lennon took a wet wipe out of her purse and covered her finger with it and rang the doorbell. She didn't want to physically come in contact with anything in fear that she might catch something. Scotland heard the bell and stopped boxing up her kitchenware. She had no idea who could possibly be at the door.

She wasn't expecting any guest but hoped it was Knight making a surprise pop-up visit. Excited by the thought of seeing him, she ran down the stairs. To her dismay, when she opened the door she found Lennon standing before her. It never failed. Lennon always caught her when she was at her worst. *Can I look decent around this bitch at least once,* she thought.

"What the hell do you want and why are you at my house?" Scotland's nostrils flared.

"Hello, Paris, France," Lennon sneered.

"Not today, Satan," Scotland groaned. "Not today. You must wanna get yo' ass beat again?"

"We got beef, friend?" Lisa questioned sitting up.

What people didn't know was that Lisa kept a burner hidden inside her robe.

"Nah, I'm good, girl. She ain't about that life," Scotland assured.

"So you think you've won, huh?" Lennon ignored her sarcasm.

"Won what?"

"Knight?"

"I'm sorry. I didn't know we were playing a game." Scotland said sarcastically. "What were we playin'? This ghetto chick about to steal yo' man, bitch? 'Cause if so, I won!" She cheered, cocking her head to the side.

"You think you're soooo funny, don't you, Bonquisha? Well the jokes gonna be on you, homegirl, when Knight leaves you and comes running back to me," Lennon retorted.

"Girl, Knight don't want you."

"Knight and I have history. We share a past, common goals. You're a fool if you think all of that can just be swept away in a matter of a month. He's known you for five seconds, sweetheart. You're nothing but a new play toy. He'll have fun playing with you for a while but eventually he'll get bored and throw you away. Knight is mine. It's just a matter of time before he returns home to me. So enjoy it while you can, sweetheart, 'cause this shit will never last. You will never fit in. You will never be me. I will always win." Lennon grinned from ear to ear.

"Bitch, if you don't get yo' dumb-ass off my porch," Scotland snapped furiously. "This ain't the damn Young and the Restless."

It was taking everything in her not to reach out and choke Lennon again. But she wasn't going to give Lennon the satisfaction of calling the police on her.

"Don't bring yo' ass over here no more!" Scotland warned as Lennon walked off.

"I won't have to, honey, because Knight will be back at home with me." Lennon exclaimed getting inside her car.

Scotland motioned for her to suck it and slammed the door shut. She tried to act like she wasn't fazed by Lennon's visit but she was a little bit shaken. What if she was only a temporary rebound? It would kill her if Knight changed his mind and went back to Lennon. Scotland inhaled deeply. She couldn't let Lennon sike her out. No man would buy a house for someone if they weren't sure about them. Lennon was just talking shit because she was mad. Scotland had nothing to worry about. Knight was hers.

It had taken a few weeks of shopping and ordering furniture, appliances and electronics for their new home but Knight and Scotland had finally gotten it done. Things that they'd ordered from IKEA, Home Goods, Restoration Hardware, Wal-Mart and Target were piling in by the second. Although Knight had the money to have custom furniture designed and flown in from around the world, Scotland refused.

She'd lived her entire life barely getting by and now that she was with a man that had money she wasn't going to go overboard with spending large amounts of money. She believed in living under their means so they could have money for a rainy day, vacations and their future kids if they decided to have any. Scotland liked the designer frocks that he laced her with but she was still gonna shop at Forever 21, H&M and Urban Outfitters. She refused to get sucked into the pitfalls of having money.

Scotland stood in the center of their living room pinching herself. She couldn't believe that this was her life. She had everything she'd ever prayed for: a man that loved her wholeheartedly, a beautiful home that she didn't have to struggle to afford and the best thing of all, she felt complete.

All she had to do now was get her career on track. She insisted on getting a job so she could help out with the bills but Knight refused her offer. He only had one request, and that was that she finish writing her book. Scotland felt so blessed to have someone in her corner that supported her dreams. She also encouraged Knight to start working towards his dreams of owning his own restaurant. He told her he would and she couldn't have been more pleased.

Life for Scotland was blissful. Nothing could ruin her vibe or tarnish her spirit. It was a gorgeous Saturday afternoon. The sun was shining. The house was coming together. Everything was good, that was until her friends arrived. She'd invited them over to see the new crib and meet Knight. She hadn't seen them in weeks. She was overjoyed when they pulled in front of the house. Scotland skipped down the steps and greeted them at the car.

"What up, bitch?" La'Shay got out and hugged her. "You look cute."

"I am?" Scotland looked over her outfit.

She wore her hair up in a messy ponytail. A white scarf was wrapped around her head and tied in a bow. Since it was the end of October, she rocked a red and black checkerboard flannel, white tank top, cut off jean shorts and Dr. Marten boots.

"Thank you. I just threw something on."

"Hey, boo." Tootie got out the back seat.

"Hey, love." Scotland squeezed her cheeks. "Where is my baby?" She referred to Tootie's son.

"He's at my mama's house."

YaYa got out the driver's seat and slammed the door. She'd had a long morning at the shop and did not want to use her lunch break to come see Scotland show off her house. They were hardly ever around each other anymore and when they were, all she wanted to do was brag and show off shit. YaYa could watch reruns of Cribs if she wanted to see rich people and all of their overpriced, over the top, tinker toys.

She was starting to feel like she barely knew Scotland anymore. She was turning into the bougie, egotistical, braggadocios chicks they talked about. YaYa adjusted her five dollar bug-eyed shades over her eyes and hung her MK bag from the crook of her arm. She slowly switched around the car.

"Hey, Hollywood!" Scotland stared at her intensely.

She could sense YaYa's stank attitude coming from a mile away.

"Hey," YaYa replied dryly.

"Give me a hug." Scotland approached her awkwardly.

YaYa gave her a one-arm hug and stepped away quickly.

"What's wrong wit' you?" Scotland screwed up her face.

"I'm tired and my head hurt." YaYa walked past her.

"Mmm… ok." Scotland ignored her brush off.

She didn't have time for YaYa and her negative-ass attitude. Lately, negative was all she'd been. Scotland hoped she wasn't jealous of her newfound love and happiness. It seemed like when she was down and out everything between her and YaYa was good. For years she said she wanted nothing but the best for her but Scotland was starting to sense that wasn't true.

"Bitch! He copped you a new car too?" La'Shay ran over to Scotland's brand new Mercedes-Benz G-Wagon.

"Yeah," Scotland smiled brightly.

"Aww, bitch, we 'bout to kill it in this!" La'Shay ran her hand over the black exterior.

"I know! I can't wait to see the look on everybody face when we pull up in this mufucka, especially Murda. That nigga been hittin' me up like crazy lately," Scotland confessed.

"Word?" YaYa said surprised.

"Yes, but I am not stuttin' his ass. That nigga is so tired to me now." Scotland flicked her wrist dismissively. "Come on; let's go inside so y'all can see the house." She led them up the stairs.

"Ladybug, this house is beautiful!" Tootie gasped looking over the front of the house.

"Girl, how much this shit cost? This gotta be like half a mill." La'Shay looked around in awe.

"I don't know." Scotland linked arms with her. "He won't tell me. All I know is that it's paid for in full and it's ours."

YaYa couldn't contain her laughter as they walked inside.

"What's so funny?" Scotland asked as they strolled into the kitchen.

"Is your name on the deed?"

"No." Scotland's face burned red.

"Then it ain't yours. It's his. You gon' learn one day, li'l girl." YaYa giggled pleased with herself.

"Don't mind her. She's just pissy that you found a good come up and she didn't," La'Shay pursed her lips.

"But I'm not with Knight for his money. I would love him with or without it," Scotland said honestly.

"And that's where you gon' fuck up," YaYa declared. "If the dough runs out, you run out the door with it. Cute kitchen though." She admired the marble countertop.

Before Scotland could give her a piece of her mind, Knight interrupted their conversation.

"Baby! Where you at?" He called from the other room.

"I'm in the kitchen!"

Knight met up with her. He didn't know that her people had arrived. He wore no shirt, just a pair of basketball shorts and Jordan sneakers. The girls' eyes immediately grew wide as he entered the kitchen. Knight's body was mouthwatering delicious. Tootie had never seen an eight pack in real life before. La'Shay eyed the imprint of his dick in his shorts. It was thick and long. She had to swallow hard so she wouldn't drool.

"Baby, why you ain't got no clothes on?" Scotland said embarrassed.

"I didn't know we had guests." He wrapped his arm around her neck and pulled her close.

"I told you my sister and my friends were coming over."

"Yeah, but you didn't say what time."

"Whatever; it don't matter. Knight, I'd like you to meet my sister, YaYa, and two best friends: La'Shay and Tootie."

"Oh, girl, he fine." La'Shay arched her brow.

"I told you," Tootie blushed.

"You gotta brother, cousin, uncle, daddy?" La'Shay bit her bottom lip and twisted her right leg from side to side.

"I do," Knight chuckled. "He would probably dig you too."

"So when you break her heart you know we gon' be the ones to pick up the pieces, right?" YaYa spat leaning up against the kitchen island.

"What?" Knight said caught off guard by her comment.

"I mean, I know this shit won't last but obviously my sister don't. She thinks you really do love her but eventually you'll get tired of playin' house and dump her."

"YaYa, what the fuck is wrong wit' you?" Tootie asked stunned. "Why would you say something like that?"

"'Cause it's true and you know it!" She said shocked that no one agreed with her.

"Yo, yo' sister trippin'. Handle that. I'm about to go grab us something to eat." Knight eyed YaYa with disdain as he kissed Scotland on the forehead before leaving.

"You know he's runnin' 'cause it's the truth, right?" YaYa insisted.

"I don't know what your deal is, bitch, but you gotta go. I am sick of you." Scotland pointed to the door.

"This nigga got you sprung. You're really choosing him over me? I'm your sister. I've been there for you since day one." YaYa said in disbelief.

"I'm choosing happiness, YaYa. I don't need no hating-ass bitch cock blockin' my joy; so if you can't be happy for me, then I don't need you in my life and that's real talk."

YaYa stood silent and looked at each of the girls. They were looking at her like they hated her. Tootie and La'Shay weren't backing her up. She stood alone in her theory and disdain for Scotland's choice in a man. She'd exposed herself and took it too far. Even though she didn't want to, she had to swallow her pride and make things right.

"Look, I'm sorry. I just got a lot going on and I took it out on the wrong person. I was totally out of line," she apologized. "Shit has just been really hard lately."

Scotland sighed heavily. She felt horrible. She'd been so wrapped up in her own life that she'd forgot to ask her sister or the girls how they were doing.

"What's going on? You need to talk?" She asked truly concerned.

"Nah, it's something I gotta deal with on my own."

"Well, I'm here if you need me." Scotland rubbed her shoulder.

"You don't have to go through whatever you're going through alone. I'm here for you. We're all here for you," Scotland guaranteed.

"Yeah, bitch, 'cause you've been trippin' lately." La'Shay sneered still not feeling her.

"Your house really is dope though." YaYa admired the huge kitchen and all of the stainless steel appliances. "You did good and I really, truly am happy for you."

"Thank you. That means a lot coming from you," Scotland smiled. "Now let me give you all a full tour of the house."

Scotland and Knight's home was 5,000 square feet and included 5 bedrooms, 6.5 baths, a state-of-the-art kitchen, large media room, a 4-car garage and a separate guest quarters in the back. They even had a swimming pool, Jacuzzi and an oversized patio. Knight encouraged Scotland to decorate the house however she pleased. He trusted her taste. After consulting a home decorator, she went with a downtown, urban-chic décor. Once the tour was over, the girls stood on the porch talking about people on Instagram when Knight returned with Chinese takeout.

"Y'all hungry?" He asked stepping onto the porch. "I got enough for everybody."

"We're actually about to leave but it smells so good," Tootie inhaled the mesmerizing smell.

She wanted badly to stay and get a plate.

"The devil is a liar. I will not go off my diet." She exercised her willpower.

"Where you get it from?" La'Shay asked.

"Lisa's, of course," Knight obliged.

"Ok, you got yo' hood pass." La'Shay gave him a pound.

"Knight, my bad for earlier. I didn't mean to disrespect you like that," YaYa clarified. "I'm just overprotective when it comes to my sister. I don't want her to get hurt.

"You good."

"Well, we're outta here, girl. I gotta get back to the shop." YaYa air-kissed Scotland's cheek.

"Thanks for coming by." Scotland hugged them all goodbye.

She and Knight stood on the porch and watched as the girls piled into YaYa's car.

"So what did you think of everyone?" Scotland wrapped her arm around Knight's waist.

"La'Shay and Tootie were mad cool, but ya' girl, YaYa...she a live one, ma. I don't wanna talk negatively about your sister but I would watch her if I was you."

Scotland allowed his words to sink in as YaYa blew the horn and pulled off.

"IF I COULD... FORGET HIM; I WOULD."

-JAZMINE SULLIVAN, IN LOVE WITH ANOTHER MAN

CHAPTER 19

Scotland never thought the day would come when a man would take her home to meet his family. She felt honored that Knight thought enough of her to do so. She'd dated Murda off and on for two years. He never once mentioned taking her to meet his family. She didn't know much about his family at all. She figured he didn't talk about them because of his lifestyle.

She respected that he wanted to keep his family safe and didn't press the issue but that was her past. Knight was her future. He was a man of his word. Everything he ever told her was true. He treated her like a queen. He hung off her every word. The past month with him had been nothing short of a fairytale.

They were comfortably set up in their new home. While Knight worked, she stayed home and worked on her book. Lennon had been causing a little ruckus at work but it was nothing Knight couldn't handle. Scotland offered to fuck her up again but Knight said he was good. He figured Lennon would eventually move on and find her next victim.

Scotland hoped so because she didn't want any more problems out of Satan's daughter. Being that it was Thanksgiving and it was their first holiday together, Scotland went all out in the looks department. For her makeup, she rocked a Kylie Jenner inspired face. A grey, Missguided, French inspired coat hung off her shoulders. Scotland rocked a two-piece, slate grey, furry crop top and skirt that matched her hair perfectly.

The black, Louboutin Pigalle six inch heels she wore were the most expensive thing on her body. They were her most prized possession. She'd obsessed over them for years and now owned a pair of her own. Scotland looked edgy and fashion forward as usual. Knight thought she looked stunning.

The entire ride over to his mother's house, he couldn't stop admiring her beauty. He loved how her silky, deep brown, skin matched his. It was almost as if she was an extension of him. Her chiseled cheek bones and full, pouty lips mesmerized him. He'd never seen a woman more exquisite than her. He was blessed to call her his woman. Choosing Scotland was the best decision he'd made in a long time. Every time he lay next to her at night and awoke with a kiss from her on his face he thanked God.

Sure, she wasn't the most educated or experienced in a lot of things but none of that mattered. He loved her just the way she was. He encouraged and supported her aspirations and cheered her on in the process. He was her biggest cheerleader. He made her feel comfortable with being exactly who she was. He saw her heart and how big it was. Scotland prayed that the love they shared would last a lifetime.

After almost a thirty minute drive, Knight and Scotland arrived at his mother's house. Knight had bought her a gorgeous mini mansion in St. Charles, MO. His mother, Ms. June, and his twin sisters lived there along with his nieces and nephew. Scotland nervously took one last look at herself in the rearview mirror before getting out.

"If you look at yourself one more time. I told you, you're good," Knight chuckled as his phone began to vibrate. "My mom is gonna love you." He checked his phone.

It was Lennon calling. He didn't know why she was calling him. They had nothing to discuss. Knight forwarded her call to voicemail and placed his phone back inside his pocket.

"I'm just so nervous. I've never done this before. You think I'm overdressed?" Scotland examined her outfit.

"No, now come on." Knight got out the car.

Scotland didn't budge. Her legs wouldn't move. Knight stood in front of the car and looked at her like she was nuts.

"Man, if you don't bring yo' ass on."

"I change my mind. I'm not coming in. I'ma just stay out here in the car," she pouted.

Knight walked around to the passenger side of the car and opened the door. He poked his head inside and said, "What's the problem?"

"You just called off your wedding and now you show up with me. Yo' mama gon' think I'm some home wrecking ho."

"You are," Knight joked.

"Really?" Scotland glared at him not amused.

"I'm just playin'," he laughed. "My mama ain't trippin' off that shit. She ain't like Lennon no way. She gon' be happy I'm wit' anybody but her. Now come on.

My stomach growling like a muthafucka. I can smell my mama greens from all the way out here."

Scotland exhaled and placed her hand inside his. Seconds later she was entering his mother's home. Ms. June had a warm and inviting home. It was immaculately decorated but it still had an old school vibe to it that put Scotland at ease. Ms. June was a big woman but was beautiful no less. Her hair was natural. She wore it in a low cut. She possessed big, brown eyes and a smile that could light up the entire world.

"There's my big head baby." She held her arms out for Knight.

Knight walked into his mother's embrace and gave her a huge hug.

"Mama miss you. Let me take a look at you." She stepped back and examined her oldest son. "You a little on the skinny side. Mama gon' have to fatten you up."

"You trippin'; I'm swole." Knight flexed his muscles.

"Chile, please. Put that li'l arm down. You gon' hurt ya'self." Ms. June waved him off. "Now introduce me to this pretty young lady." She focused her attention on Scotland.

"Mama, this is my lady, Scotland. Scotland this is my crazy mama, Ms. June." Knight introduced them to one another.

"It's a pleasure to meet you." Scotland extended her hand for a shake.

"Uh ah," Ms. June smacked her hand away. "We hug around here." She wrapped her arms around Scotland. "I've heard so much about you."

"Really? You have?" Scotland asked surprised. "I hope only good things."

"Yes, honey." Ms. June ended their embrace. "My son tells me everything. Thank you for making him so happy."

Scotland couldn't find the words to convey her emotions. All she could do was grin and smile.

"Where is Omari?" Knight asked taking off his coat.

"He didn't wanna come 'cause you were gonna be here. It's all just so petty. I really hope you two get it together. Y'all are brothers. Y'all shouldn't be fighting each other," Ms. June spoke sadly.

"That's him. I ain't got no problem with Omari. I just don't like some of the choices he makes," Knight replied. "He needs to grow up and stop wit' all that thug shit. It's wack as hell."

"Well, all we can do is pray for him. Now, enough about that. Come on so I can introduce Scotland to the rest of the family." Ms. June led them into the dining room where his sisters, nieces, nephew, best friend and his girlfriend were.

Scotland said hello and hugged everyone. She was surprised with how open and welcoming his family and friends were. They treated her like she was one of the family. Over dinner they all laughed and talked like old acquaintances. Knight's sisters told old stories about when they were kids.

Scotland soaked up every moment. After dinner they all ate dessert in the family room. A fierce, competitive game of Spades was being held. Knight and his friend Amir were playing against his sisters Mya and Sierra. Scotland sat on the couch eating a piece of strawberry cheesecake. She watched as Knight played. He'd just made another book when his sister Nicole sat next to her.

"You wanna see some pictures of Knight when he was little?" She asked.

"Yes!" Scotland said excited, putting down her plate.

"Not the baby pictures," Knight groaned, throwing down a card.

"Yeah, nigga, she about to see you ain't always been cute."

"Whatever, I'm handsome." Knight winked his eye at Scotland.

"Handsome now, you was an ugly-ass li'l boy," Nicole teased.

"You was ugly, dog," Amir agreed.

"Man, forget you and play the card." Knight threw up his middle finger.

"Ok," Nicole flipped open the photo album. "Here is a pic of Knight when he was first born."

"Aww you were so cute," Scotland gushed.

Knight had the chubbiest cheeks when he was a baby.

"This is him when he was around three." Nicole pointed to a pic of him on Halloween.

He was dressed up as a cowboy. Knight had on a cowboy hat, button up shirt, vest, sheriff badge, jeans, chaps and cowboy boots. He held a silver gun in his hand. It was by far the cutest thing Scotland had ever seen.

"Well, I know what somebody's gonna be for Halloween next year," Scotland remarked.

"Straight up? You gon' do me like that?" Knight laughed.

"I couldn't help it," Scotland grinned, blowing him a kiss.

"Oh, you gotta see this one. This is me, Knight and our baby brother, Omari, at Six Flags. I think Knight was around fifteen on this pic."

Scotland looked at the picture and saw that Omari looked oddly familiar. Before she could really look at the picture, Nicole turned the page.

"This is Knight and Omari a few years ago before they fell out."

Scotland's heart stopped beating. She stared at the picture and wondered how she was still alive. It was as if she'd seen a ghost. *No, it can't be,* she thought examining the picture. *It can't be,* she prayed to God. But no amount of praying to God was gonna change the fact that Knight's little brother Omari was Scotland's ex-boyfriend Murda.

The rest of the night she was as quiet as a church mouse. She couldn't comprehend that the only two men that she'd ever loved were brothers. They were complete opposites. Knight noticed that she'd become withdrawn and called it a night. On the ride home Scotland gazed out the window wondering what she was going to do.

If she told Knight the truth, he was sure to end things with her. What self-respecting man would want to be with a woman that had fucked and sucked his brother? Knight wouldn't stand for it. He'd be totally grossed out by it. Hell, Scotland was, so she was sure he would be too.

Her fairytale love story was over. Things had been going too good. The shoe was sure to fall off the other foot at some point and now it had. Knight would never look at her the same way again. She was tainted now.

"Babe."

"Huh?" She responded sluggishly.

"You a'ight?" Knight asked worried about her.

"Nah, I think I'm coming down with something." She lied unable to tell the truth.

"You wanna stop and get some medicine?"

"Nah, I'm just gonna lie down when we get home." She avoided eye contact with him.

"You sure you're good? You liked my family and everything, didn't you?"

"Of course. They were beyond welcoming. Thank you for bringing me."

"You're a part of the family now. I told you, I'm in this for the long haul."

Hearing him talk about their future crushed Scotland. She had to tell him.

"Knight, I have to tell you something." She turned and looked at him.

"Sssssshhhh…it's been a long day. You're not feeling good. Let's not talk about anything heavy tonight. Let's just go home and chill, a'ight?"

Scotland let out a sigh of relief. Knight was right. It wasn't the right moment to tell him. They'd just had a wonderful day together. She didn't want to ruin that for him. She'd tell him when the time was right.

"SHE IS A STRANGER. YOU AND I HAVE HISTORY OR DON'T YOU REMEMBER."

-ADELE, RUMOR HAS IT

CHAPTER 20

Scotland couldn't sleep at all that night. She tossed and turned the whole night through. She found herself staring absently into the dark replaying the thought that Murda and Knight were brothers. She would've never thought that they would've even known each other let alone be siblings. The two were complete opposites.

They looked nothing alike which meant they must've had different fathers. Their personalities were completely different. Murda was arrogant, selfish, inconsiderate and often cruel. Knight, on the other hand, was compassionate, thoughtful, supportive and loving. Scotland didn't know how she was going to deal with this. Knight was the love of her life.

Although they'd only known each other a short amount of time, she knew they were meant to be together forever. But when he learned that his little brother was her ex, he was going to leave her without a doubt. No man wanted to envision another man dicking his woman down, especially not his brother.

She needed help sorting her mess out so she called up her girls and told them they had to have an emergency meeting. The following night she and the girls met up at Friday's for dinner. Tootie was still in her work scrubs while the other girls were dressed casually cute. The four women sat inside a booth awaiting their food and the tea Scotland was about to spill.

"Girl, I'm about to tear these ribs up." Tootie licked her lips hungrily.

"What happened to your diet?" La'Shay asked.

"Girl, I got tired of feeling like I was near death every day. I had to eat something with a high calorie count." Tootie snorted with laughter.

"Bitch, I knew that shit wasn't gon' last," YaYa said, arrogantly.

"Shut up, hater." Tootie waved her off.

"So, what's going on? Why was it so important that we meet tonight?" YaYa questioned Scotland while taking a sip of her soda.

"I'm in trouble, y'all." Scotland's hands shook uncontrollably.

"What's new?" YaYa griped.

"What the hell you do? You done fucked up with this man already?" La'Shay remarked. "I ain't even got a chance to meet his brother yet."

"Speaking of his brother, that's the problem." Scotland said on the brink of tears.

"His brother?" La'Shay furrowed her brows confused.

"What his brother do?" Tootie asked perplexed as well.

"Ruined my life. That's what he's done," Scotland responded.

"How?" YaYa questioned wishing she'd just spill the tea.

"Ok, so I'm at his mother's house yesterday for Thanksgiving and everything is going great. Now mind you, the brother isn't there because him and Knight don't get along. I meet the rest of the family and they love me. We're getting along great and then it happened." Scotland paused for dramatic affect.

"What?" Tootie asked on the edge of her seat.

"His sister sits next to me and starts showing me old family photos. As she's going through the pictures, I see a pic of Knight's little brother, whose name is Omari, when he was a kid. I'm looking at the picture and I'm like, I know this muthafucka from somewhere. Then the sister shows me a pic of Knight and the brother from a few years ago and I damn near faint."

"Why? Tell us, bitch!" La'Shay said barely able to breathe.

"Knight's little brother Omari...well we know this nigga. Omari is none other than Murda," Scotland confessed.

"You lyin'?" Tootie said in disbelief.

"Get the fuck outta here," La'Shay gasped.

"Are you sure?" YaYa asked dancing with glee on the inside.

"I'm dead fuckin' sure," Scotland responded. "Y'all, I was a wreck the rest of the night. I didn't know what to do. Hell, I still don't know what to do."

"Now I see why you called this emergency meeting," La'Shay sat back stunned. "That's some bullshit."

"Well, you know your relationship is over, right?" YaYa gloated.

"That's why I need y'all help. I cannot lose this man, especially not behind some bullshit like this," Scotland was damn near about to cry.

"Maybe he'll understand, friend." Tootie tried to comfort her. "You had no idea they were brothers so it's not your fault. He can't be mad at you."

"Girl, bye," YaYa shook her head. "It's a wrap. If he's a real nigga, he's going to drop her ass as soon as he finds out 'cause that shit goes against the code. Men are territorial. They like to put the woman they wife on a pedestal. Niggas love fuckin' wit' chicks that they know ain't nobody else had. So when he finds out that his brother not only use to fuck wit' his current bitch, but fucked her too, it's a wrap," YaYa declared.

"He ain't gon' wanna be wit' her ass no more. He ain't gon' be able to get that shit outta his head. Think about it. Anytime he and Murda get into it, the first thing Murda gon' say is that's why I fucked yo' bitch! Don't nobody wanna deal with that shit. And he done left his fiancée to be wit' her too? Man, it's really gon' be over," YaYa laughed uncontrollably.

"Thanks for the encouragement," Scotland shot sarcastically.

"I'm just keeping it 100 wit' you 'cause I don't want you to get yo' hopes up."

244

"You gon' tell him; 'cause I think you should," Tootie urged.

"Absolutely not," YaYa cut Scotland off before she could speak. "Scotland, don't listen to her. If you wanna keep yo' nigga you better keep yo' damn mouth shut," she advised.

"You sure? 'Cause I really don't' wanna lie to Knight. I love him too much to do that to him," Scotland said unsure.

"Fuck love!" YaYa retorted indignantly. "You in survival mode right now, bitch. And besides, you ain't lyin'. Ain't nobody asked you shit, so you don't know shit. You got it?"

Scotland swallowed hard. The thought of losing Knight was like the thought of committing suicide. She didn't want to exist without him. He meant too much to her. She knew that telling him about Murda was the right thing to do but YaYa was right. What Knight didn't know wouldn't hurt him.

He and Murda didn't speak anyway. Scotland would have more than enough time to build up the courage to eventually tell him the truth. It just wouldn't be now. She was going to take YaYa's advice and keep her mouth shut.

Everything in Knight's life was on an even keel. He was on cloud nine. Nothing was out of place or causing havoc to his frame of mind. His family adored Scotland like he knew they would. She was perfection in his eyes. He knew his family would see her the same way too.

245

What Knight didn't know was that a love like they shared could ever really exist. He was over the moon beyond the stars in love with her. She made him happy on every level. Scotland didn't give a fuck about material things or keeping up with the Joneses. She stayed in her lane and created her own path.

She treated Knight with the upmost respect. She allowed him to be a man. She never tried to emasculate him. What he appreciated most about her was that even though he could afford to financially take care of her, Scotland wanted a career of her own. She'd been working tirelessly on her first novel. He loved what she'd come up with thus far. She was an amazing writer.

The way she used her words to weave together a story was spellbinding. He had no idea why she hadn't pursued writing earlier in life. Being an author was her calling. She was naturally gifted at it. Knight knew she had a best seller on her hands.

The more confident she became in her writing skills, the more confident she became in fitting into his life. He was happy that he could show her that there was more to life than what was handed to her. Scotland now knew that whatever she wanted out of life, she had to fight for in order to get it.

Knight sat at his desk going over his schedule for the day. Although he'd started hating coming to work every day, he loved his office. He put a lot of energy in making sure it represented him well. His walls were stark white. He had wooden floors. Behind his desk were three black and white photos and a long, sleek table where his computer, phone and other electronics sat. On his actual desk were several books, files and paperwork.

His office chair was black and weaved like a basket. Two black, high back chairs sat in front of his desk. On the wall to his left were several photos of his family. He'd began responding to emails when he heard a light tap on his door. He looked up and found Lennon standing there. She was dressed in a red, Donna Karen, long-sleeve, cold shoulder dress. A black leather belt was wrapped around her waist, accentuating her curves.

Her short pixie cut was perfectly styled in tiny ringlets and her signature, ruby red lipstick shown bright from her lips. None of that hid the fact that he could tell she'd been crying. Her eyes and cheeks were puffy. She looked miserable, more miserable than usual.

"Can I come in?" She asked somberly.

"If you've come to argue and start a bunch of nonsense, then no." Knight focused his attention back on his schedule.

"I didn't come here for that. I actually tried calling you during the holiday but you didn't answer."

"Yeah, 'cause I was wit' my girl and my family."

"Like I said, I'm not here to argue. I'm officially waving the white flag. I just need to talk to you for a minute. It's really important." Her voice shook slightly.

"Make it quick."

Normally Lennon wouldn't tolerate his brash attitude, but today she had no choice. Lennon closed the door behind her and took a seat opposite him. She sat on the edge of the chair and looked at Knight. He looked happier than ever which pissed her off.

How dare he be so happy without me, she thought. It bugged her that he could be happy with a ghetto piece of trash like Scotland. *What could she possibly have that I don't,* she wondered. But none of that mattered in the grand scheme of things. The news Lennon had for Knight was sure to rock his and Scotland's entire foundation.

"What is it? Talk." Knight sat back in his seat and glared at her.

"Listen, I know that I messed up things between us. Everything that happened was my fault," Lennon spoke softly. "I see that now but it's obviously too late."

"You damn right about that."

"I want you to know that I did love you though, Knight. I know I had a weird way of showing it but I did love you. I still do love you and I know that you don't love me anymore and that's fine. I just don't want it to be awkward between us. We have to work together and see each other every day and I don't want any unnecessary tension."

"Me either," Knight agreed. "You're the one that's been acting crazy."

"And I apologize for that."

"I accept your apology," Knight said after a pause.

"Good, that means a lot to me, especially since I'm pregnant with your child," Lennon said with ease.

"You're pregnant with what?" Knight chuckled.

"I'm pregnant, Knight," Lennon said seriously.

She was in fact pregnant but Knight wasn't the father; Paul was. She'd told him about the pregnancy but he flat out refused to leave his family. He and Maggie didn't have a prenup. If they were to get a divorce she was sure to take half of his fortune. In Paul's mind, it was cheaper to keep her.

He loved Lennon but he couldn't risk his money or his career. Lennon agreed. She didn't want him to leave his family either. It wouldn't be in either of their best interest if he did. Her father would have a heart attack if he knew she was carrying on an affair with one of her white, married coworkers.

She had to keep the identity of her baby's father a secret. She figured that since she was so light, if the baby came out more on the white side, she'd be able to play it off because of her skin complexion. Soon she'd be showing and people would naturally assume that Knight was the father because of their prior engagement. Telling Knight he was the father was her only choice. Knight stopped laughing once he noticed that Lennon wasn't joking. Pissed, he hung his head back and willed himself not to scream.

"How far along are you?" He finally asked.

"Three months."

Fuck, Knight thought. She wasn't lying. The last time he'd touched her was the morning he left to go to Miami which was three months prior.

"Look, I don't want anything from you. I just thought you would want to know." Lennon stood up. "I'm truly sorry for everything that has happened." She willed herself to cry.

Suddenly a stream of tears flowed from her eyes. Lennon grabbed a few tissues from off Knight's desk and dabbed the tears away.

"I know it doesn't mean much now but I really do love you, Knight. It hurts so bad knowing that you no longer feel the same. I know you care for Scotland but she's practically a stranger. We had something real. Don't forget that. Anyway, at this point, I just want us to be great co-parents. You know how to reach me if you wanna talk." She turned her back and headed towards the door.

An evil smile traced the corners of her lips as she left out. By the stunned look on Knight's face, she knew she had him right where she wanted him. He believed every lie she'd told. Once again, like a Phoenix rising from the ashes, Lennon Whitmore had pulled herself out of another debacle. Nothing or no one could stop her. She was invincible.

"I'M JUST SAYIN' YOU CAN DO BETTER AND I'LL START HATIN' ONLY IF YOU MAKE ME."

-DRAKE, MARVIN'S ROOM

CHAPTER 21

Kendrick Lamar's *Good Kid, M.A.A.D City* CD played softly as Knight finished cooking dinner. He was preparing one of his favorite meals: shrimp and grits. Heavy cream, chicken broth, onions, green peppers and garlic were just a few ingredients on the countertop. He and Scotland had barely spoken two words to each other since he'd come home from work. They both were enthralled in the secrets they were holding.

After the bomb Lennon dropped, Knight spent the rest of the day in a deep trance. He thought when he left Lennon that he'd be able to start his life over with a clean slate. He wanted no parts of Lennon but now he had to spend the rest of his life dealing with her. He didn't know how he was going to tell Scotland. She hated Lennon. She wouldn't be able to live with the fact that his ex-fiancée was carrying his baby.

Scotland was sure to bounce and Knight honestly couldn't blame her if she did. From the moment they met, it was one drama-filled moment after the next. Nobody wanted to deal with that. Scotland had been through enough. She'd been so happy. He didn't want to take that away from her but he vowed to never lie to her. Knight placed dinner on the kitchen island.

"Babe, dinner is ready," he announced.

"Ok." Scotland rose from the couch and walked slowly to the kitchen.

Ever since she'd learned that Murda was Knight's brother, she'd barely been able to look him in the eyes. She now knew what it felt like to be Lennon every day. She felt like an evil snake keeping such a secret from him. She felt rotten to the core.

She knew she was being selfish by not telling him but the fear of losing him overwhelmed her. It kept her up at night. She hadn't been able to eat either. The secret and fear haunted her.

Scotland washed her hands and sat down. Knight sat on the opposite side of the island. The energy between them had never been so awkward. Neither was able to look the other in the eye. They said grace and began to eat in silence. Knight scooped up a spoonful of grits. He stared off into space and swallowed it.

Scotland took a sip of wine and held it in her mouth. It took her a minute to swallow because she was so deep in thought. She wanted so bad to open her mouth and spill the beans. The truth was right there on the tip of her tongue. She could tell him that Omari was her ex and let the chips fall where they may. She loved Knight dearly but she'd be able to survive without him, at least she hoped so. Knight cleared his throat which caught Scotland's attention. She immediately snapped back to reality and swallowed the wine.

"So how was your day?" She asked.

"Lennon's pregnant," Knight blurted out unexpectedly.

"What?" Scotland repeated losing grip of her wine glass.

The glass fell to the floor and shattered. Wine and small pieces of glass splattered everywhere.

"She told me today." Knight tried to gage her reaction.

He knew that she wasn't going to take the news well. He expected for her to be shocked but he couldn't tell if she was mad or not. Scotland had a blank expression on her face. She just sat there frozen stiff staring at him.

"Say something." He urged frantically.

Scotland sat quiet. She couldn't find the words to express how she was feeling. Here she was holding onto what she thought was a huge secret and he was holding onto an even bigger secret. She hadn't seen this coming. She thought that they'd gotten Lennon out of their lives. Now she held an even bigger presence in their world. The first thought that came to Scotland's mind was that Knight had cheated on her. She was gonna kill him. She was going to skin him alive if he had.

"How far along is she?" She asked barely speaking above a whisper.

"Three months." Knight's voice cracked.

"So she got pregnant right when we first started fuckin' around?" Scotland put two and two together.

"Yeah."

"So the baby's yours?" She blinked repeatedly trying to come to terms with what she'd heard.

"Yeah." Knight hung his head ashamed.

"Mmm." Scotland looked down at her hands.

They were shaking uncontrollably. Her chest felt like it was about to cave in. With each breath she took, it was getting harder and harder for her to breathe.

"I need to step outside." She got up wearily from her chair.

"Where you going?" Knight asked getting up as well. "It's cold as hell outside."

Scotland ignored him and headed towards the door. At that moment, she didn't give a fuck about anything. She didn't care that it was 20 degrees outside. She simply needed some air.

"Hold up! We need to talk about this." Knight followed behind her.

Scotland ignored him and continued to walk.

"Scotland!" He grabbed her arm afraid that if she left out the door she'd leave for good. "You can't just run away. We gotta talk about this."

"I don't need to talk about shit!" She spun around and shot him a look that could kill. "This is your fuckin' problem not mine!"

"What the fuck you mean this my problem?" He threw her arm down.

"I'm not about to argue wit' you, Knight." Scotland turned and gave him her back. "Y'all go ahead and be a happy fuckin' family. I don't even care." She threw up her hand tiredly.

Learning that Lennon was pregnant, on top of knowing that Murda was his brother, were all signs that their relationship wasn't meant to be. YaYa and Lennon were right. She'd always be the side bitch. He would always choose Lennon over her. It was only a matter of time before they got back together.

"What that mean?" Knight questioned.

"It means I'm done. I'm not dealing with this shit."

"So that's it? Knight got in her face. "You just done?" He questioned flabbergasted.

"Yep! Now move!" Scotland pushed him out of her way and unlocked the door.

The cold, crisp, winter air hit her like a ton of bricks. Scotland welcomed the cold air. Snow covered the ground.

"Don't disrespect me and just walk away." Knight followed her outside.

"Don't disrespect you?" Scotland looked at him like he was crazy. "You got a whole baby on the way with another bitch and you gon' tell me not to disrespect you? Boy, please. You got me fucked up. I'm not dealing with this shit wit' you. Been there, done that and I ain't doing it no more. This is obviously a sign that we need to end this so let's just end it now before shit gets worse."

"I can't believe you just wanna end it like that. When shit get tough you just wanna bounce? So I guess all that shit you was talkin' 'bout how much you love me was a bunch of bullshit," Knight mean-mugged her.

"Oh, I love you," Scotland assured folding her arms across her chest. "Don't get it twisted. I'm just not down to have my heart ripped to shreds every time the wind blows."

"Nah, you couldn't love me, 'cause if you did, you wouldn't give up so easily. But if that's what you wanna do, do it. I don't give a fuck. I ain't chasing nobody."

"Explain to me how you mad? You're the one wit' a baby on the way wit' your ex not me," Scotland quipped furious.

"I understand that, but if I wanted to be wit' Lennon, I would be wit' Lennon! What about that don't you get?" He barked.

"I don't want her! I want you! She's pregnant and I understand that hurts you but I can't change the past. I'm not gon' abandon my child. You know how I was brought up. I would never do that to my kid."

"And I don't expect you to!" Scotland yelled back. "But I know me. I ain't gon' be able to play mama to a baby that ain't mine, especially not to a baby by a bitch like Lennon. I can't do it. I won't do it. We were supposed to have our first kid together." Her bottom lip quivered.

"I know." Knight scooped her up in his arms. "But as you can see, life don't always go as you plan. God brought us together for a reason. We ain't going through all of this shit for nothing. I told you this is a forever thing. You may wanna leave but I ain't lettin' you go. We gon' figure this out." He held her in his arms and tried to calm her fears. "I'm willing to do whatever it takes to keep you in my life."

It was pitch black outside. Murda closed his eyes and laid his head on the headrest. A cold wind blew through the air but it was toasty as hell on the inside of his car. He donned a black, puffy coat with a fur hood. The heat was on but the warm mouth wrapped around his dick was what really heated him up. He fully enjoyed the sensation of a wet, hot tongue stroking his dick as snowflakes fell from the sky.

No one was outside. An eerie quietness swept through the block. The only sound he could hear were the slurping noises as he got his dick sucked. Murda gripped the back of YaYa's head and imagined that it was Scotland there with him instead of her. He missed the fuck outta her. She'd never gone this long without talking to him.

He'd hit her up numerous times to no avail. She hadn't bothered to return his calls once. Maybe he'd done her dirty one too many times and she'd finally had enough but Murda wasn't going to give up. Scotland was his and she always would be. She was in her feelings extra hard but with a little persuasion, wining and dining, he was sure she'd change her mind and be back on his team.

In the meantime, he'd continue to occupy his time with YaYa. She seemed to like being Scotland's substitute. YaYa bobbed her head up and down. She relished the taste of his long, caramel dick in her mouth. Murda tasted like the sweetest candy the world had ever created. Every chance she got to be in his presence she took full advantage of it.

For years, she'd been trying to secure a place inside his heart. The night she and the girls met him, YaYa was sure he would want to holla at her. To her surprise and dismay, he liked Scotland instead. She didn't understand what exactly it was he saw in her. Sure, Scotland was cute but in YaYa's eyes, she looked ten times better. She had a better body, prettier face, was smarter and had more going for herself.

With all of that being said, everybody always saw something special in Scotland that caused her to win them over. YaYa looked at it as a pity thing. Everybody always felt sorry for her 'cause she was adopted but YaYa grew up with hardships too and nobody ever felt sorry for her. YaYa was sick of it. She was the one who deserved the attention.

She wanted a man to fawn over her like Murda and Knight did over Scotland. It was mind-boggling to her that Scotland could attract two niggas that were fine, had paper and didn't mind spending it on her.

She was sick of Scotland coming out on top. She was sick of her batting her eyes, flashing her megawatt smile and getting exactly everything she wanted. It was YaYa's turn to have it all and she was going to start with having Murda all to herself. They'd been fuckin' around for nearly just as long as he and Scotland had been fuckin' around.

When Scotland pissed him off, he came running to her. When he got tired of his other hoes, he came running to her. When he needed a stash spot, he used her crib. When he wanted to fuck or get his dick sucked he hit her up. When he needed a third chick for a threesome, she was his chick of choice. YaYa was down for whatever. She hoped that eventually Murda would see that she was the woman for him.

Everything he needed in a woman was instilled in her. She didn't nag or complain. She let him be him. YaYa knew that niggas weren't shit. They were gonna lie and cheat. She just had to play her position and play it well. She wouldn't stress him over seeing other chicks. All she cared about was him making her his main bitch.

It was time for Murda to push Scotland to the side and make her his top priority. YaYa worked her wet tongue around the tip of his penis then worked her way down to his shaft. The tip of his dick hit her tonsils. Coughing, she gagged on his dick. She tried to ease her way back up but Murda kept her head there.

He was on the brink of busting a gigantic nut. Drool slipped out the corners of YaYa's mouth as she tried her hardest to breathe. Murda released his grip on her head and finally let her up for air. YaYa gasped for air and licked her lips. She loved when he got rough with her.

"You like that shit, huh? You want me to spit on it?" She asked with glossy eyes.

"Mmm hmm." Murda pushed her head back down.

Now was not the time to talk. He was right on the brink of nutting. YaYa swallowed his dick whole and worked her head up and down at a feverish pace.

"Suck that dick." Murda bit into his bottom lip. "Make me cum. Work that tongue."

YaYa did exactly as she was told and continued to work her magic.

"Ohhhh… shit. I'm 'bout to cum." Murda massaged the back of her head.

"You ready to cum, daddy?" YaYa purred.

"Yeah... make me cum, Scotland." Murda answered absentmindedly.

YaYa paused. *This nigga did not just say that,* she thought.

"Why you stop?" Murda tried to push her head back down.

"Did you just call me Scotland?" She sat up straight.

"What you talkin' about?" Murda grimaced not in the mood for a bunch of questions.

"You just called me Scotland."

"No, I didn't."

"Yes you did," YaYa challenged.

"Yo you buggin'. C'mon on, finish. My dick going soft." Murda held his dangling dick in his hand.

"Nah, I'm good." YaYa shook her head pissed.

"You serious?"

"Yeah." YaYa replied with an attitude.

Normally she wouldn't have tripped but she was over him obsessing over Scotland. She wasn't the one that held him down. She wasn't the one for him and she was going to make sure he knew it.

"I don't know what the fuck done got into you tonight," Murda zipped up his jeans. "You trippin'. How you just not gon' finish suckin' my dick? That's some disrespectful-ass shit right there."

YaYa stared angrily out the window at the snow. She felt just as small as the snowflakes from the sky. The jealousy she had for Scotland consumed her.

"I can't believe that you just sat up there and called me that bitch name," she hissed.

"She a bitch now?" Murda asked laughing, amused by her anger. "That's your sister. You ain't shit."

"Yeah, she is a bitch," YaYa rolled her neck. "You would be callin' her a bitch too if you knew what I knew. Everybody think that she this Miss Goody Two Shoes… but she's not. Scotland is just as scandalous as the rest of us," she spat.

"Damn, it's like that? I thought y'all were tight?"

"She cool," YaYa shrugged dismissively. "But we can't be that tight if I'm here wit' you. We been kickin' it now for almost two years, Murda. I been your ride or die bitch but you too busy being stuck on stupid for her ass and she fuckin' yo' brother!"

"Get the fuck outta here," Murda cracked up laughing. "Scotland don't even know my brother. She don't know nobody in my family."

"Have I ever lied to you?" YaYa stared at him.

Murda studied her face. YaYa wasn't joking around. She was being dead serious.

"Your brother's name is Knight, right?" She arched her brow.

"How you know that?" Murda screwed up his face.

"I told you. She's fuckin' yo' brother." YaYa ran down the whole entire story of how Scotland and Knight met.

She told him how they'd moved in together and how she'd gone to his mother's house on Thanksgiving and learned they were brothers. She told him how she knew and still hadn't told Knight the truth. Murda couldn't believe his ears. He never brought any of his chicks around his family.

He never bought any of his chicks around his family because he barely went to visit them himself. His brother didn't approve of his lifestyle and chose to love him from afar. Murda always felt like his mother loved Knight more than him. He was her golden child. He could do no wrong. Murda, on the other hand, was constantly in trouble. He stayed away from his mother because he hated the look of disappointment in her eyes when she looked at him. Murda would never measure up to Knight, and for that, he despised his brother. Knight had it all. Murda would be damned if he got Scotland too.

"So my brother doesn't know?" He asked with venom in his voice.

"No, I told her not to tell him," YaYa verified.

"Cool."

"ANYTHING BUT US IS WHO
WE ARE."

-KANYE WEST FEAT. JOHN
LEGEND, BLAME GAME

CHAPTER 22

Scotland and Knight tried to go on as if things were still normal between them but it wasn't. Things had drastically changed. The closeness they once shared was fading away with each day that passed. She no longer looked at him the same. All she saw was a man she wanted to give her all to but couldn't.

She felt stupid for thinking that their love affair would stand the test of time. From day one the universe was against them. Maybe she should've listened when YaYa and Lennon said it wouldn't last. They obviously saw a flaw in their relationship that she didn't. The only thing Scotland knew for sure was that they couldn't continue on pretending that everything was alright.

Things between them had changed drastically. Her heart broke every time the word baby was mentioned. Whenever she saw a baby commercial or an ad in a magazine, she got upset. How was she supposed to deal with knowing that he and Lennon would have their own little family? She figured it was God's way of punishing her for messing with a man who had a woman.

Scotland had selfishly placed her wants and needs in front of what was right. Now she was suffering the consequences of her actions. But what was she supposed to do when everything about her and Knight said they were meant to be? Being with him felt too good to let go.

She had to make a decision about their future sooner than later because she couldn't keep the secret that Murda was her ex much longer. The only reason she hadn't spoke up yet is because she knew that Knight would give up on them too as soon as he found out. Scotland wasn't ready for that so she kept silent and quietly worked through her fears.

That day, she and Knight paced the aisles at Target. Normally during that time of the year, Scotland was full of the Christmas spirit but not this year. She felt like the walking dead. She pretended like she was having the time of her life while they searched for gifts for his nieces and nephew. She must've been doing a great job at it because he seemed to believe her act. They had two carts full of toys and clothes. Scotland couldn't help but to think that the following Christmas they'd be picking out gifts for his son or daughter.

"What you think about this?" Knight held up a toy gun.

"For who; your nephew?"

"Duh," Knight answered. "Hold up." He stopped to check his phone.

He'd just received a text message. Knight read the message and groaned.

"Who is that?" Scotland asked wondering what his problem was.

"Lennon. She gotta a doctor's appointment next week and want me to go wit' her."

Scotland inhaled deep and rolled her eyes.

"You gon' go?" She questioned picking up a John Cena action figure.

"Yeah." Knight placed his phone back inside his coat pocket.

Scotland turned her back and shook her head. She was already starting to feel like an outsider. She needed their shopping excursion to be over ASAP.

"Now back to this gun." Knight tried to change the subject. "You think I should get this for my nephew?"

"I personally don't think kids should play with toy guns but that's just me. Do what you wanna do tho. That's what you gon' do anyway." Scotland quipped not in the mood to shop anymore.

"What's that supposed to mean?" Knight shot angrily. "I played wit' toy guns all the time when I was a kid and look at how I turned out."

"Exactly." Scotland said sarcastically as her phone rang. "Hold up; I have a phone call of my own to take." She shot with an attitude, walking away.

"Hello?"

"Scotland, how are you?" Mrs. Frasier asked cheerfully.

"I'm good. How are you?" Scotland smiled, happy to hear from her.

She hadn't talked to Mrs. Frasier in a minute.

"Remember you don't work for me anymore. Call me Maggie," Maggie insisted.

"How are you, Maggie?" Scotland giggled.

"As good as I can be. I guess," she sighed.

Scotland could hear the uneasiness in her voice. Mr. Frasier must've still been up to no good.

"What's going on? How are the kids? I miss them so much."

"Busy asks about you every day. They like their new nanny but she's no you."

"Awww," Scotland poked out her bottom lip. "Tell her I said hi. We need to get together for lunch or something so I can see them."

"I have an even better idea. You know next month is Liam's birthday. He'll be turning three. We really want you to be there when he celebrates his birthday."

"You mean you and the kids want me there. I know damn well Mr. Frasier doesn't want to see my face and you know I don't wanna see his," Scotland said with a laugh.

"I don't care what Paul wants. I want you there. It wouldn't be the same without you. You're family."

Scotland smiled at the notion. It was sweet of Maggie to see her that way. Scotland felt appreciated.

"I'm sending out invitations soon so I wanted to make sure you'll be on the list of invites."

"Sure, I'll stop by for a minute," Scotland replied.

For Busy and Liam she'd tolerate seeing Mr. Frasier's smug face for a few hours.

"Oh thank you-thank you." Maggie said with glee.

"The kids are gonna be so happy. Oh, and I heard about you and Knight becoming a couple. Congratulations, girl; he's a good guy."

Scotland gazed over her shoulder at him.

"Yeah, he is."

"You think Knight would want to come? The kids really like him."

"Only if I come."

"Ok, well, be looking for your invitation in the mail. It'll be addressed to you and Knight. I look forward to seeing you, Scottie."

"Me too, Maggie." Scotland ended the call.

"That was Maggie? Paul's wife?" Knight questioned ear hustling.

"Yeah, she was calling to invite us to Liam's birthday party next month."

"You gon' go?" Knight responded.

"Yeah, but I'm not going to stay long. The only reason I'm going is because I miss the kids."

"Speaking of kids, let's go over into the baby section." Knight pushed the carts in that direction.

"For what?" Scotland turned up her face.

"So we can look at some stuff for the baby." He signaled for her to come on.

"What would possibly make you think that I would want to go look at baby stuff wit' you for a baby that ain't mine? Do you know how fuckin' insensitive that is to me?" She asked heated.

"I thought we got past all of that," Knight sighed annoyed.

"Just because I haven't left yet don't mean shit. My feelings still remain the same," Scotland made clear.

"I know it's fucked up but it is what it is. Lennon is pregnant and the baby is mine. I'ma be in my kid's life so you gon' have to be a big girl and put on yo' big girl panties and deal wit' it," Knight shot, sternly.

Scotland shot him a look that could kill. If they weren't in public she would've hauled off and slapped the shit out of him.

"You know what?" She centered herself. "I don't have to deal with this shit. Finish shopping by your damn self. I'ma be in the car!" She stormed off, leaving him standing there.

"Excuse me, Knight. You have a visitor." His secretary knocked on his door nervously.

She was giving him eye signals that resembled a person being held up by gunpoint.

"Who is it?" Knight questioned.

"He says he's your brother. His name is Murda." His secretary said afraid for their safety. "Should I call security?" She whispered.

"No," Knight chuckled. "It's ok. Send him in."

"Ok." She backed out of the room.

Seconds later, Murda glided through Knight's office door dressed like the ultimate thug. He rocked a blue, puffy, goose down coat with fur around the hood, a blue, hooded sweatshirt, white tee, Gucci belt, baggy, denim jeans and Tims. A diamond, Cartier watch gleamed from his wrist. Murda's eyes were low. He was high as hell. The smell of marijuana followed him as he entered his brother's office. He'd never visited Knight at work. Bougie white people and Murda didn't mix.

"Omari," Knight stood up and buttoned his Tom Ford suit jacket.

"It's Murda, man." He corrected him.

"You know I'm not callin' you that."

"Whatever, man," Murda declared.

"What brings you here? You ain't in any legal trouble are you? You know that's the only time I see you." Knight stepped around his desk to greet him.

"Nah, I'm straight. I just came to see my brother; is that such a crime?" Murda gave him a one-arm hug.

He hadn't seen Knight in over a year. Knight disapproved of his career choice. Murda got sick of him always trying to throw down his throat how smart he was and how he was throwing his life away. A regular nine-to-five would never suit him. It wasn't his thing. He would never be a suit and tie nigga. The streets were his board room. He was the CEO of the drug game in St. Louis. No other nigga could compete with his squad. He used to wish that his brother would accept his lifestyle but the older and richer he became, the less Murda gave a fuck what his brother thought.

"No, not at all." Knight hugged him back.

Although he would never admit it, he missed his brother. When they were kids he did everything in his power to protect him. Knight was the father Omari never had or knew. Knight took pride in taking care of him. He just didn't understand where he went wrong with him. Knight started to notice a change in Omari when he went to college. Without Knight there constantly on him, Omari went wild.

Murda didn't understand why Knight was so surprised that he took up the dope game. He introduced his brother to the game. Yeah, he'd told Murda not to follow in his footsteps but then contradicted himself and took him on runs with him. Why would Murda work his way through school, owe Sallie Mae, be a slave and work his ass off for another man when he could make fast money on the streets? Selling dope, in his eyes, was the obvious choice.

"I'll admit; I'm surprised to see you." Knight sat on the edge of his desk. "Last I heard, you didn't fuck wit' me."

"I don't but I figured, let me go see what this nigga is up to." Murda strolled around Knight's office.

"As you can see, I'm doing good. What about you?"

"You know I stay on top. Can't shit bring me down." Murda looked at an old family photo that hung from the wall.

He was trying to gage whether or not Knight knew about him and Scotland yet. Judging by his mannerism, he didn't know a thing, which was perfect for Murda. He looked forward to being the one to make his brother's entire world come crumbling down. Knight always thought he was so much better than Murda. He always tried to act like he had a better job, home, cars and women than him. Murda couldn't wait to burst his bubble. While Knight thought he was over there doing it, little did he know, but his new chick was nothing more than community pussy.

"You know Mommy missed you on Thanksgiving."

"I went by to see her the next day." Murda sat across from him.

"This little division between us is really wearing on her."

"I know," Murda said mildly. "That's why I'm here. I think it's time we squash this li'l beef of ours."

"That's the thing tho… I ain't got no beef wit' you, little brother. You the one that got a problem wit' me. Now, do I like the moves you make? No, but that's your life. I ain't got shit to do wit' that as long as it don't affect Mommy, Mya, Sierra and Nicole. All I ever wanted was the best for you. I tried to help—"

"But I don't need your help, dog," Murda cut him off.

"Except for when you get in a jam," Knight challenged.

"But you act like I ask you for help all the time. I ain't asked you to do nothin' for me in years."

"You haven't. I'll give you that," Knight agreed.

"For Mommy's sake, I really wanna work this shit out wit' you. She ain't gettin' no younger so we need to fix shit," Murda reasoned.

"That's all I ever wanted." Knight dapped him up.

He'd been praying for this moment for a long time. He missed having his little brother around. Now that he was about to be a father he really wanted him around.

"Knight," Mr. Whitmore entered his office.

Knight was surprised to see him. Mr. Whitmore barely ever visited his office.

"Yes, sir?" Knight stood up.

"Wow, it smells like a weed dispensary in here." Mr. Whitmore fanned his nose with his hand. "You two haven't been smoking in here have you?"

"No, sir. Of course not." Knight replied nervously.

"Ok good. How are you today, son?"

"I'm good. Let me introduce you to my brother, Omari."

"Nice to meet you, young man." Mr. Whitmore tried to shake his hand.

Murda didn't even bother to stand up.

"What up?" He reached over his shoulder and gave him dap instead.

Knight inhaled deep. His brother never missed an opportunity to embarrass him.

"Can we speak freely?" Mr. Whitmore asked because his brother was there.

"Sure." Knight gave the ok.

"I know that things between you and Lennon are quite strained right now but for the sake of the company and my unborn grandchild, I would really appreciate it if you two could just set your differences to the side and work together. The company's Christmas party is approaching and I really need the both of you there. A lot of our clients are going to be there and we need our two best agents on the floor shaking hands and kissing babies," Mr. Whitmore said with a laugh.

"Of course, I'll be there," Knight assured.

"And I mean no disrespect when I say this, but I think it's best for everyone if you... leave," Mr. Whitmore's voice trailed off.

He hoped Knight would catch the hint.

"I understand and I agree." Knight nodded his head at the suggestion that he leave Scotland at home.

"Bring your brother with you instead," Mr. Whitmore suggested.

"Y'all gon' have some brown liquor and chicken wings?" Murda asked seriously.

"We should," Mr. Whitmore laughed.

"Bet." Murda nodded his head.

"Well, it was nice meeting you, Omari. I'll leave you two now to finish your conversation." Mr. Whitmore declared leaving.

"Thanks for stopping by, Mr. Whitmore." Knight waved goodbye.

Once Mr. Whitmore was gone, Murda turned to Knight and said, "So, hold up. You and the bougie bitch ain't together no more?"

"Nah." Knight ran the story down.

"So you really diggin' this Scotland chick, huh?" Murda played dumb.

"Yeah, that's my baby. I can see myself marrying this girl."

"You saw yourself marrying the bougie bitch too," Murda countered.

"I know but it was always something off between me and Lennon. With me and Scotland it's a sure thing. Li'l mama the truth. She been rockin' wit' me hard from day one and the fact that she still holding me down knowing I got a baby on the way shows me that I can trust her."

"Trust her, huh?" Murda massaged his chin. "Remember what Chris Brown said. These hoes ain't loyal."

Knight cracked up laughing.

"You silly, dawg."

"That's what's up tho." Murda stood up. "I'm happy for you, bruh, and I'll most definitely swing through the party."

"You do that."

"KISS ME NOW SO YOU WON'T RUN OUT OF BREATH."

- JOHN LEGEND, HOLD ON LONGER

CHAPTER 23

"Oh my God," Scotland closed her eyes and savored the flavors in her mouth.

It was like an explosion of flavors was going off in her mouth.

"This white chicken chili is fuckin' delicious," she relished the taste.

Christmas was right around the corner. It was a cold December Sunday. She and Knight had done nothing but lie around making love in front of the fireplace. Scotland sat in just her panties and bra on the living room floor, her back rested against the couch. Knight sat beside her. After working up a massive appetite, Knight got up and fixed them a big pot of white chicken chili. Scotland had never had it before.

Knight was a beast in the kitchen. Every other night he prepared a different cuisine. He knew how to cook a wide range of meals from southern to Chinese. Scotland hoped that he would finally take a leap of faith and start his own restaurant or food truck. The man could make a meal out of nothing.

"You like it for real?" He asked rubbing her thigh.

"Yes! I told you it's good as hell. You need to make this for us at least twice a month. I demand it." Scotland leaned over and kissed the side of his face.

It seemed like ages ago since they shared a quiet, peaceful moment. They weren't arguing or thinking about all the bullshit going on in their life. For the first time in a long time, they allowed themselves to just be. The fire place roared and crackled before them; SIR's *Love You* played softly creating a tranquil mood.

Knight wished they could be like they were in that moment every day. He wouldn't have it any other way. All he wanted was to spend every day of his life loving her. He was placed on earth to love her and he knew it. Only God could create something so beautiful. Scotland was heaven sent. She was his best friend. Knight bit and kissed her shoulder. Scotland squealed in delight.

"I love this," he admitted.

"Me too." She eyed him lovingly.

Scotland placed her bowl down. She took his bowl from out of his hand and straddled him. She gazed deep into his eyes and wrapped her arms around his neck. Knight palmed her ass cheeks. Scotland never wanted to stop looking at his face. The mere sight of his warm, brown eyes and charming smile made her day. He was perfect in her eyes.

If it was up to her, they'd never leave the house. When they were alone the troubles from the outside world didn't matter. All that mattered was them and their undying love for one another. He was everything she wanted and more. The way he looked at her made her proud of what they had begun. This was what real love felt like. It was peaceful, quiet and plentiful.

Scotland would love him forever. With him she was full. She would go to the edge of the earth and back just to prove her devotion to him. She couldn't hold it in any longer. She had to tell him the truth. Tears welled in her eyes. She knew once she opened her mouth the moment would be lost. It would all become a distant memory of what they could've been.

"Baby, what's wrong?" Knight asked as a tear slipped from her eye.

"I just..." She held him tight.

Knight held her close as she cried. He placed his head in the crock of her neck. He knew what the problem was. Lennon being pregnant was really stressing her. Knight felt like shit. Seeing her cry killed him.

"Everything is gonna be ok. Lennon being pregnant isn't going to change anything between me and you. You're my baby. You're my big baby," he joked, massaging her back.

Knight made her look at him. He cupped her face in his hands. He'd never seen her look so sad.

"Knight I—"

"Shhhhh... it's ok." He wiped her tears away with his thumbs.

"I understand but everything is gonna be ok. We gon' be straight, a'ight? I ain't going nowhere and neither are you." He gently pulled her face towards his. "I love you."

Knight sensually kissed her lips. Scotland wanted to speak but all of her thoughts had suddenly become lost in translation. Knight's kisses enveloped her. She somehow had forgotten the English language. Knight had placed his dick inside her. All of the air in her lungs had escaped. His stroke game was driving her insane. Now wasn't the time to tell him. She'd find the courage to another day.

Lifetime's *Bring It* was on while Scotland lay across the bed working on her book. She was only a few chapters away from being done. She was dying with anticipation to send the manuscript off to publishers. The book was filled with love, sex and drama. She'd put her all into it. All she had to do was figure out a title and find a literary agent. She couldn't submit her manuscript to a major publishing company without one.

Tons of ideas were swarming through her brain as she wrote in her notebook. She was at home alone and deep in thought. Knight was gone for the evening. He was out for a work meeting which gave Scotland enough time to work in peace and quiet. Whenever he was around she immediately became distracted. She often found herself wanting to live in his arms and love on him.

They'd gotten things semi back on track. She couldn't have been more pleased. Knight was never her enemy. He was her friend and the man she adored. Once they were all the way good, she would tell him about Murda.

She just needed more time before she confessed. She didn't want to rock the boat. They'd just barely got through the tidal wave of bullshit that had washed up from nowhere. With her feet kicked up in the air she continued to work on her book. Suddenly her phone started to ring. The ringtone alerted her that it was Murda calling. Scotland lie frozen stiff with fear. She hadn't heard from him in weeks. She figured he'd finally gotten the hint and moved on.

As the phone rang she debated on whether or not to answer. Her mind was telling her to ignore him but her gut was screaming for her to pick up the call. Scotland reached over and swiped to the right. She placed the phone on speaker and said, "Hello?"

"Whaaaat… you answered the phone?" Murda teased.

"I can hang up if you like?" Scotland shot back.

"Damn, what I do to you?"

"What haven't you done to me?" She responded dryly.

"What you doing? You miss me?" Murda quizzed.

"Workin' and no."

"You sure about that?"

"Very."

"That's fucked up. You just hurt my feelings," he grinned, getting inside his car.

"Lies; your feelings can't get hurt 'cause you don't have none."

"So now you gon' tell me how I feel. I've obviously been callin' you for a reason."

"Yeah, why have you been callin' me?" Scotland died to know.

She needed to know if he'd figured out that she was dating his brother.

"That's what I wanna talk to you about. Come meet me for drinks."

Scotland paused. Nothing about meeting Murda for drinks was enticing to her. She was fine just where she was at. Knight would be home after a while and she wanted to be there when he arrived.

"I don't think that's a good idea."

"Why not? You got a new man or something?" Murda played coy.

Scotland let out a sigh of relief. He knew nothing. *Thank you, God,* she mouthed.

"As a matter-of-fact, I do."

"Well, if yo' man gon' get mad cause you're having drinks with an old friend then that's on him. I ain't got nothin' to do wit' that. I'm just tryin' to wrap wit' you about some shit that's been on my mind. I wouldn't be bothering you if it wasn't important."

Scotland knew Murda like she knew the back of her hand. He wasn't the type of dude to sweat a chick. There had to be something wrong for him to be hittin' her up so much. Although she was done fuckin' with him for good, she couldn't forget that he'd been there for her in her time of need. If he needed to talk she could at least do that for him. She would meet up with him for a quick second and see what he had to say. Maybe she could even build up the courage to tell him about Knight and possibly get his blessing. That way, it would be easier when she told him.

"A'ight; where you wanna meet?"

"EVEN THOUGH I'M DOING WRONG, GIRL. YOU CAN NEVER MOVE ALONG GIRL."

-TREY SONGZ, ME 4 U - INFIDELITY 2

CHAPTER 24

Although she no longer was checkin' for Murda, there was no way in hell Scotland was going to meet up with him and not be snatched. She hadn't seen him since her birthday. She had to show him that she was doing better than ever now that she'd cut him out of her life. She wanted to make him regret every time he played her to the left, cheated on her, lied to her or abused her trust. After that night, he would live the rest of his life regretting how he mistreated her. Scotland would go down in history as the one who got away.

After much debate, she decided to wear a black, suede and leather, peplum jacket that she wore as a top, leather leggings with three zippers at the knees and black, suede, pointed toe pumps. She carried a black Celine bag that Knight bought for her. Her long, ombre, gray weave had a tousled bed head affect to it. Her makeup look consisted of a cat eye and a plum, matte lip.

Scotland drove at a snail's pace down Washington Blvd. She and Murda were meeting at Lucas Park Grille. Traffic was a muthafucka. It seemed like everybody and they mama were out that night. The cold December weather wasn't stopping anybody from kicking it. Scotland finally made her way up the busy strip and gave her keys to the valet.

Murda stood waiting for her out front. Scotland took in his navy blue pea coat with gold buttons, brown t-shirt, charcoal gray jeans and Tims. He looked gorgeous. Scotland had almost forgotten just how fine Murda was.

Despite her disdain for him, her attraction for him was still there.

Murda hoped that she couldn't tell that his dick was hard as she switched over to him. Scotland was always pretty but now she looked like a super model. She had an air of confidence about her that she hadn't had before. Sex appeal oozed from her veins. A peaceful glow shined from her cheeks. Seeing her only solidified his feelings for her. He had to get her back. She belonged to him. He was determined to remind her of that.

"Damn," He looked her up and down lustfully. "You look good than a muthafucka." He opened his arms for a hug.

"Thanks." Scotland leaned forward and embraced him.

Normally she would've melted in his arms but she felt nothing. Murda would never measure up to Knight. He didn't know how to love a woman. He was young and still trying to play the field. He had no problem loving and leaving a trail of broken hearts in his path.

"Come on." He placed his hand on the small of her back. "Let's go inside. It's cold as fuck."

Scotland reached behind her back and politely removed his hand.

"Oh, it's like that?" Murda chuckled.

"Yeah, I told you. I gotta man."

"My bad. I respect that." Murda held his hands up in a freeze position.

As they neared the door, Scotland noticed a big-ass sign that said "Restaurant Closed. Private Party Inside".

"We gon' have to go somewhere else." She stopped dead in her tracks. "They're closed for a private event."

"I'm on the guest list," Murda grinned, opening the door.

"Oh." Scotland shrugged, stepping inside.

The place was packed with white and black professionals. The people at the private party were not Murda's type of crowd.

"Who do you know here?" She turned to him and asked.

"My brother invited me." He replied with ease.

Scotland's eyes grew wide with fear. Her mouth instantly became dry. Frantically, she searched the room with her eyes for Knight. She didn't see him but she did see Paul in the distance. She was confused. Knight said he had a business meeting that night. He didn't say anything about a Christmas party.

"Yeah, I know all about you and my brother." Murda said into her ear.

"That's why you brought me here?" Scotland's bottom lip quivered.

"I brought you here 'cause I wanted you to see that nigga ain't the one for you."

"You don't know what you're talkin' about. Me and your brother love each other." Scotland shot back.

"He love you so much but he ain't tell you about tonight. He ain't tell you 'cause he's here with her." Murda pointed in Knight and Lennon's direction.

The two of them were standing side-by-side sharing a good ole hearty laugh with some of their top-tier clients. There was no tension between them. Knight seemed to be enjoying her company immensely. All of the hatred he claimed to have for her had completely disappeared. He and Lennon looked like two love birds.

Scotland's entire body became hot. Sweat had begun to form on her forehead. He'd lied to her. Why hadn't he told her about the party? Was he ashamed of her or was he still in love with Lennon?

"Knight ain't like me and you. This is the life he wants. He like tap dancing for these bougie muthafuckas. You think he gon' be able to move up the ladder wit' somebody like you on his arm? You're not good enough for him but Lennon is. She's carrying his baby. It's only a matter of time before he stops fuckin' wit' you and go back to her." Murda continued to break Scotland down.

Scotland looked at Knight with what felt like a billion tears in her eyes. Every word that Murda spoke was like a stab to the heart. She hated to admit it, but he spoke the truth. Knight couldn't possibly love her as much as he claimed he did. If he did, he wouldn't have lied. Lennon was right; she would always come out on top. Scotland would always be two steps behind playing catch up.

The death glare Scotland was giving Knight must've bore through his skin 'cause he could feel her eyes on him. Nervously, he looked around the room in search of who was staring at him. His eyes immediately landed on Scotland.

He spotted her standing by the door. Tears streamed down her face. He quickly wondered how she knew where he was. Then he spotted his brother standing next to her. Confused, he excused himself and headed their way. Scotland wiped her face as he came near. She'd be damned if she let him see her cry. He'd made her look stupid enough.

"Baby, what you doing here?" He tried to kiss her on the cheek.

Scotland quickly sidestepped his attempt and moved back. Caught off guard by her reaction, Knight looked back and forth between her and his brother.

"You here with my brother? Y'all know each other?" He asked confused.

"She ain't tell you?" Murda grinned devilishly. "We used to go together."

"What?" Knight questioned completely stunned.

"Why didn't you tell me you were gon' be here tonight?" Scotland finally spoke up.

"Nah, fuck that. You used to fuck wit' my brother? I thought you said you didn't know my brother?" Knight glared at her.

"I didn't know he was your brother. I know him by Murda not Omari. I didn't figure that out until Thanksgiving when your sister showed me a picture of y'all," Scotland's voice trembled.

"So hold up. You've known this since Thanksgiving and ain't said shit?" Knight became enraged.

"I was going to tell you, but when were you going to tell me that you're still in love with Lennon?" Scotland asked calmly.

"Don't try and flip this shit around on me. You've been fuckin' my brother!"

"I used to fuck with your brother; used to!" Scotland snapped.

"And how long have you known this?" Knight asked Murda.

"Uhhhhhh… a few weeks," He answered nonchalantly.

"So you knew when you came to my office to see me?"

"Yeah," Murda nodded his head on the brink of laughter.

Knight could see himself reaching out and choking the shit out of his brother. At that moment, he would gladly spend the rest of his life in jail for murder. He couldn't understand why Omari hated him so much. What type of human being would go to such lengths to cause so much pain? Knight was so caught up in his emotions that he didn't notice that everyone in the restaurant was staring at them. Lennon stood back enjoying every second of it. Mr. Whitmore on the other hand wasn't pleased.

"Knight, what is going on? You're causing a scene." He asked embarrassed by Knight's unprofessional behavior.

"I'm sorry, sir. Me and my girl are having a problem." Knight ran his hand across his head frustrated.

"I thought I told you not to invite her?"

"Excuse me?" Scotland fumed. "So you are ashamed of me?"

"Mr. Whitmore, can you just give us a minute?" Knight pleaded.

"Handle this," Mr. Whitmore warned.

"Why the fuck are we even together if you can't even bring me around?" Scotland asked feeling her heart break into a million pieces.

Knight didn't know what to think or what to do. His head was spinning with questions.

"Yo, I can't believe you right now. I trusted you and this is how you do me?" He paced back and forth.

He was trying his best to keep his composure and not spazz out. Lennon sauntered over, placed her hand on his shoulder and said, "Knight, honey, are you ok?"

Scotland quickly noticed that she had a small bulge in the bottom of her stomach.

"This ain't got nothin' to do with you so you can just walk yo' li'l frail ass back over there." She instructed smacking her hand away.

"This has everything to do with me. Knight is the father of my baby!" Lennon shouted unwilling to back down.

"Bitch, fuck you and that baby!" Scotland got in her face.

"What you say?" Knight ice grilled her, pushing her back.

"You know I didn't mean it like that." Scotland tried to clean up her mess.

"Nah, you meant it just like you said it." Knight's heart dropped. "You ain't gon' never accept this baby. I don't even know why I thought you would. And you been smashing my brother? I'm done. This shit is a wrap, cuz."

"How many times do I have to tell you that I used to mess with him," Scotland declared, feeling herself about to lose it.

"It don't matter. You knew and you kept it a secret so I'm done! Here I am thinkin' she the bad guy but you ain't no better than her!"

"That's how you feel?" Scotland said deeply hurt.

"Yeah it is." Knight nodded his head.

He was through with the conversation and with her.

"I think it's best you go."

Scotland's eyes became clouded with tears. She could barely see. This had to be a nightmare. Knight hadn't really turned his back on her. He'd promised to love her forever. She was his baby. He was her man. In a matter of minutes, all of that had gone out the window. He'd dismissed her as if she were nothing.

Everyone had warned her that this would happen but she'd foolishly believed that love would outweigh any obstacles brought their way. Scotland gathered herself as best as she could and left without saying a word. She wasn't going to beg him to stay. He'd already thrown her away. She would never be able to recover from that. Murda followed her out the door.

"Scotland, wait up!" He jogged after her.

Murda wasn't expecting it but Scotland spun around on her heels, reared her hand back and slapped fire out of his mouth. She'd hit him so hard that blood trickled out the side of his mouth.

"You set me up," she hissed. "Why? What did I ever do to you?" She cried.

"You didn't do nothin'." Murda tried to comfort her. "I just wanted you to see that my brother ain't the right one for you."

"And you are?" Scotland dodged his attempt to console her.
"Yeah." Murda stood puzzled by her reaction.

"You are fuckin' insane. I don't want you! You have an I.Q. the size of a Ritz Cracker. I want him!" She pointed towards the restaurant. "And now because of you that's ruined, so let me make this clear." Scotland got close enough that he would be able to read her lips.

"Don't call me and don't text me. If you see me out in the street, look the other fuckin' way. I want nothing to do with your tired, pathetic-ass."

Murda swallowed hard. He hadn't seen things ending this way. He'd cooked up in his mind that Scotland would come running back to him. The look of venom in her eyes proved otherwise. She hated him. Having made herself crystal clear, Scotland gave him her ass to kiss and signaled the valet.

"THIS IS WHAT IT FEELS TO BE THE ONE WHO'S STANDING LEFT BEHIND."

-MELANIE FIONA, WRONG SIDE OF A LOVE SONG"

CHAPTER 25

To say that Scotland was depressed over her breakup with Knight was an understatement. She was so distraught that she didn't even return to their house that night. She couldn't bear to see his face. Her worst fears had come true. He'd left her and now she was back at square one. All she could imagine was him and Lennon running off into the sunset and her being left behind with nothing.

She was so sick of being the one left alone. With Knight she thought she'd finally found a life companion. How could something so innocent and pure end up so ugly and full of hate? He hadn't even attempted to call her once. Had she read him and their entire relationship the wrong way? Had she once again made a relationship out to be more than it really was?

What she couldn't figure out was how Murda knew about her and Knight. She was so wrapped in her hate for him that night that she hadn't thought to ask. The one thing she knew for sure was that the pain in the center of her chest hurt like hell. It was unbearable. Scotland felt like she was losing her mind. A million what if's and whys filled her head. The only person she trusted herself to be around was Tootie. She wouldn't judge her or say I told you so. She'd welcome her with open arms and allowed her to sort through her feelings.

Scotland closed herself off to the outside world. For days she lay on Tootie's couch staring at the wall or sleeping through the pain. She didn't want to face reality. Scotland knew she couldn't hide out at Tootie's forever.

She'd have to face Knight eventually. She just didn't know how she'd muster up the strength to do so.

She didn't want to accept that things between her and Knight were truly over. She tried to pretend that it was all a bad dream but each day that passed with no sign of communication from him brought her back to reality. She still loved him so he had to still love her. A love like what they shared didn't just fade away in a matter of days. But maybe Knight had never really loved her at all? Maybe he was just infatuated with her?

Little did she know, but the girls were planning an intervention. Scotland lie on the couch curled up in the fetal position trying to fall asleep when Tootie, La'Shay and YaYa came storming in. They had snacks and Lime-A-Rita's and were ready for girl chat. Tootie clicked on the light. Scotland groaned and placed the covers over her face.

"Can you please turn the light off?"

"No, bitch! You need to get up!" Tootie pulled the covers from off her. "Got my damn living room smelling like corn chips!"

"Uh unh." Scotland tried pulling the covers back. "Give me my covers back," she whined.

"Give the girl her damn covers back." YaYa exclaimed plopping down on the love seat. "I don't feel like hearing her damn mouth."

"Here!" Tootie threw the comforter back at her.

"Thank you." Scotland wrapped herself in the cover. "Where is RJ? I wanna give him a hug."

"I just dropped him off at my mama's house so we could talk to you."

"You look like shit, girl." La'Shay looked at her like she stank, which she did.

She smelled like she hadn't taken a bath in days. Scotland's weave was all over her head and matted together. Dried up makeup and tears adorned her face. The girl looked terrible.

"I hope you didn't come here to make me feel better 'cause you're doing a pretty shitty job at it." Scotland rolled her eyes.

"I told the girls to come over because we're all worried about you." Tootie sat beside her.

"Speak for yourself." YaYa opened a box of Cheez-Its. "I told her dumb-ass this was gon' happen but everybody just thought I was being a hater."

"You are a fuckin' hater." Scotland shot back not in the mood.

"Y'all stop," Tootie pleaded popping open a can of Lime-A-Rita. "Scotland, we know you're hurting but you can't stay on my couch forever. You have to figure out what you're gonna do."

"But in the meantime, you gon' have to take a bath." La'Shay covered her nose.

"Fuck you!" Scotland threw a beaded throw pillow at her.

"I just need a few more days to get myself together. My whole world is upside down right now. I don't know

299

what I'm going to do. I just miss him so much." She began to cry. "I should've never listened to YaYa. I should've told him the truth as soon as I found out."

"Don't try to blame this shit on me," YaYa shot as Tootie passed her a drink.

"You could've told him the truth as soon as you found out but who's to say that things wouldn't have still ended up this way?" La'Shay reasoned. "I mean, I know that you love him but I don't see how it was ever gonna work out. You used to mess with the man's brother and he got a baby on the way with his ex-fiancée. There really ain't no upside to that."

"You're right," Scotland sadly agreed. "I could never accept that baby no matter how hard I tried. I just thought that love would pull us through."

"You sound like a fuckin' Hallmark card. Bitch, this ain't an episode of Dawson's Creek," YaYa interjected.

She was fed up with Scotland's pity party.

"Life ain't a Disney move, bitch. You ain't fuckin' Julia Roberts and Knight for damn sure ain't Richard Gere."

"YaYa, be compassionate to your sister," Tootie advised.

"Nah, fuck that! I've been running to this bitch rescue her entire life. She's always involving herself in some dumb shit then wanna cry about it later. I told her from the jump the shit wasn't gon' work but nah, she ain't wanna listen to me. So fuck it. Let her ass hurt. Let her cry 'cause she deserve it. She brought all this shit on herself."

As venom spewed from YaYa's mouth, Scotland couldn't help but to think back on just how Murda knew about her and Knight. The only people who knew the truth were YaYa and her friends.

"You told him didn't you?" A light bulb went off in Scotland's head.

"Told who what?" YaYa remarked annoyed by the sound of her voice.

"You told Murda about me and Knight?"

"I sure did." YaYa didn't hesitate to tell the truth.

"YaYa, why would you do that?" La'Shay asked stunned.

"Cause he deserved to know. I'm sick of fakin' and frontin' for this broad. I ain't liked yo' ass since Mommy and Daddy adopted you. I'm so tired of you and your Little Orphan Annie routine that everybody falls for. Ain't nothin' special about you, bitch. You're weak and pathetic. You're basic. I don't see what either of them niggas ever saw in you, especially Murda. You ain't no down as bitch. I am! Murda was supposed to be mine, not yours."

"So that's what this is about? You mad over some dick?" Scotland snatched the covers from off her and stood up. "You mad 'cause that nigga didn't want you?"

"Oh he wanted me a'ight." YaYa rose.

Both girls were face-to-face.

"We been fuckin' for almost two years. Now what?"

Scotland didn't even realize that she'd done it but she'd knocked the shit outta YaYa. She'd hit her so hard that her nose had begun to bleed. YaYa wiped her nose. As soon as she saw blood she went ballistic. She reached out and wrapped her hands around Scotland's neck. She tried to choke the shit outta her but Scotland was quick on her feet.

She swatted YaYa's hands away and kneed her in the stomach. YaYa doubled over in pain. Scotland didn't waste any time wailing on her. She hit her with several blows to the head before La'Shay and Tootie broke up the fight and pulled her off of her.

"Uh unh, let her go!" YaYa attempted to lunge for her.

"Hit her if you want to and it's gone be World War III up in this mafucka,' La'Shay warned.

"Really, La'Shay? That's how it is? You gon' take her side?" YaYa's chest heaved up and down.

"Bitch, there ain't no sides to this! You wrong as hell! Scotland is my girl! She's supposed to be your sister; but if you don't rock wit' her, then you don't rock wit' me!"

"Yeah," Tootie agreed. "Now get yo' crazy-ass up out my house!" She gathered YaYa's things for her and threw them out the door.

"Fuck all you hoes! I don't need y'all!" YaYa spat storming out.

"Fuck you too! I barely liked yo' ass anyway!" Tootie slammed the door behind her.

"I can't believe that scandalous-ass ho," La'Shay fumed, wanting to fuck YaYa up.

"Here I was thinkin' this bitch really looked at me like a sister and she been fuckin' Murda the whole time." Scotland fell back onto the couch. "You gotta be careful who you run with. You never know who wants your life. Shit, now I see how Blac Chyna feels."

A few days later, Scotland finally returned home. She was tired of pretending that the end wasn't coming. The only thing she was doing by hiding out at Tootie's house was prolonging the inevitable. But facing Knight had been even harder than she thought. As soon as she walked in their bedroom and saw his face she broke down in tears.

There he was, lying on the bed watching television, as if he didn't have a care in the world. Scotland wanted nothing more than to run and lie in his arms. Knight wouldn't even give her eye contact. Unable to see her cry, he left and went downstairs. He couldn't mentally handle her tears. Knight was emotionally fucked up. He didn't know what they were doing. He knew they both were upset. They both had every right to be. They'd both fucked up. That still didn't stop him from loving her.

He just didn't know if loving her was enough to keep them together anymore. She'd committed the ultimate betrayal. He couldn't just forgive her and move on as if nothing had happened. He didn't want to but he had to say goodbye. It was best for the both of them.

They'd rushed too fast into a relationship. They barely knew each other. Maybe if they would've taken their time and gotten to know each other better things would've been different. Maybe then they wouldn't be in this mess. But they were and there was no changing what had already occurred.

They'd both lied and kept secrets from one another. Knight couldn't really expect her to put her emotions to the side and support him while another woman carried his child. That would be selfish of him to ask her to. As she packed her bags he sat idly by the door waiting for her to leave. Knight glanced over at the Christmas tree.

Christmas had come and gone. The engagement ring he bought her still lied under the tree. Seeing the box made Knight remember the love they once shared. He thought about running up the stairs and stopping her but his pride wouldn't allow it.

He was still mad that she hadn't told him about Murda. He felt that if she could keep something that important from him then what else would she do. He couldn't take the chance of her betraying his trust again. Trust was important to Knight and he'd completely lost his trust in Scotland. She'd betrayed him in the worst way. There was no going back and fixing it. Their relationship was over. He had no choice but to let her go.

Tearfully, Scotland finished packing her things. The things she couldn't fit in her car Knight would have to have movers bring to Tootie's house. She'd taken longer than needed to pack in hopes that Knight would stop her but he never did. *How did we end up here,* she thought as she packed up pictures and old love notes he'd written her?

When she'd met him she was broken and he was scared but somehow they made it work. They hadn't left each other's side since that day at the park. He was supposed to be the man she married; so what happened to second chances? She wanted to make peace. Their love was too much to give away. If he gave her the chance, she'd calm his fears; show him that she was trustworthy.

Scotland was fully prepared to beg her way back to him but changed her mind. She was done being weak. If he didn't want to be with her anymore then oh the fuck well. It was his lost. She knew she was a good woman. She never meant any ill will towards him. She only kept the secret because she couldn't see herself without him. There was nothing that she could say or do to make him see that so she grabbed her bags and headed down the steps.

Scotland stopped at the door and took one last look at Knight. If he said he loved her she'd turn around and stay but Knight said nothing. He wouldn't even look her way. Crushed, she placed her key down on the bench beside him and left without saying a word.

"YOU CUT ME DEEP, BITCH."

-KANYE WEST,
"BITTERSWEET POETRY"

CHAPTER 26

It was the day of Liam's birthday party. Knight boarded the elevator to Paul and Maggie's floor. He never imagined that he'd be attending the party alone. Only a few weeks had passed since Scotland left. They'd only spoken once and that was via text. He'd offered to get her an apartment but she refused his offer.

Scotland didn't want any more of his handouts. She'd survived 28 years without him. She'd get back up on her feet without his help. Knight was fine with that. He just wanted to know that she was safe and out of harm's way. It hurt him deeply the next time he tried to reach out to her and was hit with the fact that she'd changed her number.

It damn near killed him. Knight got off the elevator with the gift he and Scotland had picked out for Liam in his hand. The only reason he was even attending the party was because he wanted to run into her. They needed to talk. He couldn't spend another day without her. Knight never expected that when she left she'd take pieces of his heart with her.

The last few weeks without her had been torture. He couldn't do anything but think about her. He couldn't even concentrate at work. He was sick without her. Like a fiend on a drug, he longed for her touch.

Without her he was going loco. All he did was drink his pain away. He was over the fact that she used to mess with his brother. None of that mattered anymore. She was his and he needed his rib back so that he could function properly.

Knight could hear the loud sound of children crying and laughing as he walked down the hall. He was dressed casually in a black leather jacket with a black, hooded, unzipped jacket underneath, Homies t-shirt, black, fitted jeans with a rip at the knee and Chuck Taylor's. Standing at the door, he nervously knocked.

"Come in!" Maggie yelled over the noise.

Knight opened the door and walked inside. As soon as he entered he almost ran into a little kid. Toddlers were running around everywhere. Maggie and Paul had a houseful. Cars decorations were all over the living area. Maggie had gone all out. She had a Cars cake, cookies, cupcakes, water bottles, napkins and cups. Everywhere Knight turned there was something Cars related.

"Knight! What a surprise." Maggie said pleased to see him.

"How you doing, Maggie?" He gave her a formal hug.

"These kids are driving me nuts but other than that, I'm great." She answered looking disheveled.

Maggie's hair was out of place and she was out of breath from running after the kids.

"Is Paul here?"

"No," Maggie diverted her attention elsewhere. "He had to get some work done at the office."

"On a Saturday?" Knight quizzed, knowing damn well that was a lie.

Paul never came in on the weekend to work.

"That's what he said." Maggie shrugged her shoulders trying not to get upset.

She didn't know any father that would willingly miss his sons' birthday.

"Is Scotland here?" Knight scanned the room for her.

"No, she called this morning and wished Liam happy birthday. I'm surprised you even came."

"To be honest, I thought she was going to be here," Knight said disappointed. "How is she doing?"

"She's doing good. The move to Chicago has been great for her." Maggie tied one of the kid's shoes.

"Chicago?" Knight said perplexed.

"You didn't know she moved to Chicago?" Maggie asked hating to be the bearer of bad news.

"Nah." Knight said feeling like he was about to die.

"I helped her get a book deal. It took us no time. My editor loved her book and signed her right on the spot."

"Wow," Knight said stunned. "That's what's up. I got to read what she wrote. She has a banger on her hands."

"Yeah, it's a damn good book."

"I'm happy for her." He said solemnly.

He wished he could share in Scotland's triumph. They'd stayed up plenty of nights talking about her getting a book deal.

"Where she staying at in Chicago?"

"I wish I could tell you Knight but she swore me to secrecy," Maggie replied, regrettably. "She really just wants to concentrate on her book and getting her life back on track."

"I can respect that." Knight handed her Liam's gift. "Look, I'ma get up outta here."

"You sure?" Maggie eyed him concerned.

Knight looked like he was on the brink of tears.

"Yeah." He assured waving goodbye.

Knight walked back to his car in a daze. He was happy that Scotland had reached her goal but the realization that she'd moved on without him was too much to bear. He thought after a while they'd be able to see each other and work things out. Now she was gone and he had no way of getting to her.

After leaving the party, the idea of returning home to an empty house wasn't so appealing to Knight. Being in that house without Scotland made him depressed. Even though she wasn't physically there, the memory of her haunted him every which way he turned. He didn't know how much longer he would be able to live there without her.

Knight drove around aimlessly for an hour trying to figure out his next move. He had to get Scotland back. Letting her go had been the biggest mistake of his life. Now he didn't know if he'd ever be able to see her again. He prayed to God he hadn't lost her for good. He wouldn't be able to live with himself if he had.

Unwilling to go home, Knight decided to head to the office. He figured burying himself in his work would take his mind off of Scotland. After parking his car in the garage he entered the building and headed to his office. No one was there except for the janitors and security. It was so quiet he could almost hear a pin drop.

Knight wasn't so sure if peace and quiet was what he needed anymore. The silence was deafening. He was just about to turn and leave when he heard the sound of Paul's voice. *This nigga really is at work,* Knight thought, standing outside his door. He just knew Paul had lied to his wife. Paul was inside his office but the door was cracked halfway open.

"Oh my God!" He sighed heavily. "If Maggie calls me one more time, I'm going to flip my lid," he complained.

"I can't believe you missed your son's birthday party," Lennon laughed.

She sat on his desk before him with her legs wide open. She and Paul had just finished having sex and were now eating takeout and shooting the breeze.

"You are such an asshole."

"I wasn't an asshole a minute ago when I was going down on you on this desk." He gripped her waist and kissed her thigh.

Knight furrowed his brows. He couldn't believe what he was hearing. Lennon and Paul were having an affair. He wondered how long it had been going on. *She better not have been fuckin' him while I was wit' her,* he thought.

"You sure wasn't," Lennon purred.

"You have to slow down on all the food though. Your baby bump was kind of getting in the way," Paul frowned.

"Excuse you," Lennon mushed him in the head. "I'm eating for two now."

"Don't remind me," Paul shot sarcastically.

"You better get on board and act like you're excited about this. This baby is going to be here in the spring. I'm going to need your help."

"That's what you have Knight for," Paul countered.

"Poor thing. He's so dumb. Knight's going to be there, sure, but I'm still going to need your help. You're not going to do me like you do Maggie. You're going to be present in our baby's life."

Time suddenly stood still. An eerie sound pierced Knight's ears. He could hear the sound of his heart beating slowly through his chest. He'd never had a panic attack before but he felt like he was having one. Knight didn't even realize that he'd balled up his fist and pushed Paul's door open. It was as if he was having an outer body experience.

His feet were moving but he had no control of himself. Paul and Lennon didn't even see him coming. They didn't realize it until it was too late. Lennon was startled when Knight appeared out of nowhere and grabbed Paul by his throat.

"Knight, what are you doing here?" She shrieked jumping back.

Knight couldn't answer her. He was too busy punching Paul in the face. His fist pounded his eye repeatedly. Paul couldn't even fight back he was so caught off guard.

"Knight, let him go!" Lennon yelled trying to pull him off of Paul but Knight was too strong.

"Get the fuck off me!" Knight furiously pushed her away while still holding onto Paul's throat. "You lied to me, bitch!" Knight barked seeing red.

"Knight, I can explain! Just please let him go!" She begged terrified for their life.

"Fuck you!" Knight pulled Paul out of his chair and dragged him across the floor.

Paul was so disoriented by the blows to his face that he couldn't even put up a fight.

"And you was just gon' go along wit' the lie!" Knight said to Paul.

He viciously let him go and kicked him in the stomach.

"You two ruined my life!" He kicked Paul over and over again until he coughed up blood.

"Knight! Stop! You're gonna kill him!" Lennon cried hysterically. "Somebody help! He's gonna kill him!" She yelled out the door.

Two security guards quickly came running to her aid. They both grabbed Knight by the arms and pulled him back.

"Get off of me!" He yanked his arms away.

"Baby, are you ok?" Lennon kneeled down on the floor and checked on Paul.

She didn't even care that she'd destroyed Knight's life or hurt him. All she cared about was Paul's wellbeing. His entire face was swollen, his lip was busted and he couldn't stop coughing up blood. Knight was sickened by the sight of them.

"Look what you did!" Lennon sobbed uncontrollably.

"You two crazy muthafuckas deserve each other!"

"You're going to jail! I'm going to press charges against you!" Paul groaned.

"I don't give a fuck what you do! Both of y'all can suck my dick!" Knight hit'em with the middle finger and stormed off.

"I WAIT IN THE RAIN BUT I DON'T COMPLAIN 'CAUSE I WAIT FOR YOU."

-INGRID MICHAELSON, ALWAYS YOU

EPILOGUE

Everything in Knight's life had changed drastically but the one constant that remained was his desire to have Scotland back in his life. After learning he wasn't the father of Lennon's baby, he quit the Whitmore Agency. Knight didn't want to spend another day around those people. He hated going to work every day anyway.

Paul kept his promise and pressed charges against him for assault and battery. Knight was charged and ordered to pay his medical expenses and perform five hours of community service. He took the punishment on the chin with glee because Paul and Lennon thought they were gonna win. They thought he was going to spend time in jail.

When they didn't get their way, they tried suing him but the lawsuit was thrown out of court. Knight was stunned that a person would go so far just to make another human being suffer. Paul and Lennon were wicked people. He guessed they had to make him hurt because they'd lost everything.

When Maggie learned about the affair and the baby she immediately filed for divorce. She was done being humiliated and mistreated by Paul. Since they didn't have a prenup, she received a large settlement, their apartment, one of their cars and child support. She was also awarded full custody of the kids.

Mr. Whitmore was none too pleased when he found out about his daughter's dirty deeds. Lennon had shamed their family in ways that could never be repaired. She'd gone against everything he'd engrained in her. She was not an appropriate representation of the Whitmore's or the Whitmore Agency, so her father not only disowned her but fired her as well.

Paul was fired as well. When Knight found out, all he could do was laugh because like the old saying goes: you never win when you play dirty. Murda and YaYa were arrested after the police raided YaYa's home and found several kilos of heroin. The feds had been surveying them for months and had built an extensive case against them. Murda called his brother for help but Knight didn't have anything for him. Murda would have to suffer the consequences and deal with his choices.

Knight was concentrating on his own life. Being a sports agent wasn't his calling. He was destined to be a chef. Cooking was his passion. Whenever he got in the kitchen, he felt at peace. Cooking was cathartic for him. It gave him a chance to vibe out and think.

It had been six months since he quit the agency. During the day, he spent his time going to culinary school. At night he worked on plans to open his first restaurant. He was happy with where his life was heading. The only thing missing was Scotland. If he had her everything would be perfect.

Knight was over their separation. They'd been apart far too long. Her first novel *Paper Heart* had just been released. The book went straight to #1 on the New York Times Best Selling List. The entire book was based on their relationship. When Knight read about her hardships and how she felt about him, it made him love her even more.

He had to see her. With no way to contact her, he went to her website and saw that she was having a book signing at the Barnes and Noble on the Magnificent Mile in Chicago. Knight knew that would be his only chance to see her so he bought a plane ticket. Her book signing was from 2:00 to 5:00p.m. Unfortunately, Knight's flight was delayed because of inclement weather.

He didn't get to Chicago until 4:45p.m. By the time he hopped into a cab and made it to the book store the signing was over and Scotland was gone. As he stood at an empty table where Scotland once was, Knight couldn't help but feel defeated. He'd missed her by a matter of minutes.

Knight swallowed his anger. He didn't care if he had to fly to every one of her book signings. He was going to find Scotland. All he needed was one opportunity to tell her how much he loved her and wanted her back. Knight stepped outside into the humid, July, afternoon rain. It didn't even matter that he didn't have an umbrella. The rain washing over him was the tears he wanted to cry. With his hands in his pockets, he started down the street when he heard a familiar voice call his name.

"Knight!" Scotland called out.

Knight turned around. Scotland came out of the book store looking like an angel. She stood underneath a black and white polka dot umbrella. She looked well rested and refreshed. She'd lost the long gray weave and now wore her hair short. Both sides of her hair were shaved off.

The top was dyed a pastel pink color and coiffed to the back. The new style framed her beautiful face well and highlighted her round eyes, high cheeks and full lips. She wore a bold, red lip, big, gold, drop earrings, gold, statement necklace, white crop top, white, wide-leg trousers and nude, flat sole, sandals. Knight prayed to God that she wasn't a figment of his imagination. He'd dreamt of this moment too many times for it not to be true.

"Scotland, is that really you?" He asked as the heavy rain clouded his vision.

"Yeah, silly." She sauntered towards him.

"Hi." He caressed the side of her face with his hand.

"Hi," she smiled.

"I just left from inside. The manager told me you were gone."

"I know. I was in the bathroom, so she'd thought I'd gone. When I came out she told me that a fine, black brother with a bald head was lookin' for me. I figured it could only be you. What are you doing here?" She beamed, excited to see him. "Are you here on a business trip?"

The sound of rain tapping on Scotland's umbrella mirrored the beat of Knight's heart. Now was the time to tell her how he felt. He could finally tell her how he'd wait a lifetime just to see her smile, how life without her wasn't worth living, how from the moment they met his heart had chosen her. With her he felt no pain. She completed him.

"I came to see you. Baby, I'm sorry for letting you go. I fucked up but if you give me another chance I—"

Scotland placed her index finger up to his lips and silenced him. He didn't have to say another word.

"You had me at hello."

Made in the USA
Charleston, SC
02 December 2015